The Chronicles of Jaydür

Book One

The Lost Voice

L.F. Oake

Dedication

To Pyra...the spice to Jaydür.

Also, to every kid who dreams of being a writer.
Jaydür began when I was thirteen years old.
You got this.

The Chronicles of Jaydür

Book One

The Lost Voice

L.F. Oake

Table of Contents

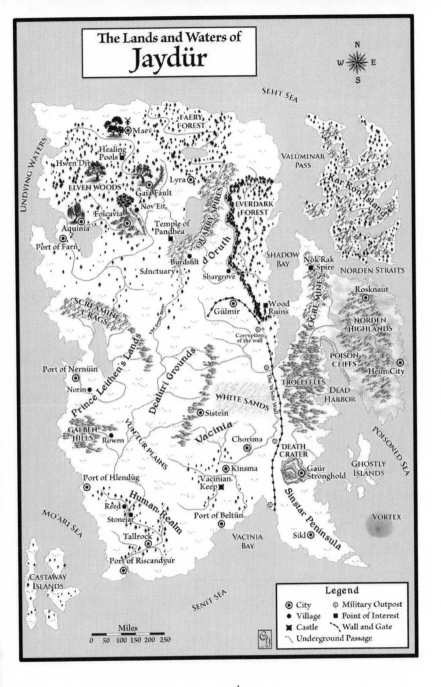

The Lands and Waters of
Jaydür

SEHT SEA

FAERY FOREST

Maev

Healing Pools

Hwen'Dit

ELVEN WOODS

Lyra

Gaia Fault

Nov'Eit

Folcavia

Aquinia

Temple of Pandhea

Port of Farn

Burdsfilt

Sanctuary

Shargrove

SCREAMING CRAGS

Gülmir

Wood Ruins

Corruption of the wall

QUARRI SPIRES

d'Oruth

EVERDARK FOREST

SHADOW BAY

Nok'Rak Spire

NORDEN STRAITS

Rosknaut

NORDEN HIGHLANDS

VALÜMINAR PASS

Kar'Ron Island

UNDYING WATERS

Port of Nernüin

Norin

Prince Leithen's Lands

Dealuri Grounds

The Steed River

WHITE SANDS

Sistein

GALBEN HILLS

Rowen

Vacinia

Chorima

VÜN'TUR PLAINS

Kinsma

Port of Hlendüg

Human Realm

Reed

Stonejar

Vacinian Keep

Port of Beltün

Tallrock

MO'ARI SEA

Port of Riscandyür

CASTAWAY ISLANDS

SENIT SEA

OGRE MINES

The White Wall

TROLLEFELLS

DEAD HARBOR

DEATH CRATER

Gaür Stronghold

GHOSTLY ISLANDS

VACINIA BAY

Sikl

Simstar Peninsula

POISON CLIFFS

Heim City

POISONED SEA

VORTEX

Legend

⊙ City
⊛ Military Outpost
● Village
■ Point of Interest
⚔ Castle
╲ Wall and Gate
⌇ Underground Passage

Miles

0 50 100 150 200 250

Chapter One
Heartlessness

Caia Foriei gasped at the harrowing *crack* of an arrow splitting a tree branch near her head. She looked over her shoulder—it came closer than she would have liked. Since when were goblins that good of a shot? And on horseback!

"I believe you now!" Solin Rahngwa, Caia's best friend and fiancé, called from his horse behind her. "The barrier is down!"

That was a first. Solin was not one to admit defeat so quickly, but after three minutes of being pursued, he'd given in.

"I'm glad we could come to an agreement!" she called in return while sliding one of her own arrows from the quiver at her side and nocking it onto her bow. "Get down!"

Solin leaned down onto his horse's neck as Caia sent the arrow over his head to plunge into the jugular of one of the three pursuing goblins. A resounding shriek from the creature rang through the woods.

"If there are more, they will have heard—" Solin's words turned to an abrupt *ungh* of pain.

"Solin!" Caia cried. She urged her horse to the left to leave more room for Solin's horse to come beside her. "Solin, are you shot?"

Pain contorted his features. "Yes," he winced, pointing over his shoulder to the arrow protruding from his back. "I've never been more shot in my life!"

Grabbing the arm of his tunic, Caia pulled him toward her to drag him onto her own horse.

"No, no!" he cried. "I can stay upright! I'm all right! By the Highest, just keep going!"

A bolt of white light suddenly shot past Caia on the right, followed by the death screeches of the second and third goblins behind them.

Stiff from his injury, Solin looked to Caia for an explanation of what was happening. She had nothing to offer him but wide eyes and a slack jaw. With the threat of the goblins gone, Caia stopped the horses and surveyed the area. The shadows of the white birch forest were dense and deep beneath the late afternoon sun. Caia could not see the green, gnarled faces and hooked noses of the goblins, but their skill in camoflauge was renown. If they were hiding, the elves might not be able to see them. Though it was quiet, she felt eyes on her and Solin, but the sense of threat that followed the dark creatures was no longer present.

"Hello?" she called out, but the forest was quiet.

Solin groaned as he tried to turn for a look.

"Don't move," Caia scolded him. "Someone is out there. He's watching us."

"How do you know it's a 'he?'"

"I don't know; I just do."

The horses jumped in surprise when a man suddenly stood before them. Caia reached for an arrow, knowing the stranger was too close for a ranged weapon. She should have gone for Solin's dagger. No matter—she could make do with anything sharp in hand.

"Lands be damned," Solin swore in his surprise. "Where did you come from?"

"We should get that arrow out," the stranger replied beneath the shadow of his hood. Even with the black leather mask covering his mouth, his voice was clear and smooth. His eyes, glowing an unnatural teal as if imbued with some kind of magic, caused Caia's skin to rise like gooseflesh. She swallowed hard.

"Who are you?" Caia asked, eyeing the black jerkin he wore. One arm—his sword arm—was sleeved and gloved, while the other was bare up to his shoulder. "And why should we trust you?"

The man laughed and his hidden smile crinkled the corners of his eyes. A glowing blue symbol like branches of a tree appeared beside his left eye as if being drawn in that moment with an invisible pen, then disappeared just as quickly. Truth dawned on Caia, and she dismounted, mouth agape.

"You," she started, having trouble finding her words. "You're a *Sapient*." Speaking the word seemed like a sin in and of itself. It was an ancient term, from the days of early creation.

The man bowed his head and walked to Solin's side, where he offered his hand in help. A white tree was on the back of his jerkin, and swirling letters of old script marked the outer edges of his hands and pinky fingers, glowing the same teal color of his eyes. Caia couldn't read the language, but she recognized it as the ancient scribblings marked throughout the books she studied since she was told of the bloodline—books often put aside for daydreaming and extra hours spent in the woods with Solin.

Solin took the man's proffered hand and winced as he was helped from the horse. "Thank you," he said to the man, then looked to Caia for clarification. "But…Sapient?"

She carefully gestured to the script on the man's hand, unsure what was customary or polite when speaking about someone of such authority. "He wears the script and the tree of the *Rehnedhen*—the spirit world. No one carries those symbols without first crossing into the realm."

"I am here to escort Caia to Sanctuary." he said with a slight bow of his head.

Caia lowered her eyes to the ground but could feel

Solin's eyes on her back. Solin had always insisted that no one would come for her after so much time had passed. "No one can possibly know who you are," he had said. "And it would take a lot of effort to hunt you down."

But Caia knew better. She knew how the leader of the slit-eyed, gray-skinned sinstarians, Glim'Ruk, had tracked down her family long before killing the first Voice of Apan. She knew the only things holding them back from taking her were the living Voices that still held power—until now. If a Sapient was there, that could only mean *all* of the Voices were now dead, and the truth was laid bare for all of Jaydür to see—the ethereal barrier created by the elves to keep the descendants of the Voices safe was now gone, and the sinstarians sent in the goblins in swarms.

The Sapient slipped his finger into the ripped fabric where the arrow entered Solin's back, above the shoulder blade. Solin writhed in pain as the man pulled some of the tender flesh to the side, studying the wound.

"Oh good," he said. He took hold of the shaft and pulled the arrow right out of Solin, who howled in agony.

"Solin!" Caia cried. She looked up to the Sapient with wide eyes. "Was that necessary?" she asked.

The man eyed the tip of the arrow. "It's hardly a sharpened stick. Clearly these goblins are not the ones worth our concern. But more are coming. Now stand still." He dropped the arrow and placed his ungloved hand an inch or so away from the wound. A white glow radiated from the man's palm, up his forearm beneath his gauntlet and to his elbow. The skin around the wound sizzled and smoked as the Sapient's magic cauterized the site. Solin gasped and cried out as his flesh sealed shut, stopping the flow of blood.

"You will heal," the man said. "As for you," he turned back to Caia, "you have your weapon, your cloak, and your horse. You have need of nothing else." The Sapient's eyes trailed over Caia and an uncomfortable sensation came over her. It was difficult to tell if he was simply studying her or if there was more to his gaze. Until then, reading a person's intentions through their eyes was not a complex thing for her to do. In fact, her ability to do so with acute accuracy was something she took pride in, so the inability to do so *now* was somewhat distressing for Caia.

"I suppose the Elder should know I am here." The Sapient cut his gaze from Caia and looked at Solin. "Boy—you are tasked with letting your master, Dy'Mün, know I have the Voice with me. We will reconvene at his cottage."

Solin eyed the man warily. "Dy'Mün is not our 'master.' He's our professor."

With a hand on Caia's shoulder, the man gently urged her southward. "As far as you know. You be sure to pass on the message." He passed Caia a sidelong glance as she opened and closed her mouth in shocked silence.

"Wait," Solin interjected. "You really think you can just appear, ogle my fiancé, and snatch her away right from under my nose? How do we know *you're* not the enemy?"

The Sapient stepped toward Solin. "If I were the enemy, you would have been dead before you even knew I was here." He ripped off the mask, revealing a face of a much younger-looking man than expected. "I am Archai, guardian Sapient of the Voices. I've witnessed the rise and ruin of kings and kingdoms for ages. I was present for the birth of language. The very course of the moon and stars has grown dull in my time." Solin's eyes widened with recognition as he stepped back with every step Archai took forward. "*You* have no power here."

"Solin, let's just consider this all for a moment," Caia started, torn between who she should stand with. Solin was her everything, but a Sapient came from the heavens with an authority no mortal could comprehend. Everyone knew Archai's name from stories and history books. Clearly, though, history and authority did not matter to everyone.

Solin squared his shoulders and walked forward until he stood nose-to-nose with Archai. "I don't give a damn who you claim to be. Until I have proof, Caia is under my protection as my future wife."

"Not anymore, she isn't." Neither one noticed Archai's hand on the hilt of his sword until he flung up the butt of it in a swift blow to Solin's head, rendering him unconscious. He turned to Caia. "Now, we go."

"Solin!" she cried, hurrying to Solin.

Archai stopped her with a hand around her arm. "That way," he demanded, pointing a finger in the opposite direction, but Caia wouldn't have it.

"No! Let me go! He's hurt!"

In an instant, Archai's arm was thick around her waist as he lifted her, tossing her over his shoulder like a sack of wheat. Each of Archai's long strides carried her farther away from Solin until she couldn't see him anymore.

"He'll be fine," Archai explained in a much too casual tone as he walked steadily south. "Give him a moment. He'll wake."

"Put me down!" she demanded, pushing against his back to lift herself up. "Who do you think you are!"

"I told you. I am Archai, guardian Sapient of—"

"I demand you put me down!"

He laughed, clearly pleased with himself, as he dropped Caia to her feet. She immediately attempted to pass by him, but he blocked her and, with a frustrated breath, reassured her. "He's fine. I swear it. But you must come with me."

Catching Archai's eyes, Caia searched him for

some sign of danger or dishonesty. This time, she did not struggle to find what she looked for. The Sapient, to her satisfaction, was being truthful.

"Caia! Caia!" Solin's desperate voice filled the air.

She wanted to cry out to him, to let him know she was all right, but Archai hushed her.

"He is not my charge to protect," he said.

Caia's heart was in her throat. Dy'Mün's warnings rang in her memory along with the reality of the situation. This would not be the only separation from Solin. Caia knew what the arrival of a Sapient meant. Years were spent being taught the history of her bloodline, and the small fraction of a possibility that she would be called to give up her life for the life of a Voice, but Caia never believed it. And here she was, with goblins seeking her out to take her life. It wasn't fair that Solin was in danger because of her. He took an arrow to the shoulder because of her. As much as it pained her to think of their current separation, Caia knew Solin would be safer if he returned to their village.

When she finally calmed, Archai asked, "Do you know where Nov'Eit is?"

Clearly the man knew where he was going when he first began carrying her away, but she played along. "Yes," she replied, pointing south.

"Lead the way, and tell me what you already know of the Voices."

With another glance back, Caia nodded. Solin would go searching for help—likely from Dy'Mün. He would be all right. He had to be. Regardless, her stomach soured at their separation.

"The bloodline began on my father's side," she began. "Some hundreds of years—"

"History is no longer important," Archai cut in. "Tell me what you know of your fate."

Caia looked up with a clouded gaze. He stood more than a head taller than her, his broad shoulders only adding to his size and intimidating presence.

"My fate?" she repeated, unsure exactly what he was asking. "My fate now that the Voices are gone? Or my fate if I fail my calling?"

"What is expected of you?"

Caia swallowed hard. Her throat was beginning to itch with thirst. "To keep balance."

"By doing what?"

Words came with great difficulty at the question. For years, she was taught exactly what Archai was asking her about, but her reply simply would not form. "By making sure..." she paused, thinking twice on her words.

"By keeping watch," Archai interjected. "By making sure the wars are kept to a minimum. By aiding the inhabitants of Jaydür with their struggles. Emotional. Physical. Spiritual. You will be a mediator between the people. But you also have a new task—something the first Voices did not do. You are going to walk amongst the people and bring back their belief in the Voices. Darkness overcomes the hearts of people without hope, and you will soon see proof of this. People have changed without the Voices."

With her heart in her throat, Caia kept her focus before them. They were nearing Nov'Eit, a village less than a mile from her own that ran along the Seven Mile River. Blue flags marked Nov'Eit as a fishing village and helped travelers decide whether or not it would be their next best stop. It was a wonder the village flew such a flag—Nov'Eit was known to like its privacy.

Children screamed jovially as they splashed at the edge of the water and their mothers smiled at them. How simple life seemed for these people. No one had expectations of them like she had. No one feared what was to come. No one even *knew* the Voices were dead. And according to what she had just heard, some people in Jaydür no longer even believed in their existence. It wasn't a difficult concept to grasp, considering Caia's personal ties to the deities—and the obvious existence of the Sapient man walking alongside her. But there they were, passing home after home in a village full of people who were too busy to notice an immortal man among them.

"There." Archai gestured to a small mud-patched hut past all the rest.

Caia nodded and made her way to the home. It was a distance away from the majority of the homes, which made her feel slightly uncomfortable. Yes, Archai was a Sapient, but he was also the man who rendered her fiancé unconscious, and now brought her to an isolated place.

"Why are we coming here?" she finally asked. "Dy'Mün knows this place?"

Archai's hand gripped the hilt of the sword at his side. Caia noticed its silver pommel and matching blade, the grip wrapped in a blue leather cloth beneath a gold cross guard. The weapon stood out against the black clothing he wore. "It is one of Dy'Mün's many homes. I chose the most populated of them all, so if Glim'Ruk comes looking, he will have to go through the village to get to you."

Archai's words stung, overwhelming the surprise that Dy'Mün held ownership over multiple homes that she did not know about, let alone one so close to her own village. "You mean we would sacrifice this village for me?"

Archai nodded and held his gaze firmly outside the window above a small table with two chairs. "You sound shocked."

Caia rubbed her arm and looked down at her feet. "No, not shocked. But afraid. These are good people."

"Even good people sometimes have to make sacrifices."

"Making a sacrifice is not the same as *being* the sacrifice. Especially when they don't know they're being put up as one."

Archai's brow wrinkled just slightly as he stared at Caia as if searching her eyes for something. Holding his fixed stare was uncomfortable for her, as she was never the one on the receiving side of a probing gaze. She crossed her arms and asked, "Well, what are we doing now then?"

"Preparing you for Descent," he replied. "You cannot remain in Jaydür."

Caia snapped to attention. "What do you mean? Jaydür is the *world*. How can I not be in the world?"

"There are other worlds," Archai replied. "Worlds that can better hide you than we can. Your very skin reeks of the Voice's blood. We need to remove you to a realm lower than ours—somewhere magic is scarce and difficult to detect."

The room turned into a confusing blur as Caia thought about his words. The Sapient sounded like a madman. "What other worlds?"

Archai gripped her upper arm and gently pulled her down to the seat by the window. "I think it would be best to wait for Dy'Mün before we discuss details." He looked over her head into the village once again.

Caia followed his gaze, her mind reeling. A dirt road led away from the hut, through the village, and down into the woods where Caia and Archai had come from. Solin would be coming from the same road, if he was looking for her. Caia wondered how he was doing. If he had opted to find Dy'Mün the way Archai told him to, the professor would have surely calmed his nerves by now. She really was in no danger; Caia knew that now. But still, that didn't remove the overall fear and confusion of all that was happening.

"Another world," she spoke under her breath. "I suppose I'm not *that* surprised."

"And you shouldn't be," Archai replied monotonously. "You were raised knowing where you come from, were you not? The concept of other realms is nothing unusual."

Caia sucked in a deep breath as Solin came into view on the dirt road. He rode on his horse, Sam, with the injured shoulder slumped and his elbow leaned onto the saddle. Dy'Mün was close behind, looking even more harried than usual. She stood and wiped her damp hands on her leggings. "But Solin," she started as she looked nervously to Archai, "he doesn't know anything of the sort. This won't be easy for him."

Of all the things Archai could have responded with to make her feel better, he chose to shrug instead. That alone made Caia's stomach sink. This man couldn't care less about Solin.

Solin's voice called in the distance, and Caia saw Dy'Mün's mouth moving through his bushy gray beard and mustache, the telltale sign of his familiar muttering. Caia couldn't even smile at the memory of jokes she and Solin had made about the professor, saying he would breathe in so much of his hair while speaking that he would opt to chew on his tufts rather than finish what he had to say.

The door flew open, crashing against the back wall as Solin hurried in. "Caia!" he exclaimed at the sight of her. He ran toward her, but Archai stepped between them. "You have no part in this. You can go."

"What?" Caia said in surprise.

Solin straightened his back and forced his shoulders back with a slight cringe. "I told you, I'm not leaving her."

"Sapient," Dy'Mün cut in with a slight croak in his voice, "I truly hoped we would not be meeting in person."

"I am elated to see you, too, Elder Dy'Mün," Archai retorted with a smile he clearly attempted to restrain. "I've come to understand, though, that your students are completely unaware of why I am here. Seeing as you're all on the verge of being murdered in your sleep, this comes as a surprise to me."

Solin's hands clenched into fists at his side. "We know why you're here. The Voices are dead."

Archai looked down his nose at Solin when Dy'Mün huffed and passed by them into the home. "Sapient," The professor said, "Leave them be. Solin is free to stay for now."

Archai's nose wrinkled into a light snarl as Solin pushed past him into Caia's arms. She rested her head on his unwounded shoulder when he asked, "Are you all right?"

"I'm fine." She looked up, noticing the purple bruise forming on the side of his head from the hilt of Archai's sword. "How are *you?* I'm so sorry. I tried to stay with you, but…"

Solin's eyes flicked to Archai, who still stood by the window with Dy'Mün, his arms crossed, and his face relaxed as if he had no cares in the world. "It's all right. He didn't hurt you, did he?"

Caia shook her head. "Not at all." Her voice lowered and she drew Solin in for a tighter embrace, whispering into his ear, "He's nothing like I imagined a Sapient would be." She looked to Archai again.

"And he's *really* Archai? The man from the books?"

Caia nodded. "So it seems." With a shift of her gaze, she found Professor Dy'Mün tugging at his beard with sad eyes on her. There was something behind the green eyes highlighted by those thick gray eyebrows—as if he held information or understanding of something to come. The old man straightened his back and walked briskly to the other side of the hut where a chest was pushed up against the wall. A tattered gray tapestry was draped over the dark wood, which Dy'Mün grabbed and carelessly tossed onto the ground. "The Voices of Jaydür have been dead for longer than you know," he said, fumbling through the chest. A deep clanking came from whatever he was doing, and Caia was surprised to see her professor pull out clay cups and a kettle. His movements were rapid as he spoke, as if he was having difficulty keeping up with his own thoughts. "We were able to keep it under control, as the southeastern realms did not realize what happened. But now, the sinstarians are out to tip the scales." Dy'Mün made his way to the fireplace where a tube poked out of the wall, the opening clogged with a round cork. "Which they can do if they get hold of any of the young Voices."

"But even without having a Voice in their grasp, Jaydür has weakened," Archai said, watching with curiosity as Dy'Mün popped out the cork. Water splashed out of the tube, filling the kettle Dy'Mün had taken from the chest. Archai went on, though his words were spoken more slowly and broken. "The world is…already suffering as…balance is…interrupted." Archai finally stopped and gestured to the kettle. "I'm sorry, but Dy'Mün, what are you doing?"

"I'm making some damned tea," Dy'Mün replied through his teeth with clear restraint. "What does it look like I'm doing? We cannot leave until the others get here, and we have a long journey ahead of us."

"So sit and relax yourself," Archai suggested.

Ignoring the Sapient, Dy'Mün looked back to Caia and continued. "The new Voices of D'Irdda and Mae'Ehr are older than you and Naoni and spent many years preparing themselves for this day, though we hoped it would never come. But they are still only two of the four. We need all four for true balance."

At the mention of her friend's name, Caia stepped away from Solin with fresh panic. Naoni Arduun was a folcavian descendent of the Voice of Folc and first choice to become the new Voice, even though her elder sister also bore the *eled'hwen,* or, the elven light. When Dy'Mün first disclosed their ancestry some years back, Naoni's sister grew frightened and disappeared the next night.

"Where is Naoni, anyway?" Caia asked. "Is she safe?"

Dy'Mün nodded, moving the kettle to the fireplace, where he conjured an orange spark from his palm to start a fire in the firebox. He so rarely used magic that Caia was always astonished to see it. "She is making her way here with your father. They're gathering a few essentials to bring while I rode here ahead of them. Naoni has not drawn the eyes of Glim'Ruk the way you have, so she is not being hunted. I'm not even entirely sure *why* he caught sight of you in the first place. Regardless, we have a short time to discuss our plan. Mae'Ehr and D'Irdda cannot hold the realms together themselves, so they are in hiding while we Elders are working to keep what balance we can. If you and Naoni do not unite with your sister Voices, all of Jaydür will be a wasteland."

A breath of relief flowed from Caia's lips at the thought of Naoni's safety. Solin stepped up beside her and took her hand in his before asking, "So what's the plan, then?"

Archai's attention was quickly on her hand in Solin's. There was a glimmer of something in his eyes—something she didn't quite expect. He seemed threatened.

"The first step is to lessen the load," Archai replied, snapping his gaze up to meet Solin's. "The boy remains with Caia's father as we move forward." His words came cold and swift, like a winter's gust blowing out a small warm fire.

Solin cast glances at Archai and Dy'Mün, as if expecting the professor to counter the Sapient's words. "What is he saying?" he asked Dy'Mün. "I'm staying with Caia. Tell him I'm staying."

Dy'Mün turned back to the chest and took a small tin canister from which he removed five thick cuts of what Caia recognized as *dafne* roots. "We have a long way to travel, and I am fine with you accompanying her for the next few days, but where Caia is going afterwards, you cannot follow."

"The more who follow, the more I have to split my attention," Archai snapped. "I will not waste my energy on a mere boy."

Solin dropped his gaze to Caia, then to the floor with a furrowed brow. Caia could tell he had a million things he could say, but like her, he abhorred confrontation. Even more than that, what could possibly be said to sway a Sapient?

Caia took Solin's hand and gave it a squeeze. After so many years together, Solin knew how much she respected and loved him. No Sapient would change that.

Archai let out a snort of dismissive laughter at her motion just as screams rang from the distance. Caia ran to the window to find her father, Atar, and Naoni coming from the path leading to the home. On the other side of the village, a gray throng of sinstarians came upon them like a storm.

"Dy'Mün!" Naoni called. Her sword was in her hand, but she was not foolish enough to think she could take on a horde by herself. She leapt off her horse and burst through the door with Caia's father.

Atar slid the wooden crossbar across the door and turned to the professor. "Do you have weapons here?"

Dy'Mün moved to a door Caia hadn't noticed; it was the same color as the walls of the hut. Behind the door was a shallow closet hiding a slew of weapons, ranging from swords to spears and arrows. "They are sinstarians?" he asked Atar while handing him a sword.

"Yes. There may be goblins, but we did not stop to look. They crested the hill just as we entered Nov'Eit." Concern was clear in his expression, and fear shone bright in his eyes. "There are many of them, Dy'Mün."

Screams rang from the village amid the snarls and shrieks of the sinstarians. Caia stepped back and clutched her chest, terror stabbing at her core like a cold dagger. All those people…

Dy'Mün looked to Archai and replied to Atar. "The young Voices will make it." He handed a short sword to Solin. "We have a Sapient with us."

"By the Highest," Atar said softly, his eyes locked on Archai. His eyebrows raised as he lifted a hand to his mouth in shock just before a thud sounded against the door and everyone turned to face it. The air in the home grew heavy and Caia wondered for a second if she was dreaming. She squeezed her eyes tight, hoping she would wake from the moment and realize it was all a nightmare.

Instead, the windows behind them crashed in, and the group formed a circle, facing every side of the hut. Caia looked to Solin, who returned a despairing gaze.

"We'll be all right, Caia," he said with an attempted half-smile. "I love you."

A huff of frustration left Archai as he wielded his sword and made for the doorway. The blade spun in his hand, cutting the air with a whistle. The young elves exchanged glances.

As the goblins tore through the door, Archai swung his sword, spilling the bellies of three creatures at once, then he kicked down what was left of the splintered wood. "Come," he called.

Naoni sent an ear-to-ear grin to Caia, who was fixated on the gore in front of them with wide eyes.

Solin grabbed their hands and they all hurried after Archai. When they exited the home, they were met with something none of them could have fully anticipated: dead bodies mottled the village ground in every direction, as far as eyes could see. Caia's gaze followed the running rivers of red, and she stepped back with a hand to her mouth as the muddied blood of an innocent squelched beneath her boots. They were all slaughtered like sheep, simply to get to her.

Her lungs heaved for breath as she recognized the faces of those she'd known all her life. Bowi, the blacksmith; Gëniv, the herbalist; beneath a toppled feed wagon were the bodies of the Nornin twins—not yet six years old—face down in the mud.

A battalion of sinstarians intertwined with goblins came at them from all directions but the east, weapons and bindings at the ready. They must have planned on taking the girls alive—Caia would not allow that. With tears in her eyes and her heart all but torn, Caia strung an arrow and took aim.

Archai turned at her side and looked down at her with curious eyes.

War cries echoed through the village as the enemy made for the small group. Caia took one long breath to regain control of her anger before releasing an arrow. She would hit her target, no doubt. The feathers of the arrow brushed past her cheek as it sliced the air and plunged into a sinstarian's heart. After that, the faces were all a blur as she impaled goblin after sinstarian, sinstarian after goblin.

Behind her, Solin joined Naoni, who spun and sliced at will. His movements were short and fast in comparison to the folcavian's fluid, dance-like motions and together, they staved off a wall of goblins.

Archai leapt into the air as massive white wings erupted and spread from his back. He was quickly made a fresh target for archers, but with every swing of his sword or gesture of his hand, a blue and white light discharged from him and annihilated arrows and attackers alike.

The elves gaped in wonder at the Sapient but didn't slow their attack.

Dy'Mün and Atar were side by side, armed with staff and sword, slaughtering any creatures close enough for a face-to-face kill.

Death was everywhere and still coming. The battalion drew so near that every arrow Caia launched, she retrieved from the bodies and used again. Suddenly her weapon was wrenched from her hand and a sinstarian grabbed her from behind, dragging her away into the multitudes. She screamed against the gray bloodstained hand of the monster that took her, knowing that none would hear her cries within the howls of war. Dozens of pairs of snake-like eyes looked down at her from long, gray faces.

"Do not kill her! We need her alive!" a mingling of voices cried out amid cackling.

One creature threw her to the ground and bound her hands at the wrists with metal bindings and chains. She fought against them until her arms and legs burned from the effort when a blinding white light shone through the wall of her attackers. The laughter turned to high-pitched shrieks and bellows through the momentary blindness. Caia felt the earth leave from beneath her, but she saw nothing beyond a wall of white.

The smell of rain filled her nostrils and made her skin tingle, but she didn't know what was happening or who lifted her. She twisted and squirmed fearfully against the hold.

"Stay still," Archai demanded. "Your sight will return in a few moments. I am sorry, but I had no choice."

A breath of relief escaped Caia's lips as wind beat against her face and she asked, "Are we flying?"

"Yes, we are."

Caia greatly wished she could see and hoped her sight would come back before they landed. She knew of no one who wouldn't relish the opportunity to fly, and there she was, face against the wind. It was not long, though, before the wind stopped, and her feet were dropped to unmoving ground. Archai took her elbow and led her on.

"You wait here," he said, lowering her down to sit against a tree. "No one will see you if you stay put. I will find the Voice of Folc and bring her as well."

Caia nodded in agreement, though she felt it strange that she and Naoni had already taken on the titles of the Voices. She tried to blink away the seemingly perpetual light. A slight sense of fear twinged in her chest at the thought that whatever happened to her sight would not be fixable. *But Archai said it would fade.*

Archai. She thought about him for a moment while she yanked at the chains around her wrists. She would have never thought opportunity would arise to meet a Sapient, even with her knowledge of her bloodline. But there she was, her life in the hands of an immortal being. Part of her was utterly thrilled with every interaction with him. How could she not be? He was a *Sapient.*

A cold wind stirred through the trees, and Caia perked her ears attentively, the chains clinking with her every move. There were no clashing blades or cries, but silence in its stead. Was it the silence of victory or defeat? Sadness consumed her once again as the faces of those lost flashed before her mind's eye.

Finally, and to Caia's relief, she heard horses in the distance. From the sound of it, there were four, which gave her the hope that all survived—unless they were riders of the enemy. Thinking twice on rising from behind the tree, Caia remained low and listened closely, attempting to pick up on any voices.

The horses stopped nearby.

"Where is she?" Solin's voice rang out. He'd never sounded so surly, but hearing him was a relief, regardless.

"Here," she replied, using the tree beside her as support to stand. Without her sight and with her wrists still chained together, her balance was off.

Solin hurried to his fiancée and embraced her. "Are you all right? They got you? Did they hurt you?" he asked, shaking the chains in a panic. Her eyes looked toward him, but she couldn't tell if she was looking at him. It was as if she couldn't focus. "How do we get these off? What's happened to your eyes?"

"It'll fade," the voice of Archai suddenly spoke from the left.

Solin turned to face the Sapient. "What is it?" The stress in his voice was clear.

"It is a light spell. I had little choice," Archai went on. Rock crunched beneath footsteps as he neared. "Move," he ordered Solin. Caia blushed at the sensation of Archai's hands as he held her firmly by the sides of her face. "I'm not going to hurt you," he assured, obviously noticing her discomfort.

Caia tried offering a smile. "Elves are not accustomed to such closeness. We believe it improper unless coming from a loved one—especially a touch of the face."

"Right," Archai replied shortly. Caia could sense the judgment in his tone. "Do not blink," he directed.

Entirely uncertain of what was supposed to happen, she gasped at the sudden air that crossed her left eye. Archai's breath came stronger and she couldn't help but do what he bid her not to. Her eyes fluttered wildly at the sensation. With her face still in one of his hands, his other one held the eye open.

The sensation was uncomfortable, and Caia grasped and pulled at Archai's hands, trying to free herself.

"What is he doing?" Solin asked from the side.

To Caia's surprise, sight in that one eye cleared as if a fog were lifted from it. She blinked in wonder when she was able to see Archai's teal gaze. Without another word, he held her other eye open and did the same until both eyes were clear of the blinding light.

"That was amazing. Thank you," Caia said as Archai slid his sword from its scabbard and cut through the metal bindings, showing just how unnatural even the power inside his blade was. He pulled down his hood, revealing hair as silver as the sword in his hand. With an arrogant grin, he bowed slightly.

"You're welcome."

"Now, we are all here," Professor Dy'Mün said, looking around. "No one is injured beyond a night's healing? Good. Archai, you've arrived just in time. Our initial plan to meet you in Sanctuary would not have panned out."

Archai nodded, closely examining the new Voices

once again. "I sensed trouble, so I came out to find Caia."

"Yes, though we still need to get the girls to Sanctuary," Dy'Mün confirmed.

Archai's eyes lighted upon Caia's wrist, and he lifted her hand in his to look closer.

"What is it?" Naoni asked, breaking a heavy silence that came with Archai's focus. Caia had nearly forgotten she was there.

"Right," Archai replied absent-mindedly, ignoring Naoni's question. He faced Dy'Mün. "Elder, I give you leave of the Voices. I can handle them from here. We'll be off to Sanctuary."

Atar exchanged glances with Dy'Mün. "Are we leaving the girls?" he asked in something of a panic.

Dy'Mün knocked his staff on the ground, sending up a puff of dirt. "Archai, your reputation with women precedes you. Focus on the problem at hand and not the view! These are not like your pathetic maidens coming to you for companionship. Have I made myself clear?"

Atar swallowed hard and took in a deep breath. "What are you saying, Dy'Mün?"

Archai looked sidelong at the old man, seemingly more humored than annoyed at the response. "Dy'Mün, I know exactly what is at risk here. I am simply thinking of their safety," he offered, though Caia saw no truth in his eyes.

"I know what you are thinking," Dy'Mün said,

then spit at Archai's feet. "'Leave of the girls,'" he muttered. "How daft do you think I am?"

Atar rubbed a hand down the side of his smooth face. His concerns likely matched Caia's own—what kind of man were she and Naoni being entrusted to?

Professor Dy'Mün looked to the east. "We will take them to my cottage near the foot of the mountain for the night. It is hidden well enough from sight, and there are soldiers nearby, which will be advantageous."

"Why are there soldiers?" Naoni asked.

"And how many cottages do you have?" Caia added.

"I have many places I call home. As an Elder, I must have a place to rest no matter where I am in Jaydür," he explained. "As for why there are soldiers, well, a fortress belonging to Prince Leithen is near there," he replied.

Naoni turned to Caia with cocked brows and a mischievous smile cracking her plump lips. "The Prince? Oh my."

Dy'Mün puffed, clearly agitated by Naoni's response. "I do not know whether or not the prince is there himself, but it does not matter. His soldiers are present year-round. Come, we must hurry before it is too dark to make camp," he said. "It would be wiser if we not stay the night so close to the battleground."

"I agree," Archai added, gesturing toward the elf prince's lands. "Let us go, then."

The group followed after him and Caia looked up at her father, who gave her shoulder a squeeze. "You gave us quite a scare when we lost sight of you," Atar whispered.

"I'm sorry," she replied with a soft smile as she shifted her quiver around her waist. She wondered, briefly, what happened to her bow. Last she saw it, the horde dragged her away just after snatching the weapon. The memory of the gray hands and faces of sinstarians nauseated her.

"Don't blame yourself. I'm just glad you're safe." He paused and watched the Sapient walk alongside Dy'Mün. "And Caia? Please be careful. And wise."

Caia smiled as he stepped forward to join the men in the front, then turned to Naoni, who nudged her.

"Quite the revelation with the Sapient, hm?" Naoni whispered. "With a sullied reputation for women, I've not yet decided whether to be offended by his brash attentions or to be charmed."

Atar looked over his shoulder with a glower. "Your mind should be on more important things," he snapped. "And more honest men."

"Where's the fun in that?" she whispered, then giggled the troublesome giggle she was known for.

Caia laughed as she followed the group. One by one, they each found a horse and Caia quickly realized she was the only one lacking. Solin came up on, Sam, his own horse, and offered Caia his hand to ride with him. She smiled and squeezed onto the saddle behind him, tossing a glance back to Nov'Eit. The life she'd led was gone, along with the people who'd filled it. Whatever smile touched her face fled quickly, replaced by a controlled grimace—nothing more than a mask that covered the twisting agony that writhed within her and darkened her spirits.

Night came quickly, giving the group little time to distance themselves from what was left of Nov'Eit. Using the Seven Mile River as a guide, they continued on well into the night before finally settling down in a deep ravine. With the height of the trees on each side, limited smoke would be detected from a campfire. The group remained by the river for some time to wash their blood-stained hands and clothes. Caia finished and started toward the camp when Solin stopped her.

"I don't want you to be alone with him," he said, gesturing toward Archai at the camp.

Caia followed his eyes and frowned. "Solin, he can't be avoided. He's my guardian now."

"You heard what Dy'Mün said. Archai is known for things we should not accept. The way he looks at you and Naoni—it worries me."

"Solin," Naoni called. "Can I have your washing stone? Mine's chipped."

Solin passed it over as Caia gave his other hand a squeeze. "Don't worry, Solin. Of all people, you know best that I can handle myself." With as soft a smile as she could manage, Caia leaned in and kissed Solin on the cheek, then made her way to the camp where Archai sharpened his sword beside the fire. His attention flicked to her as she sat across from him, then went back to his blade. With the rest of the group still at the river, it seemed the opportune moment for Caia to speak what she had on her mind.

"Thank you," she said over the crackling of the fire. "For saving my life. And for what you did with my eyes."

Archai looked up through his lashes but said nothing.

Caia knit her brows together, unsure of what his silence meant, but continued on. "I wasn't sure I was going to make it. If not for you, my life would surely be lost."

A splash came from the river, momentarily distracting Caia.

"It's all right," Archai finally replied, his voice deep and thick. "You'll have the rest of eternity to make it up to me."

Caia frowned, not certain she understood what he meant by that.

"Don't mind him," said Dy'Mün as he came up from the side. "In all the centuries I've known him, he has not changed."

"All of eternity?" Caia repeated.

Dy'Mün frowned at the girl. "Are you so unaware

of your fate? Yes," he said. "As a Voice, you will be like Archai—one of the Terehn."

Solin and Naoni arrived with Atar not far behind. Wonder brightened up Naoni's orange-toned eyes. "So they're real," she said, interrupting the conversation as she took a seat beside Caia.

Archai's attention fell on the brunette. "Am I not sitting here before you? Are you telling me you doubted our existence?"

"I think, in a way, everyone has," Solin replied. "If the Terehn are never seen, how are we to truly accept their being?"

With that, Archai pulled a knee against his chest and leaned forward with interest. "Tell me, do you doubt the existence of the Highest Power?"

Solin frowned. "Well, no, but—"

"No, you don't. But rather, you give it power over you and your lives. This unseen spirit has earned your respect and ever-listening ears. But one of the Terehn walks beside you, sits beside you, and even lights the fire that makes you warm, and still you doubt our existence. On top of all that, you refuse to take my advice and are still here, yapping at my heels."

"Archai," Dy'Mün barked, watching as Caia and Solin exchanged wordless glances. "You must be more understanding. Immortals are easy to doubt. Even though elves live hundreds of years, they can, in fact, die. The minds of those whose life is limited cannot comprehend the vastness of forever, let alone the soldiers of forever."

"How long have you lived?" Atar asked Archai. The light of the flame flickered across his pale face.

The man didn't bother looking up at him as he replied, "I wish I knew."

Caia, Solin, Naoni, and Atar responded with wide eyes and slack jaws.

"How do you not know?" Naoni asked in a tone of unimpressed disbelief.

Dy'Mün answered, "It is impossible to know for sure. Archai was present at the inauguration of the original Voices."

"And all this time," Archai chuckled, looking up at the girls, "you did not even know I existed."

"You say we are to become one of the Terehn," Caia continued. "How can one simply become an immortal?"

Dy'Mün leaned toward the fire, holding his gray beard away from the flames with one hand and using the other to light his pipe as he replied. "No one completely understands the way any of it truly happens. It is in the hands of the Highest Power." He paused for a moment in thought. "Also, you are but the second generation of Voices. Never have we gone through this before. What happens to you will be just as new to us."

"You could have kept that to yourself," Naoni snipped. "As if nervousness about all of this was not devouring my spirits enough, you have to go and tell us you're just as oblivious."

Caia sent her friend a scolding look. Naoni did have the tendency to peel one's flesh with her opinions. She replied with an innocent "what have I done" expression in response.

"And what have you been doing all of these ages?" Atar asked. Caia was pleased with his question. A turn in conversation was due before anyone grew more distressed with thoughts of what was to come.

Archai, though, was not pleased and slid his sword into its scabbard before turning all of his attention to the group. "I guarded the Voices," he said shortly, as if hoping to end all of the questions. His tone was that of a high person speaking to an illiterate one, but as soon as he realized what he'd said, he dropped his eyes to the ground and softened his tone. "It is what earned me the name 'Guardian,' after all."

A silence fell over the group. As if aware of their thoughts, Archai rose to his feet, took his sword and made his way to the river. "You must rest. I will keep watch."

As he disappeared into the darkness of the wood, Caia and the others were left facing one another, each uncertain of what to say next.

It was Solin who asked the next question aloud. His eyes focused on a fading ember that jumped from the fire as he whispered, "Can we trust him?"

Dy'Mün took a puff from his pipe and leaned

back against a large rock. "Archai may be arrogant, but I would trust him with any of you, no matter what mistakes were made in the past with the Voices."

"Should we not fear another mistake?" Solin went on, looking up. "Is there no one else we can call on for help?"

Caia wanted to shush him but at the same time, she respected Dy'Mün's opinion on any matter and was curious to hear his response. These were things she needed to know, as uncomfortable as they were to speak of.

"The man has lived for thousands of years," the wizard reminded them. "Learning from mistakes is one thing Sapients never fail to do."

"The fact that they're gone…that's a pretty significant mistake," Naoni muttered.

Caia watched Solin's reaction to the response and took his hand before he could burst out with another uncomfortable question. She looked up at him with a weak, fabricated smile. She wanted desperately to hide the feelings of uncertainty and fear that grappled with her heart, but there was one fear that she had to confront that was hurting her most. Without turning her eyes from Solin, she asked in a quiet voice, "What is to happen to Solin when I become a Voice?"

Four pairs of eyes quickly rose to Caia as all were caught off guard by the question. The promise held between Caia and Solin was so concrete that none but Dy'Mün thought to suggest any change.

The fire hissed as a breeze passed through it in the silence.

"He'll live on," the wizard replied, just loud enough to be heard over the flames. "I have no doubt he will find a wife and settle down."

Solin's eyes remained frozen on Caia. After a moment, his hand squeezed hers while he cleared his throat. Rising to his feet, Caia gripped his hand more intensely.

"Solin," she started.

"Caia, it's fine. I'll come back." And with that, Solin wandered into the forest opposite Archai. Caia stood and watched him leave the clearing.

"Leave him," Dy'Mün suggested. "He's coming to terms with your fate. Better he gets it out now. Sit down, Caia."

With eyes on the dark woods, she slowly took her seat beside the fire. Naoni grabbed a stone and hurled it into the flame, her jaw set and eyes bright. "Who does he think he is?" she snapped. "As if he's the only one whose life is changing."

Caia passed a sidelong glance at Naoni and noticed movement in the trees. It was Archai, guarding the area. With eyes locked on him, she jumped to her feet.

"Hey," she called after him.

With a quick glance over his shoulder, his pace slowed but his attention remained on the forest.

She quickened her own steps until she was just

beside him, craning her neck to meet his eyes. "I need to know something."

"Are you bound to him? Ceremonially," he replied, catching Caia off guard.

"What? No, I'm not."

He looked down at her with cocked brows. "Good. Then the sooner you cut him off, the better."

Caia pressed her lips into a tight line. That's exactly what Dy'Mün had told her. "As a Voice, I'm going to be powerful, am I not? Surely there will be a way to still be with him."

"These relationships you Jaydürians have are useless. Live together, die while the other continues living and thinking about what you should have done before either of you died in the first place."

"It wouldn't be that way; not with Solin. He's my—"

Archai spun on his heel. "Your 'twin soul?' Your 'better half?' Or my favorite, your 'soul mate?'"

This man was irritating Caia all the more. "Yes," she snapped. "To all of the above."

Archai snorted.

"What, like you've never been in love?" she asked.

There was a momentary pause, filled only with the sounds of brush beneath their feet, before Archai replied, "No. I have not."

The frankness of his answer froze Caia in her response. "Really?"

"I've never had reason to go looking for it, nor have I had the time. The majority of my days in Jaydür were spent in the Temple of Pandhea, and whatever women I have ever come to know did not come to me for *love*."

His response caught Caia off guard, and she opened her mouth slightly to respond, yet no words came. A snake slithered from their pathway into a pile of fallen leaves, drawing Caia's attention as she walked. Her boot caught on an unearthed root and she stumbled, only to be caught and steadied by Archai's hand on her elbow. She looked up to him and swallowed hard as she quietly said, "Thank you."

Their gazes locked on to each other, both full to the brim of things needing to be said. Caia wanted to fight for Solin to remain at her side, but Archai seemed to sense it.

"I ask for the better good," he said, more softly. "For *your* good and the good of all of Jaydür. Your attention will need to be on the survival of a planet and the people who inhabit it. You will not have freedom to chase after time spent with the man you love."

Caia looked past Archai at a dying tree, unwilling to look him in the eyes as he spoke the blatant truth.

"You do not realize it now, but when you have all of eternity, lifetimes in this world pass you by. But *he* will feel it," Archai explained, motioning to the camp. "He will feel every moment not spent together, and he will resent you for it."

A tear threatened to fall down Caia's cheek and she blinked it away. She could see it all in her mind— Solin, lonely and unhappy while waiting for her to show up every day. She could imagine the change of heart he'd surely have while all the needs of Jaydür came before him. Archai was right; with time, Solin would resent her. While a chance at life with someone else willing and able to bear him heirs was within reach, she had to help him see and take it. Her heart ached at the thought of him in the loving arms of another woman.

"Your pain will be short-lived," Archai said, as if sensing her heartbreak. "The more you focus on being a Voice, the less your mind will wander to things of the heart. Memories will remain, of course, but would you not rather leave your beloved on a positive note than on one of uncertainty?"

"I understand," she quickly said.

Archai nodded slowly, then stepped past her to continue his scouting. "I have one more thing I would like to discuss with you."

Caia hurried to keep up with him. "All right."

"You cried when you saw all those villagers lying dead in Nov'Eit," he said. "Why?"

The question seemed entirely ridiculous. "They were people of my village," Caia replied, shocked to be asked such a thing. "I've known them all my life."

"And?"

"And their innocent blood was spilled."

"And?"

"And it was spilled to get to *me*. How can you ask such cold, unfeeling questions?" she countered.

"*Cold and unfeeling* are traits you gain over time—survival mechanisms that you will need to learn. I bring you nothing but the facts that you will have to accept and things you will need to grow accustomed to. Those you love will die, and you will be left with me. We will need to learn to get along but first, you must learn to trust me and take my word as it is."

Caia shook her head, bothered by the notion of so much loss. Where a lifetime had seemed long before, an eternity sounded unendurable. "It is not that I do not trust you," she admitted, fumbling with the arrows in her quiver.

"Then you do?"

"I do because Dy'Mün claims you're worthy of it. That does not mean I like you."

The space between the two had shrunk to mere inches, and Archai moved a lock of hair away from Caia's eyes with a half-smile. "You will learn to."

Caia shook her head but refused to drop her gaze from the Sapient. He had to know his impertinence did not faze her. She would stand her ground.

"Caia," Solin's voice called from the direction she'd just come.

She stepped away from Archai. "I would not wait

too earnestly for that," she replied, then joined Solin.

As the pair returned to the campsite, the rest of the group chatted by the fire while Archai remained in the woods. Dy'Mün sighed as he spotted the two returning in the distance. "You must know, Caia, how difficult it is for us to rest when you're off wandering the woods in the dark."

"Honestly," Naoni added. "I'm sorry to see you two lovebirds in the midst of emotional upheaval, but I have a million and one questions about my fate, and believe it or not, I'm fond of getting answers and keeping my head."

Solin looked to Caia. "They're right. You've got to stay nearby. For your own sake."

"Then you need to stay with me," she quietly replied, stopping him before they were in full listening distance of the group. "You worry me when you walk away without a word. We've known each other our entire lives, and you've never left me with a cloud above my head."

"I'm sorry," he replied. "A lot of change is coming. I needed to settle my nerves."

Caia nodded in understanding, then took Solin's hand. His lack of response to her touch was a blow to her gut, but when he turned and walked away, Caia's world spun.

"*Anyway*," Naoni called out loud enough for everyone to hear. "We've traveled enough with no answers and no idea where we are going or what has happened. All I know is that Glim'Ruk killed the Voices, and we're replacing them. We're going to Sanctuary, but why? And why don't we just get rid of him? Would that not solve the problem?"

"Because we do not know where he is hiding. He has made himself scarce since he's been found out. We are going to Sanctuary because you are not safe here," Dy'Mün replied.

Caia met his eyes with a glassy stare as she sat beside Naoni. Solin took his bedroll and sat on it, some feet away from the rest of the party.

Dy'Mün went on, averting his gaze from both Caia and Solin. "You do not have the capability of protecting yourself in Jaydür, so we are sending you someplace where you cannot be detected. It is a world where magic is so disbelieved that your truth would be smothered by their skepticism."

Naoni lifted a slender hand to her lips. "Outside of Jaydür? You're speaking about another world?"

Dy'Mün nodded.

Naoni looked to Caia as if expecting shock. When Caia did not react, Naoni straightened her back and frowned. "You knew?"

"I only learned of this today," Caia replied monotonously, fumbling with her hands. Solin was just within sight, but simply looking at him made her heart ache. "I don't have all the facts, by any means."

Naoni pursed her lips in displeasure. "So what *do* we know? How does it work?"

Dy'Mün watched Caia, and his face grew soft. "Where we are heading, there is a mirror," he began, focusing his attention on the fire. "When you pass through the mirror, you will be transported to another world, called *Terra*, where you will enter as a human. You will have limited memories until we've deemed you safe to regain them."

"As humans?" Caia asked. "But what about our lives here?"

Archai stepped out of the woods and approached the campsite. The leather gauntlets on his arms cracked and stretched as he flexed his hands. "Your memories will be absorbed into a gryphon's eye— yours in one, and Naoni's in another. I will come to you at a predetermined date and bring you home."

"And what if we don't want this fate?" Caia asked, her voice croaking slightly.

The party was silent for a moment and Caia bore her gaze into the fire, watching the flames lick the air as if reaching to the skies for oxygen—a sensation Caia felt in that moment herself.

Archai's voice was thick with frustration and disgust as he replied. "Then all of Jaydür and its inhabitants will wither and die over the course of a generation."

Caia nodded, finally understanding the full scope of her situation; as she feared, there was no option in these circumstances. For someone who would be so powerful, Caia had never felt so feeble.

The flames in the fire flickered in a breeze that blew over the camp. Caia watched in thoughtful silence as darkness crawled over them and the stars shone in the sky like fragments of glass in a black sea. Archai's words would surely haunt her this night.

Chapter Two
Constant State of Learning

The barrier that protected the elvish lands for centuries was gone. Placed by the Voices during the first war between elves and man, it made sense that it self-destructed with their deaths. According to Dy'Mün, it had been gone for some years.

The wizard muttered something in a language no one recognized as they passed out of the woods and into the Free Fields. Though no one understood, no one bothered asking what he was saying either. The morning had been cold, and the hours on horseback, long. Tension between Caia and Solin was still strong, the constant anxiety over the hours of the night causing nausea for her. It didn't help that Archai had Caia ride with him rather than Solin, and Solin didn't argue the request.

Dy'Mün stopped the party when the road before them became straight, heading right into the horizon. He took in a deep breath with a slight smile. "There's nothing quite like the open road. I have a lifetime of memories with this horizon in sight." He rummaged through his satchel and retrieved three vials the size of Caia's index finger. He motioned for everyone to move in closer, then he offered one vial to Atar and another to Archai. "Each of you drink half. This is an elixir that will allow us to travel over a hundred miles within seconds, cutting our travel time extensively. Normally, it would take us nine days to make it to Sanctuary. This will take us more than halfway."

Archai held the vial in front of Caia and studied it with interest. "Is this...faery dust?" he asked with a wrinkled brow. His deep timbre reverberated from his chest into her back. She leaned in toward the quiver she held in front of her in the hopes of creating more space between herself and Archai.

"It is," Dy'Mün replied, his beard shaking as he chewed on his lip. "In the form of a draft for easier consumption."

Archai pressed his lips together tightly and took a deep breath. "And you feel this is wise to give to—" he gestured to the others, "them?" His tone was critical and somewhat demeaning.

"Hey," Naoni cut in. "You think we can't handle it?"

Archai looked sidelong to the brunette. "My lady, this is a drug. And it is a potent one at that. If you do not keep your eyes forward and your focus strong, you could end up in the Screaming Crags. Not only that, but I doubt your stomach is strong enough. What is waiting for you at the end of the ride is not pleasant."

"And still, we have no better option," Dy'Mün replied. "It's this, magic, or your form of travel. Neither of which have better risks." He drank half a vial and leaned on his horse to hand it to Naoni, who pursed her lips in thought before drinking what was left. Atar did the same, then handed his vial to Solin.

"I suppose I'll be joining you in this experience, then," Archai muttered before downing half the vial, then offering it to Caia. "If only for the sake of keeping the Voices on the right path."

Caia drank the last half, then eyed the road before them. She wondered how long it would take to feel the effects.

Dy'Mün then took what looked like small truffles out of his satchel and fed one to every horse.

"Is that the same thing?" Solin asked after finishing the second half of Atar's.

Dy'Mün nodded. "There is no need to worry. Elven horses are better equipped for this than most people are. They will stay true to the path. Now, everyone, listen. The air around you will vibrate and grow cold. When I give the word, we begin at a walking pace. Listen well for my voice, and when I say 'now,' break into a run," Dy'Mün instructed. "Above all else, *do not* turn your heads."

"Do not turn your eyes either," Archai added. "Focus on the way before you."

"Take deep breaths," Dy'Mün went on.

Caia's sight blurred as she inhaled, then refocused as she exhaled. A strange sensation tingled in her fingertips, then her elbows. Within seconds, her hips, knees, and ankles all tingled as every joint in her body turned warm.

"Start walking forward," Dy'Mün instructed, and the group moved forward with caution.

A breeze blew and Caia noticed something; the air looked like waves of paint on a canvas in hues of blue and purple.

"Eyes forward!" Dy'Mün said. "Whatever you do, do *not* look at anything around you, as tempting as it may be."

Caia could see Naoni and her horse in her peripheral vision immediately left of her, while Solin and her father were to her right.

"Now, run!" Dy'Mün called out, and everyone urged their horses forward.

The air pulled at Caia, screaming around her like a swirling wind funnel. All around her, the view blurred into streaks of light and colors. Her eyes fought against the urge to look to her side to see what everyone else was experiencing. She heard no sounds from the others amid the wailing rush of wind around them. Air surged against her face, forcing it to the side, and Caia cried out as she put all of her strength into resisting.

A slight growl came from the right, sounding like

thunder in the distance before it grew to an aggressive snarl. A gray-skinned, dog-like snout came through the streaks of light, inches away from Caia's face. Caia twisted in the saddle and lifted her arm to protect herself when a sudden gust of air knocked her off.

Caia grunted as her body slammed hard into the ground, spraying grass and dirt high into the air. She rolled over several dozen feet before she physically stopped, though her head felt like it was still spinning. Pain snaked through her arm and when Caia fluttered her eyes opened, she realized she was lying with half her face in mud. Steady rain fell, forcing her to blink rapidly against the mist. Her arm beneath her throbbed as she rolled onto her other arm, pushing herself onto her knees, which squelched in mud. She trembled with the effort.

With some difficulty, Caia lifted her eyes to the scene around her. Fields of yellow grass spread in all directions, ending in a flat gray horizon all around. There were no signs as to where she was.

"Curse it all," she whispered to herself, trying to think back on what caused her to fall from Archai's horse. "What happened?"

"You turned your head," a voice spoke from behind.

Caia spun around in surprise and lost her balance, falling to her bottom. She groaned from pain at the sudden weight on her injured arm she tried catching herself with, yet she was relieved at the sight of

Archai, sitting casually in the grass a few feet away. His eyes were closed as his face lifted toward the drab sky.

"Not on purpose," she replied, checking the arrows in her quiver. At a glance, three looked broken. "Something came at me. I'm not sure what it was. You didn't see it?"

Archai's brow furrowed, but his eyes remained closed. "What did it look like?"

Caia licked her teeth as she thought; the taste of blood was bitter on her tongue. She must have bitten herself in the fall. "I'm not entirely sure. It was something dog-like, but much bigger. It was gray, and instead of fur on its face, it had skin."

At that, Archai dropped his gaze to the ground. "That sounds like a shadow hound."

"Shadow hound?" Caia repeated. "I've never heard of such a thing."

"As it should be. Voices have no business dabbling in the Blacker Shadows. You are of the light."

Caia swallowed and wrinkled her nose in disgust at the coppery taste. "I did not dabble in the Blacker Shadows. I did as Dy'Mün instructed, even keeping my eyes forward. I only turned when this *thing* tried to bite the nose off my face." She looked at her arm and noticed discoloration and swelling around her wrist. "Wonderful. I think I've broken something," she said, flinching.

Archai stood up and stepped toward Caia. Taking her wrist in his hand, he lightly squeezed and attempted to bend her hand. She hissed in pain.

"You're right," he replied. "Hold it steady until we find a thick enough stick. We can make a splint with wood and reeds."

Caia nodded and with Archai's help, she stood up. Putting weight on her feet made her realize just how bad the fall really was; she felt like she was run over by a horse and wagon.

"Now," he went on, "if you truly did see a shadow hound, then the eled'hwen within you is stronger than we thought. A Voice can reach into the unknown at will, but seeping into the Blacker Shadows without actually trying to tap into it is a problem. We will have to address this—later. For now, we must get you back with the others."

Caia looked at the empty fields around them as rain pitter-pattered on the tall grass. "And how do we go about that?"

Archai started toward the east. "We walk. We're not all that far from where they are. We'll rest tonight, walk a few more hours in the morning, then we'll fly."

It sounded like quite a distance to Caia. She rubbed her arm with her good hand. "By the Highest, I'm so sorry," she said. "I didn't mean to get lost."

"You do not apologize. You are a Voice. Until you are away from this realm, you are in a constant state of learning. Nothing is all that bad, as long as you're not dead."

Caia nodded, though the sting of regret remained.

Archai walked through the rain with little to no sign of being affected by it. He stood as straight as ever, and his steps were high and long. He didn't speak, but Caia had a million questions on her mind now that they were alone. As much as her heart was with Solin, she found she lacked confidence to ask the questions she wanted answered most for fear of hurting his feelings.

"Archai," she began as she took larger steps until her gait was in sync with his. "Can I ask you something?"

"Of course," he replied.

His willingness to listen to her made Caia flood with excitement. She looked up at him with a smile and went on. "How long have the Voices been gone?" Of the bits and pieces of information Dy'Mün had shared, the death of the Voices was something he did not elaborate on. She wondered if he was simply not keen on discussing darker details or if he really did not know as much as she thought.

"Fifty-three years," Archai replied.

"Fifty-three years?" Caia gasped. "I thought it only happened recently."

"Fifty-three years to the day, in fact. The Voice of Mae'Ehr was the first discovered, in a ditch in the Wood Ruins southeast of here. What she was doing in the Everdark Forest, I could not tell you. That girl was always wandering Jaydür without a touch of concern for her own safety. The other Voices' deaths were discovered within days."

Awestruck, Caia put a hand to her mouth. "Who did it?" she asked. "Was it really Glim'Ruk himself, or was it one of his men?"

"Glim'Ruk, no doubt. We've seen the kills through means of scrying. Though I cannot say how he knew what would kill a Voice."

"You mean...removing her eyes," Caia said for clarification.

Archai nodded.

"But if the Voices have been gone for so long, how did Jaydür not fall into the darkness we were warned about in studies? Not that there was ever much discussion on the topic, but Jaydür is dependent on balance, and the death of *one* is supposed to spawn the darkness that creates death and disease."

"Fifty-three years did not pass unaffected," Archai replied as he scanned the distance. "In the time of the Voices' absence, tensions have risen between villages and greater cities. Monsters have been birthed. The veil between worlds is thinning."

Caia perked up at the word. "Worlds?"

"Hence, the concern in your seeing a shadow hound. We need to find out whether the creature was physically crossing over or if you were simply having a vision."

With a frown, Caia watched her feet as she walked. "It didn't feel like a vision. Though now I'm hoping that's all it was."

With nothing on the horizon to gauge how much distance they traveled, she felt like they were marching in place. The slowly darkening sky was the only thing within sight that changed, until Caia noticed a line of sparse trees in the distance.

By the time they reached the trees, the rain stopped, the clouds cleared away, and twilight painted the skies shades of purple and orange. Stars twinkled in the sky before the night even took over. The smell of rain lingered in the air.

"What will it be like?" Caia asked, finally breaking a silence that had lasted at least an hour. "Passing into another world, I mean."

Archai took in a deep breath and frowned. "We've never done this before," he replied. "I cannot say."

"But you will be there? On the other side."

He nodded. "Not always within sight, but yes."

Caia looked at the ground for a moment, then smiled. "Will I like you better then? Or will you be just as *coy* as you are now?"

"Whether you like me or not will not matter," Archai said as he passed the first tree. He ran his fingers along the bark, his deep-set teal gaze secured on her. "I'll always be there. You will be with me for all time. Unless, that is, someone removes *your* eyes."

The cold stare that accompanied his comment sent chills up Caia's arms.

"I suppose you're not one to jest with," she quietly replied. "Understandable."

"I would be quicker to jest if your life were not on the line. I do not think you and Naoni understand, Caia—I lost more than you realize. I have known the Voices since the beginning of time."

Caia bit her cheeks and moved a muddy lock of hair behind her ear. "I'm sorry."

"Do not—"

"I'm sorry you've suffered so much," she cut in, knowing he was going to scold her for apologizing. "I can't imagine what it's like to lose someone you've known all your life. Or so many lives, in your case."

Archai turned silent, a subtle wrinkle in his brow making it clear he was deep in thought. Caia wondered if she'd said something that bothered him or if he was immersed in a memory. Either way, the silence lasted until night grew and the night birds came out to hunt. The two came upon a fallen tree, where they stopped to make camp.

The surrounding trees were damp from the rain, but Archai still managed to get the branches alight for a campfire, using a white light of magic in his hands. It was something she had seen Dy'Mün do in the past.

Sitting on the tree, the fire was warm and quickly dried Caia's clothes and hair. But dry muddy hair was just as difficult to manage as wet muddy hair. Caia quickly gave up trying to clean herself up and inspected her injured arm from the earlier fall off Archai's horse. Sometimes Caia was immensely glad to be an elf. Her healing capabilities were astounding in comparison to other races of Jaydür. The discoloration around her broken wrist had faded into a light red already. Though she wouldn't be able to wield a bow for another two or three days, the bone was healing fast.

Caia lifted her eyes to where Archai was sitting a moment ago and realized he was gone. She scanned the immediate area, unsure when or how he left in the first place. And just as soon as she wondered where he was, he materialized beside her.

She blinked in surprise. "How did you—"

"Give me your injured arm," he said. Gently taking her hand, he placed a branch slightly thicker than her thumb against her inner wrist and forearm. A handful of reeds lay at his feet, which he used to tie the branch to her as a makeshift splint. "Avoid using this hand. Let it heal. It shouldn't take long."

"But how did you do that? I mean, how did you disappear?"

Archai looked her hard in the eyes. "There is no explanation that would make much sense to you now. But essentially, I am given appropriate permission to cross between the Rehnedhen, Jaydür, and other worlds as deemed necessary."

Caia nodded and looked down at her hand.

"You need rest. Sleep, and I'll keep a lookout," Archai assured.

"What about you? Don't you need to sleep, too?" she asked.

"I have other means of resting. Do not worry."

"What about eating? Do you eat?"

"I do, but you may have noticed your own lack of appetite since you drank the speed draft."

Caia lifted her eyebrows in quiet surprise. He was right. They hadn't eaten for hours, but she had no sense of hunger.

"Now sleep," he said. "Before you dwell on thoughts of food and lose sleep."

With that, Caia slid onto the damp ground and leaned her side against the fallen tree trunk. Comfortable would not be the word to describe her position, but she was exhausted and soon fell into a dreamless sleep.

The sizzle of water being poured into the fire woke Caia with a gasp, only to find Archai up and ready to leave.

"Good morning," he said. "Let us be on our way."

Caia quickly stood up, still bleary-eyed from sleep, and followed after Archai as he headed southeast.

Archai took her wrist and examined it again. There was no pain until he bent it upwards. "The muscle is still strained, but the bone is nearly healed." He lifted his gaze and looked at the way before them. "It may be best for us to fly now." Without another word, large feathered wings came from his back like a great eagle's. He slid an arm around her back and took her legs out from under her with his other arm, lifting her with ease. She gasped slightly when he pushed off the ground without another word.

Caia threw her other arm around Archai's neck, clutching him for fear of falling. The upward climb was fast and cold, making it difficult for Caia to keep her eyes open. The memory of the day she'd flown with him after he'd taken her from the clutches of the goblins and sinstarians in Nov'Eit came to mind, and Caia was simply glad she could *see* this time. When they reached a certain height, Archai flew forward rather than up, and Caia could look over her shoulder and take in the view. Her mud-crusted hair whipped wildly about, stinging her face as she tried to see.

Caia knew most would assume flying was an experience to be desired over and over again, but in reality, flying was uncomfortable. Unaccustomed to the harsh, whipping air coming from all directions, every muscle in Caia's body tensed. The pain started in her shoulders as she stiffened, then it spread to her neck. Her feet went numb after fifteen minutes or so, and her quiver jabbed into her ribcage. Caia wanted nothing more than to be put down.

"We are nearly there," he called out, and she

nodded in response, wriggling her toes in a futile attempt to return blood flow to them.

Caia gave up after another few moments and shielded her face from the wind in Archai's shoulder. She closed her eyes, thinking back on the time she spent alone with him for the last day. Part of her regretted not speaking with him more. A man with many ages of knowledge was a man she could learn anything from. She was not certain she would have much time to speak with him when they returned to the rest of their party. Swallowing hard, Caia lifted her head and looked up at Archai. As if feeling her gaze, he returned her attention.

"What is it?" he asked.

She pulled herself up enough to speak loudly in his ear. "Are we so far that we cannot walk now and still arrive before the sun is gone?" she asked.

His brow creased in thought or inquisitiveness—Caia couldn't tell which—but her stomach dropped at the sudden descent, and it didn't take long for them to touch ground.

Archai lowered her legs to the ground, yet he held his arm around her waist until she was steadied. "All right," he said. "We can walk."

Caia held on to his arms for a moment, awkwardly bouncing her eyes between his and the ground. "Thank you. My feet were losing all feeling."

Archai held Caia's attention as if waiting for her to go on. When she didn't, he said, "I assume your feet are not the reason you wanted to lengthen our trip."

With a shake of her head and a small smile on her face, she replied, "No, though I can't say it had nothing to do with it. I just—" She paused and looked ahead in the direction they were about to walk. "I just realized that we'll be surrounded by everyone else when we get there, and I may never have another opportunity to ask you what I have on my mind. I should have asked yesterday, I know. I was still wrapping my mind around all that's happened and all that's coming."

"Understandable," he replied. He glanced at her feet and held her by the elbows. "Do you have enough balance?"

Caia nodded.

"Let us walk, then, and I will answer your questions to the best of my ability."

The tingling feeling in her feet was like crawling ants, but Caia tried to distract herself with how to ask her questions. The last thing she wanted was a Sapient to think her silly or ignorant.

Archai didn't push her. He showed no sense of annoyance or urgency in their need to move, and Caia appreciated it. And yet she put that pressure upon herself until she finally gave up trying to think up some clever or intelligent way of asking what she needed to know.

"We spoke before about what is expected of me

as a Voice, like keeping wars to a minimum and being the voice of reason for those who have no sense of it. But *how* do I keep this balance? How will I know when it's time to intervene in the affairs of Jaydür's inhabitants?"

Archai rubbed his chin, and Caia noticed his growing stubble. She also noticed just how strong he seemed, from the muscles of his clenched jaw to the width of his chest and size of his arms. He was by far bigger than any elf or human Caia had ever seen.

"When you become a Voice," he began, "there will be a stage of absorption. It is the time your very essence—your *soul,* if you will—gains the understanding of the world. You will feel it within yourself when you are to intervene."

"But what if I *think* I'm feeling something and I intervene, and I make something worse?"

"Then we fix it."

Caia wrinkled her nose, and Archai smiled with his reply.

"Caia, there are many ways for you to sway the will of man. There are ways for you to use a premeditated plan to stop terrible things from happening. Similarly, there are ways for you to guide the thought of a minotaur or the desire of a young nymph. There is nothing quite so broken that you cannot fix it." Archai slowed his steps and he crossed his arms over his chest as he continued. "The important thing for you to remember is that you will not be alone in this; there are still your sister Voices, who will all undergo the same stage of absorption. No major decisions will be on your shoulders alone. It is a life of connection and communication that you are entering, not one of solitude and reclusiveness; this is a common misconception of the Voices and who they are."

There was something about Archai's voice and tone that made Caia relax. If not for him, she might have fallen into a pitiful state of anguish or despair. The very idea of being placed on a golden pedestal when one deserved nothing more than common stone was disconcerting, to say the least. And yet his answer was not quite the answer she was hoping for.

"I understand," she quietly replied.

"Is that all?" Archai asked. "Because we could fly another few minutes before we rejoin the others."

Caia parted her lips to speak but realized everything she had to say would come out sounding frail and somewhat pathetic. But at the same time, she felt it was safe to sound that way with Archai. His greatest judgments thus far were toward Solin and her ignorance about Archai himself.

"I'm anxious about joining the others," she blurted out. "The sooner we join them, the sooner there will be more expected of me. And at the same time, I feel as though my mind and heart are running in circles while I'm trying to conceptualize what's happening with my life. There is so much chaos inside of me, and being alone with *you* has calmed me. I wish I could explain it."

Archai smiled but said nothing.

"Is my confession funny to you?" she asked with a returning smile, though much smaller than his.

"Not funny at all," he replied. His voice was quieter now and held a tone of contentment. "It is just that Draì said the same thing for centuries."

Caia pressed her lips together. "Draì?"

Archai cleared his throat and the muscles in his jaw tensed. "Draì was the Voice of Apan before you."

Caia's heart sank at his words. She'd never heard the actual names of the Voices besides Poette, but Poette had a somewhat recent presence among the fae in the northeastern region of Jaydür. Stories abounded for years that the Voice had walked among the world.

Dropping her attention to her feet, Caia took in a slow, deliberate breath and said, "Draì. It's a beautiful name. The very idea that you even knew her is still baffling."

"We were close," Archai admitted. "Closer than the others."

Caia grinned facetiously. "Were you?

"Not romantically, Caia," Archai replied, his tone an awkward mix of abashedness and irritation. "We were simply friends. Her extreme empathy and love for life likely had something to do with that. I lacked the emotion she worked so hard to instill in Jaydür. I was broken to her, and she felt she had the means to fix me."

Caia frowned. "How could you say such a thing? I'm certain she didn't feel that way at all. There is nothing broken about you. Yes, you have an ego. Yes, you see the world in a vastly different light than anyone I've ever met, but it's a befitting trait. You don't seem to lack base emotions, and *that* is what makes a person a person. Everything else is just personality."

Archai's silence made blood rush to Caia's cheeks.

"Have I overstepped?" she quietly asked, and Archai shook his head.

"Not at all," he replied, stretching his back as his hand settled on the blue pommel of his sword. "I was a different man when Draì was here, that's all."

Doubt prodded at Caia, but she said nothing for fear that she had already said too much.

"Much in the way you will be a different woman when you are a Voice. That boy will hardly recognize you, and it will not be so difficult to let you go."

Caia's chest tightened. "*That boy* has been my best friend since we were children. I would appreciate some kindness toward him. This is difficult for us both."

"Kindness can get you killed in our world, Caia. Your *new* world. Balance comes with beauty and the grotesque—excitement and terror. Your life is now a life of balance, and your sweet, warm demeanor will change soon after your first task for Jaydür is completed."

Anxiety crept up Caia's gut like a spider. "What do you mean?" she asked. "What task?"

"There are many," he replied, his eyes on the way before them. "As I've said before, in the time the Voices have been gone, the veil between worlds has begun to thin. But beyond that, races have risen up against one another. As the Voice of Apan, your charge will likely be that of the people. You and the Voice of Mae'Ehr are best equipped to communicate with the people of the land as advocators of peace, which means you will help decide which wars will return balance and which will defer it. In some instances, you will decide who will die and who will live."

A gasp escaped from Caia at this explanation. Shock roiled her stomach and heated her blood. "You can't mean that!" she exclaimed.

Archai's face tensed at her response. "You have no idea what life is waiting for you, do you? You are so distracted by all this meaningless love and romance to think straight."

Caia focused on her breathing as she wiped her damp palms down her leggings and shifted the quiver around her waist. She didn't want to respond impulsively, nor be looked down on as unprepared and weak-willed, so when the two stepped out of the trees and into a field, Caia replied, "I'm learning as I go. I will do what is needed."

"That is a great answer," Archai said.

A grassy hilltop blocked the horizon, so Caia couldn't make out what was in the distance. Without a clear idea of how far they still had to travel, she turned their conversation back to the previous Voices. She needed to take the focus off her lack of preparedness.

"What was your relationship to the other Voices?" she asked as they started up the hill. "Were they as fond of you as Draì?"

Archai's smile, though a wrinkled brow accompanied it, made Caia feel slightly less tense. "Erid, the Voice of D'Irdda, was the least interested in having me close. She also caused the greatest stresses of them all. She was often a pious fool, believing she had the closest relationship to the Highest Power than any of the sister Voices." Archai chuckled as he went on. "'The ground and the plants teem with the life energy of the Highest Power,' she would say. 'And *I* was placed over that energy.' Then she would disappear for days, wandering the forests and riverbeds of Jaydür with no clue of her whereabouts. As their protector, it drove me mad."

"And the new Voice of D'Irdda? Is she as bad?"

Archai nodded. "Her name is Adeilu, and thus far, she does not show any more promise than Erid."

"Caia!" a voice in the distance called, and Caia perked to attention. She and Archai had reached the top of one hill just to see another. A small fire burned in the narrow valley between them, and the other four members of their party sat beside it.

Caia looked up to Archai and her shoulders slumped slightly. "I suppose that's all our time, isn't it?"

To her dismay, Archai nodded and grimaced at the sight of Solin. She didn't quite understand *why* he was so disdainful toward her fiancé. There had to be something more to it all.

Caia quickened her steps and threw her good arm around Solin's neck as soon as he was within reach.

"You're all right!" he cried, strengthening his embrace. "By the Highest, what's happened to your arm?"

"I'm fine. Archai stayed with me and helped me," she replied, thrilled at his new willingness to embrace her. "I fell from the horse, but I'm healing quickly."

He took a step back and took her face in his hands, pressing his forehead against hers. "I'm sorry. I'm sorry I was distant." Solin's voice quieted as he continued. "I was worried about you." His hands held her cheeks tighter. "I assumed all was well when Archai disappeared and didn't come back, but still. I hate the thought of you being out there with all of this going on."

Caia felt Archai's eyes on her and she gently pulled Solin's hands from her face, then hooked her arm around his as they made their way to the camp.

She knew the Sapient's thoughts on what should happen. She knew what had to be done, and she *did* intend on going through with what was expected. But why shouldn't she spend her last days with the man she loved?

"How long have you all been here?" she asked, doing her best to ignore Archai.

Solin looked over his shoulder at the Sapient and offered a small nod of thanks. Archai did nothing in return.

"Since last night," Solin replied with a small cough to clear his throat. "We have food. Have you eaten?"

Caia shook her head, surprised to find she still wasn't hungry. "I'm fine right now, though I would love some water."

Dy'Mün, Naoni, and Atar stood up by the fire to welcome Caia and Archai. Solin hurried to a small pack and grabbed a tin cup, filling it with water from a flask, then offered it to Caia.

"By the Highest," Naoni said with something between a laugh and sigh of concern. "You're covered in mud and you've broken a bone. When does the essence of the Voice take over your clumsiness?"

Caia dropped to the ground. With a glance and a small smile at Archai, she replied, "Very funny."

"Did I not make it clear to keep your face and eyes straight?" Dy'Mün scolded in a soft tone.

"I know. You did, and I'm sorry."

"Her mind crossed the Blacker Shadows, and a shadow hound sensed her," Archai explained. "She tried to protect herself and was sucked out of the vortex. Simple as that." He looked at her sidelong and slightly shook his head in apparent annoyance. "The hound never passed fully through. There is nothing to apologize for."

Caia rubbed her arm and licked her lips, averting her gaze. As intense a man as he was, Archai was considerably tolerant.

"What do you mean?" Dy'Mün, Naoni, and Atar asked in unison.

Caia *wanted* to say it happened by mistake but feared Archai's response if she did. But to her relief, he responded first, directing his words to Naoni.

"As the new Voices, you two will gain all of the abilities the previous Voices held. That includes the ability to see into other realms and travel great distances in a short amount of time. Being aware of the Blacker Shadows is a normal trait for the Voices." He turned his eyes to Dy'Mün and added a tone of severity to his next words. "Being put in a position where time and space cross the threshold of normalcy—like, say, by consuming faery dust—it is expected they would have a greater chance of crossing sights with the dark realm."

Dy'Mün opened and closed his mouth, clearly having something to say but seeming to lack the right words. With a puff of air that blew the hair of his mustache and beard, he replied, "When you have a better idea of how to move faster, you let me know, Sapient. Until then, I will make the decisions I feel are best."

Archai nodded his head with his lips pressed tightly together and let out a snort.

"We're just glad you're all right," Atar said. His tone was as warm and calm as ever, and Caia smiled in reply.

"Is there anywhere I could wash up?" she asked.

Dy'Mün gestured to his right, still huffing and puffing at Archai's distasteful response. "There is a stream just over the hill thanks to the recent rain, but that's the best we have until we reach our destination."

"I'll take it," Caia replied as she stood up again. "I just need this mud off my face and out of my hair."

Naoni handed her a small bundle wrapped with twine. "I grabbed this for you at a village we passed through yesterday, since we didn't have any time to pack our things when we left. They are some essentials for *proper* hygiene, and you need some attention."

Caia narrowed her eyes with a smirk. "You're just droll today, aren't you? Thank you."

"I'll show you the way," Solin started, following after her, but Archai stopped him with a hand on his shoulder.

"I think the last thing the Voice of Apan needs is a boy watching her bathe," Archai said.

Solin's eyes widened and his face turned crimson. "I only meant to show her where the creek is!"

Caia flashed him an apologetic smile for Archai's rashness.

"I'll watch over her," Archai went on. "You help everyone here prepare for our leave."

"Better yet," Naoni jumped in, passing right beside Archai, "*I'll* show her and keep an eye out. The last thing she needs is *any* man overseeing bath time."

To Caia's surprise, Archai's expression did not change. In fact, he gestured to Solin to get to work, and turned to speak with Dy'Mün and Atar.

Caia and Naoni made their way toward the creek with swift steps, and Naoni didn't wait to start asking questions.

"So, what happened out there?" she asked, bumping shoulders with Caia, who smiled in response.

"Nothing, really. I saw the shadow hound, had a rough fall, then found myself in a field, miles from here. Archai showed up quickly and we started on our way to you all."

Naoni nodded as they reached the top of the hill. "The stream is there," she said.

Caia slumped her shoulders at the sight. "You call that a stream? It's a puddle. What am I supposed to achieve here? Have you seen how much hair I have?"

"I see more mud than hair."

The two reached the stream, where Caia sat at the edge and splashed the frigid water on her face with her good arm. "By the Highest, this is cold."

"Would you rather be cold or dirty?" Naoni replied.

"Neither. Is that so wrong?"

"Here, lie down. Doing it one-armed will take too long."

Caia reluctantly did as she was told and shivered as Naoni scooped the water with her hands, pouring it on Caia's hair. The icy water nearly gave her a headache in the frigid air, but she pushed aside any complaints. This was her only option for cleaning up.

"The mud is washing out easily," Naoni said. "This may not be so bad."

Caia grit her teeth as her friend pulled at her hair in the water. She tried focusing on the familiar scent coming from Naoni—a sweet yet warm scent like a mixture of lavender and cedar. The entire Arduun home smelled that way since they were little girls. The thought of never stepping foot into that home again hurt to dwell on. There were many memories of their lives before Archai came into the picture that seemed so far away now. Sitting with Dy'Mün by a warm fire in the winter, studying and discussing history and arts would never happen again. That life was distant. That life was gone.

Naoni's next words came in the midst of a long, bored sigh. "So, did the Sapient do anything…untoward while you two were off alone?"

Caia shot up to a sitting position with wide, horrified eyes. "Naoni! What is wrong with you?"

Naoni tilted her head and smirked before pulling Caia's head back down to the water. "Oh, shut up and tell me."

"No! Archai did nothing untoward," Caia answered while Naoni continued washing out the mud. "He was a gentleman at all times and was nothing but helpful—the way a Sapient is meant to be. I was entirely comfortable with him. Does that answer your question?"

No sound came from Naoni, but Caia knew her well enough to know she wore an ear-to-ear grin. She loved drawing out extreme reactions in situations that hardly warranted them.

"I can't say I would stop him, if you ask me," Naoni prattled on. "Though, he lacks the aggression I like in my men; his face would compensate for that."

"Can we *please* talk of something else? I thought we weren't supposed to be dwelling on things of the heart when we're about to cut off all our relations?"

Naoni chuckled through tight lips. "No one said anything about things of the heart. Carnal needs can be met without emotion, you know."

Moments like these were once regarded as amusing, but enough was enough. Caia pulled her hair from the stream and squeezed out the excess mud and water. A quick look was enough to see the mud was mostly gone, so Caia began braiding her long, wet locks.

"So you're really going to do it, then?" Naoni asked.

There was an odd tone to her voice that Caia did not often hear. She turned to look her friend in the eyes, knowing exactly what she was asking.

"Yes," Caia replied, though her words were almost whispered. "I have no other choice."

Naoni swallowed as she shifted about. "And, um, how are you feeling about it?"

"I'm feeling terrible, to be honest. Like I'm breaking and I'm taking Solin down with me. And the worst part is, he *knows*, yet he remains."

"Of course he does. He loves you. And what you guys have, everyone looks for. He won't be quick to move on; I'm sure you know as much already."

Of course she knew, but it didn't make it hurt any less. Caia leaned over the water and rubbed the mud from her face. She was done speaking of it.

Chapter Three
Edge of a Sword

The fields were more beautiful than Caia expected, presenting before her and the others a vast and open land of grass below and blue sky above. But nothing was seen over the horizon until well into the afternoon when shadows turned the day cold, and Dy'Mün's cottage came into view. The sight enlivened the group like a feast for the eyes. Promise of warmth, comfort, and shelter was no more than a fancy for so long, but now within grasp, the riders urged their horses on.

The cottage walls were constructed of mud and stone with the bones of the structure made from thick planks of wood. A thatch roof blended in with the ferns that covered a small hill rising at the back of the house. From the outside, it looked as if the home was built *into* the hill.

"The horses will not wander beyond the tree line,"

Dy'Mün assured as he unbridled his horse. "Atar, would you put on some tea while I send for a messenger? Prince Leithen must know of our presence at once." Dy'Mün hurried into his cottage, gesturing for the group to enter after him.

The three young elves loosed their horses while their curiosity took in everything around them. Grass and wildflowers spread throughout the first four yards around the cottage before rising into shrubs and the start of unfamiliar woods. The surfaces of the birch trees here were gray, rather than the stark white of those in the Elven Woods. Besides the widespread birches, Elven trees wore their age in their bark, readable by the depth and length of crevices in the husk. These trees had no such telltale markings.

Dy'Mün soon exited his home and hurried to his horse, where he tied a rolled parchment to a braid in the horse's mane. He whispered, "*Altua nialcos, jedhen,*" Elvish for "Be swift in your return."

Archai walked the edge of the woods, his eyes searching deep into the forest; his mind was clearly preoccupied.

"What do you think he's doing?" Solin asked Caia, nodding toward Archai.

"Setting a perimeter," she replied, knowing somehow that what she suggested was true. "He worries, just as we do." She watched the Sapient. He was focused and alert, and she knew that nothing in the wood would go unnoticed by him. He was in his element.

The hairs on the back of her neck stood on end and she turned to Solin, who eyed her severely. "What is it?" she asked, though she knew what he was thinking.

"Selfish thoughts," he replied. "Nothing worth sharing."

"Solin, please," she said, slipping her hands into his. "We've never kept secrets from one another. Not even the darkest thoughts. Please don't make the mistake of thinking that I'm fine with everything that's happening, because I'm not."

With his eyes focused over her shoulder toward Archai in the distance, Solin took a deep breath. "I just wish so deeply that you would hate him for being here. For so long, he was no more than a faerytale. That should make his presence a thrilling thing, but instead, Archai is the one who will force us apart."

Caia looked over her shoulder. "It's not him that breaks us, Solin; it's all of Jaydür."

"Come inside, please," Dy'Mün called from his threshold, interrupting the two young elves. "The tea is on and I've some cakes and bread."

Caia followed Solin into the home, but Archai stood unmoving. "There is a biting breeze creeping through these woods," Archai said. "But there is warmth in the air as well. An inconsistency in the temperature is a warning; we must be cautious."

"Archai," Dy'Mün called after him, "come inside.

None are aware of our being here. There is much to discuss and loafing around the garden will get us nowhere."

With a frown of disdain, Archai took in the surroundings with one more sweep of his eyes before following Caia and Solin into the cottage.

They wandered through the hallway toward the kitchen, where Dy'Mün had them all take a seat at a rectangular wooden table laden with plates and sweets.

"Hurry now," he urged. "Everyone, sit." He placed a small white bowl of sugar in the middle of the table. "Forgive the meager supply. I did not expect to come back here so soon, especially with guests. But after tea, I will ride into town while you settle in for the night, and when you wake, a glorious breakfast will lead you into a morning of training."

"What sort of training?" Naoni asked, already taking a bite of sweet bread.

"Defense, mostly," Archai explained. He pulled a steaming cup of tea to him and warmed his hands around the tin. "Depending on how long we remain here we may attempt awakening your element."

Naoni's excited gaze shot to Caia, who returned the same excitement. "Can we not begin with that instead?" Caia asked eagerly.

"Of course," he said, taking a sip. "And in the meantime, we'll tie your arms and legs and drop you at the gates of Sinstar." After casting the girls a cutting glance, he continued. "There is no time to *master* such skill. What good is the power to summon water or fire if you have no ability to use it and no ability to defend yourself while trying? You are fools; we must siphon such stupidity from both of you."

That was the last Caia or Naoni desired to say to him.

"So we're no longer rushing to Sanctuary?" Solin asked, confusion in his tone.

Dy'Mün hesitated in his response and lifted his eyes to Archai. There was something there that *everyone* noticed. The professor was holding himself back from saying something.

"We will stay here for a day or so," Archai said with a tone of finality, then sipped his tea.

Night came swiftly and with it a warm current that left Archai silent and on edge as everyone bedded down for the night. He ignored any who spoke to him, and his attention shifted moment by moment between the new Voices and the surrounding woods.

The cottage was indeed peaceful as all lay in their beds. But the battle at Nov'Eit raged on in Caia's mind. Mangled limbs and severed bodies were her companions with every blink, and she eventually gave up trying to sleep. In perfect silence she rose so as not to wake Naoni, and wandered down the hall. Moonlight shone through the windows in slivers of silver, casting its brightness against the mud walls. Dy'Mün had something of a partiality for metal things, which, at any other time, would be something of interest to Caia but with her nerves on edge, every shadow they cast made her heart leap. It did not take long for her stomach to suffer from the anxiety.

Warm, damp air rolled through the front door as Caia cracked it open. Warmth was not something she expected, especially considering the typical chill of morning. She leaned her back and head against the heavy wood as it clicked shut, then searched the empty garden before her. The grass was a pallid pool in the moonlight, surrounded by trees standing like ghostly soldiers of pale shadow. Caia could not decide whether the scene was beautiful or frightening.

"You should be sleeping." Archai's voice cut through the darkness.

"By the Highest!" she replied with a startled gasp and a hand over her heart. "I did not see you there."

The Sapient stepped into the moonlight, but instead of looking at his new companion, his eyes scanned the line of trees that surrounded the cottage. "This is something of a concern, then," he quietly replied. "We'll have to work on your sense of awareness. What are you doing out here?" His back was straight and his hand rested on the hilt of his sword.

Caia breathed in a lungful of air and joined his obvious scouting. "I can't sleep," she admitted, glad she had reason to avoid eye contact.

Sam grazed by the edge of the wood and Caia took that as a good sign. If there were enemies lurking in the shadows, the horse would surely show signs of distress.

"Your mind is tormented by the dead," Archai said, finally looking at the girl. "I recall your sorrow at Nov'Eit." His gaze fell to her shaking hands as she brought them to her mouth with a nod. "In my limited experience with elf-kind, I know to be mindful of your sensitivities, but you are a Voice. Your mind is like a whirlpool, drawing on the emotions of those around you. The absence of emotion among the dead is sure to spark sorrow in the heart of a typical elf. But you are not typical and should be stronger than that." He paused for a moment and looked ahead of them again. "Caia," he continued. "Forgive me if I am wrong, but you *are* full-fledged, are you not?"

Caia's gaze shot up at his words. "Are you implying that a show of emotion is childish? You can hardly expect a person—*however old*—to overlook the abominable murder of the innocent." She tried crossing her arms, but the brace was in the way. Caia took a deep breath and forced herself to contain her feelings. "This sort of evil is something none should ever experience."

"Here," Archai said, taking her arm and unwrapping the brace. "You do not need this anymore." Caia watched his hands as he tossed the makeshift brace aside and ran his fingers over the bone. When he was satisfied enough, he let go of her and continued. "As for your emotions, you must understand that I am not accustomed to the array of them you hold. I have spent ages among those who are affected by one emotion at a time." He returned his attention to the wood. "In the short time you've stood here beside me, you've experienced a number of them. You need to gain control of your feelings and stop allowing them to rule you. I am learning that cutting out your emotion will be a trial for you."

What Archai said was true and reminded Caia with whom she spoke. "You know," she replied with a sniff, "I often forget that you are a Sapient. The very idea continues to baffle me."

Archai looked down at his sword and drew it slowly from its scabbard. "You know, I think I've had enough of doubt. Let us put an end to it. There is no way for me to help you or the Voice of Folc if you continue to dismiss who and what I am."

The blade glowed like a silver firefly and Caia wondered if it was because of the moon's reflection or if it was magic that enveloped it. He gripped the hilt and raised the blade with a deep breath. There was something in his eyes—a hint of discomfort and uncertainty—as he flipped the weapon, catching it by the other end and offered the sword to Caia.

She drew in a quick breath, unsure of what he was doing.

"Take it," he offered. "And you'll no longer be baffled."

Caia stared at the blue leather wrapped around the hilt. She could not deny her curiosity, though, and carefully reached out to take hold of the sword, unsure what it would teach her. The moment she touched the hilt, all her senses evaporated and the ground sank from her feet. A cold sensation rose up to her ankles and Caia looked down to find her feet immersed in an inch of water, but when she moved her toes, they remained dry. She turned her gaze up again and gasped at the vision. Endless sky with tinges of orange and fading pink stretched to meet a white horizon in every direction. The dawning hues darkened the higher her eyes climbed the skies until she found a black starlit pool directly above. A glass path she stood on led to a round platform surrounded by floating mirrors. From the platform, three more pathways led to different areas of the chamber. One went to a glass staircase rising up to a balcony. Another led to a large doorway made of a silvery atmosphere—a portal. The third pathway led away from the platform to a seemingly endless, unseen destination.

Aside from the wonders she could see with her eyes, Caia was overwhelmed with a sense of something no words could describe. "Forever" suddenly had new meaning. Eternity was laid out before her; the sky had no end—the water, no beginning.

Caia raised her eyes and caught movement within the glass of a floating mirror. She stepped forward, trying to focus on the image but was immediately drawn from the vision and tossed to the ground as Archai's sword was snatched from her grasp. She scrambled back to her feet, winded by the sudden extraction from the vision and leaned against the cottage wall for support. "What did I just witness?" she asked. Her eyes hungered for answers—for an understanding of the amazing sensation that came from the place she just envisioned.

"That was the Chamber of Apan," Archai replied, sheathing his sword. "Within the Rehnedhen."

"Was it necessary to force me out so violently?"

"Your eyes were wandering where they have no right to," he said. He returned his attention before them. "How do you feel now about the Terehn?"

Caia sucked in a deep breath and furrowed her brow in thought. "Connected," she said, surprised that was the first word that came to mind. She looked up at Archai, who wouldn't return her gaze. Something changed in those few out-of-body moments—there was no other way to explain the experience. The sensation of forever clung to her thoughts like threads of a spider web. "I feel an odd, *old* sense of awareness," she admitted, looking down at her hands. "A deeper sense of life. But more than that, I feel something like sadness, yet not quite that either. It's more like homesickness. As if I am far from where I belong."

"We call it *hiraeth*," Archai explained. He finally looked down at the girl who anxiously flexed and stretched her fingers. "It is a response to being in contact with the Chambers. If you were not a Voice, the reality of this world—right here before Dy'Mün's cottage—would now drive you mad. The fact that you're not currently thrashing about in anger and frustration to return to the Chamber tells me that you are more than you seem. As I suspected, you're more in tune with your position than is apparent. You're ready."

Caia looked up at Archai and frowned at his strange explanation. "What do you mean by that? What did you suspect and since when?"

"It was clear to me at Nov'Eit," he began flatly. "Your heart reaches for the people of Jaydür. Your concern did not falter when, in such a situation as that battle, most would become enraged. Take the Voice of Folc, for instance. Her life was spent beside yours. All acquaintances, friends, and family were shared between the two of you, but she did not respond to their bloodshed as you did. She succumbed to her rage without a second thought. The stupid boy joined beside her. Their reactions were not calculated. But you," Archai stopped and a quiet laugh came from his lips. "You took in the scene, processing the memories with every fallen friend, and gained control of your emotions before sending off that first arrow."

"But Naoni is a Voice as well. What of her?"

"It does not make her any less of a Voice. It just means the *essence* of the Voice—the eled'hwen—is taking residence in you more quickly. Naoni will get there when the time is right for her."

One thing in all that Archai explained to Caia made her wonder, and as guilt built within her, she asked, "Does that not make *me* the selfish one? That I did not give in to anger; that I was stayed in my grief before responding."

Archai shook his head and smiled. "That makes you the wisest of them all."

Just as Caia returned his smile, his lips tightened, his brow furrowed, and his nostrils flared. Pain shot through her shoulders as she was forced against the cottage wall. His face was inches from her own, filled with a terrifying rage. A black, blood-drenched arrow had plunged right through his shoulder, the arrowhead but a breath from her face.

"Scalt endh man!" he roared to those sleeping within the cottage just before raising his eyes and clenching his teeth. He turned his back to her and raised his sword toward the woods from which an ill-sounding screeching came. "Goblins!"

Blue and white light shot from his blade, and Caia's hair whipped wildly about in the back-current of power emanating from the sword. Archai turned and drew her against him, kicked in the door, then in the blink of an eye, shoved her through the doorway, sending her tumbling across the floor.

"Into the cellar!" he ordered when met with several pairs of startled and sleepy eyes. He turned and disappeared into the wood.

"What's going on?" Naoni called after him.

"Do not question him now," Dy'Mün advised, herding the elves toward the cellar. He tossed aside a woven red rug that concealed the doorway leading to underground. "Everyone inside. Now." The hooting resonated through the woods and Dy'Mün looked up toward the door in surprise. "How did they find us?" he asked rhetorically before entering the cellar himself and locking it behind him.

"What about Archai?" Caia cried. "We can't leave him!"

Solin grabbed her when she rushed back toward the cellar door.

"He saved me!" she went on, fighting against him. "Let me go!" She turned away, resisting Solin. "He saved my life!"

"Caia, he is doing what he was called to do," Dy'Mün explained. His hand hovered above the metal locks, pulsating with white light as he placed a locking spell upon the door. "He *will* return."

Caia shook her head. They didn't know what happened. They couldn't know how serious it was. "There's an arrow in his shoulder," she explained. "Clean through the muscle and tissue. How will he fight with such an injury?"

"Have you *seen* Archai?" Naoni replied. "I don't think a man like him is going to be stopped by an arrow."

Dy'Mün looked over his shoulder and offered a small smile. "Your compassion is heartwarming, Caia. He will be fine."

Nearly two hours went by with no sign of the Sapient. Though Caia's heartbeat slowed, her stomach still ached with fear for him. No one else seemed worried, which bothered her immensely. Sure, he was not the kindest gentleman and no, he did not have the best way with words, but he saved her life more than once and that was enough to earn her concern.

Atar looked upon his daughter sitting on the floor against the far wall. Caia met his gaze a few instances over the time they sat there. "Such lovely eyes you have," he said softly. "Just like your mother's. How proud she would have been to watch you grow into the woman you are."

Caia fumbled with her hands and frowned at the small talk—especially about her mother. No one knew what became of her after she had departed fourteen years earlier for a town by the Willow of Mae'Ehr. Caia looked up to see her father's gaze and realized how pitiful she must look. "Are you all right?" he asked, now sitting beside her. He gestured to the space between her and Solin, who paced the room. "I've never seen the two of you so distant."

Caia tossed a glance to Solin and smiled softly. "We're just coming to terms with our fate, is all."

"I see," Atar said with a nod. "And how are you handling that?"

Caia swallowed and lifted her shoulders in a slight shrug. "It hurts. We have lifetimes of plans and goals we swore we would achieve together."

Atar nodded and took a deep breath. "It is good to remember the love you two have without allowing it reign over your future. Hurt is not always bad; instead it can serve as a branding of a memory that can guide your decisions later in life."

"Or the source of long-term suffering," she replied.

"Only if you make it so. Though might I add," Atar leaned closer to whisper in her ear, "you are wearing your concern for Archai more obviously than for your coming loss. That could have much to do with this distance between you, too."

At that, Caia watched Solin as he chewed on his bottom lip while pacing the room. His arms crossed and his brow furrowed, but he didn't return her gaze.

"Archai is no threat to anyone," Caia whispered to her father in reply. "He's saved me twice in a matter of days. Does that not deserve my concern? I would think it expected."

Her father leaned his head back and took in a deep breath. "Heroism is indeed deserving of high regard. But so is loyalty. Solin has been loyal to you, and he may feel ignored or of less importance with all that is going on now."

Her father was right. Solin's emotions were wild, blazing like a lone flame in the winds of change. They both knew what the future was to claim from them—their companionship, and not just that, but their hopes and dreams were being trampled against the stones of the world with every step they took. Her heart ached just thinking about it.

"Solin," Caia called. "Would you sit with me?"

With a small smile, he made his way to her side as Atar stood and went toward Dy'Mün and Naoni. Solin wrapped an arm around her as she snaked her own around him and laid her head on his shoulder. It took all the strength she had not to let her fears stream down her cheeks.

"Are you all right?" he asked, to which she nodded with a sniff. No further words were necessary. She knew he understood what was in her heart.

The elves were shaken from their dreams by the heavy slam of a door. Dy'Mün quickly reached for his staff and blinked away the sleep, the wood creaking in his grip as someone rapped on the cellar door. Caia grabbed Solin's arm in panic, unsure whether the group could defend themselves against a swarm of goblins without Archai. Professor Dy'Mün passed Caia an inquiring glance as if she would know something he did not. She had nothing to offer but a shrug of her shoulders.

"It is safe to come out," a voice finally said from above.

Caia knew that voice! She squeezed Solin's hand and gave him an assuring smile before hurrying to the door, clambering past Dy'Mün to see what condition Archai returned in. "Are you all right?" she asked before setting eyes on him. His back was turned as he searched through kitchen drawers, the arrow still completely through his shoulder. She hurried to his side and tried to catch his attention. "Are you all right?" she asked again. "Sit down. Let me help you."

Archai seized a pair of cloths with no reaction to the girl. He gripped the arrowhead with his right hand and snapped it like a shoot from a tree. "Get that for me, would you?" he asked, gesturing to the feathered end of the arrow still sticking out of his back. Caia was in a daze and when she failed to move quickly enough, he twisted his arm around his torso and slid the shaft out himself with little more than a grunt.

Caia turned to the others who stared, mouths agape—everyone but Dy'Mün. The professor simply smiled and nodded toward Archai. "What did I tell you?" he said.

She could do nothing but watch Archai in awe.

She'd never known anyone like him.

"These goblins were not of Glim'Ruk," Archai declared, turning to face the elves. He pressed one cloth to the front wound and tossed the other to Caia, gesturing to his back. After casting a glance to the others, she pushed up on her toes and applied pressure to the back wound without a word. "Just wild scoundrels trying to earn a place within his ranks." He jerked his shoulder. "More pressure," he demanded, and she leaned into her arms.

Whatever it was that Caia expected with Archai's return, this was most certainly not it. In all the time he was gone, she'd searched her memory for any skill in healing that she might have. She remembered her mother dressing her wounds as a child but not much more than that. It would seem, though, that healing skills were not going to be needed for a man like Archai.

"We are momentarily safe from true danger," he assured. "But..."

His hesitance won Dy'Mün's disappointed frown.

Dy'Mün pressed his lips into a tight line. "We've only just settled. I will call upon the Elders and we will place a protection over the cottage," he said, but Archai quickly shook his head.

"There is no time for that. Placing such a large protection would take more than a day and as we speak, there are scouts wandering the woods. Do you not understand? The Voices are not safe here. We must leave. Now."

Frustration rang clear in the solid thump of Dy'Mün's staff on the ground. His lips tightened and his jaw flexed just before uttering, "And I thought we could have one more day of peace before the chaos. Everyone, gather your things." Then he turned and hurried off to an adjacent room.

Archai looked over his shoulder to Caia, who still pressed the cloth to his wound. "I apologize for throwing you to the ground. Are you all right?" he asked, ignoring those who were in the room with them.

Caia nodded and looked away from his teal gaze to the lesion. "I'm fine, thank you. But are you not in pain?"

"Pain is only a hindrance for those who are not well enough acquainted with it," he said, then bowed his head in what Caia perceived as thanks before walking toward the door. "Fetch a cloak, find a bow, and load your quiver. You've need of nothing more."

Chapter Four
Sanctuary

The long, empty road suddenly met with rising hills. As the fields passed them by, one mountain rose above the rest and from it came a waterfall, spilling and foaming into a lake so clear it was as if the heavens spit out the very holiness of them. A renewed energy overcame the riders after many nights spent in somber, wordless company, and they hurried to quench themselves.

"So this is Sanctuary?" Caia asked no one in particular as she studied the high mountain peaks from beside the lake. Towering and snowcapped, she'd never seen such a sight from so close a distance.

"No," Archai replied before anyone else. "Sanctuary is behind the falls, and only one who knows from where to enter can do so."

"You know where, though?" Naoni said, shaking water from her hands.

"I do, but we cannot simply enter." Archai turned

his eyes to a valley between Sanctuary's mountain and its sister peak. "We will go to the Valley of Ferici. There are safer passages."

Caia splashed water on her face. "I'd never heard that the road to Sanctuary is dangerous. Many have traveled this area and returned."

"Many were not tracked to be seized by Glim'Ruk," he retorted. "Anyone following us can see very well where we are going. It is fooling them that is the trick." Archai looked up at the group sitting beside the water and pressed his lips in a tight line. "Though I must say that with so many of us traveling, I cannot promise it will be easy. I am at a loss as to why so many of you have come this far."

Atar Foriei stepped forward and took his daughter's hand. "My dear," he began, his eyes brimming with sadness. "Archai is right. I feel as though I am a broken wheel being pulled along this adventure with nothing to offer."

Caia looked at her father with a new fear ignited. "You're leaving?"

"I've carried the risk of losing you to your calling since before you were born. I have been able to come to terms with the situation, and having spent time with Archai, I feel confident that you will be safe with him. He desires the same future for Jaydür as we all do. And I feel it would relieve you all of an added trouble if I would let you go."

"I understand," Caia began, her voice breaking.

Her heart wrenched at the sudden realization that she wouldn't see him again for what was very likely going to be a long time.

"I am confident our separation will not be forever." Atar looked to Naoni and took her hand. "You two just watch out for each other. Trust one another, and do what needs to be done."

"Well said," Archai said with his arms crossed over his chest.

Though she didn't know everything that was to come, Caia did know that there was more danger on the horizon, and if her father left, he would have more of a chance of survival. And, as he said it, they would see each other again. They had to.

She threw her arms around his neck and kissed his cheek. "I love you, Father. I will do my best," she said in a whisper. "Please be careful on your return. Go another way, in case we've left a trail."

Atar then turned to Solin and placed a hand on his shoulder. "If you so choose to come with me, I would not mind a companion in my return to the Seven Mile River. There is much to do and much to rebuild."

Solin reflected Atar's gesture, placing his own hand on the man's shoulder. He shook his head. "I will stay with Caia," he said, his attention flickering to her. "I'll make sure she gets where she must—safely."

"We will care for your daughter as best we can," Dy'Mün assured. "She is in the hands of the Highest

Power, which holds more comfort than any we can offer."

With one final exchange between the travelers, Atar took his horse and turned back to the road from which they came.

Archai urged the group back to the path and they continued their way toward the Valley of Ferici. Caia, however, could not stop fearing that she had, in fact, just seen her father for the last time.

The group moved onward and though not two moments passed, Naoni was suddenly thrown to the ground. Caia turned to find Archai straddling her, his cheek cut and bleeding. An arrow stuck—still trembling—in a tree. She looked back at the road and screamed, "Father!" A small swarm of goblins stood yards away, the lead creature with a bow in its hand. Atar was nowhere in sight. *Did he get away?*

What happened after that came with such speed that Caia could hardly feel anything at all.

Archai grabbed Naoni and Caia and in the blink of an eye, they were airborne.

"No!" Caia shrieked as the ground shrank into the distance and they rose into the sky.

"Atar is fine!" Archai cried. "He entered the other side of the woods just in time!"

Caia searched the ground for his body, unsure if Archai was telling the truth or simply saying what would make her feel better and not resist him.

Dy'Mün shouted below, thrusting his staff toward

the oncoming swarm. "Nobení fumen!" With the command, a dense smog rose from the ground like flies from a carcass, and with the Elder's bidding and a twist of his staff, enveloped the goblins. Guttural shrieks escaped through the billow, affirming that the spell had worked and its victims were wasting away.

At the foot of the mountain, Archai put the girls down and searched the stone walls of the mountains for the doorway only he knew was there. An aura of anger and frustration quavered around him.

"These cursed doors are so well hidden, even I have difficulty finding them," Archai said angrily.

"What exactly are we looking for?" Naoni asked.

"I will seek them out," he growled, looking over his shoulder. "If you wish to be of any help, you might keep your elven eyes on the area so we are not caught off guard once more." He eyed the forest and muttered obscenities under his breath.

From where they stood, the trees were more than fifty feet away. Rock and gravel paved the ground beneath them, and from behind, the walls of a mountain rose to heights that Caia had only imagined. All was quiet but for the babbling of cool water that poured through the rock and into a stream flowing toward the wood. Archai ran his hands over the sun-whitened stone until his finger slid into a crack. Fitting his other fingers inside, he pulled at the stone and it opened toward him, revealing a cave, the depth of which Caia found impossible to guess.

"Come," he called, wiping his bleeding cheek with his shoulder.

Caia turned and searched the trees behind them.

"Your father will be fine, Caia," Archai said, drawing her attention. "You cannot let the fear of losing those you love hold you back. If fear can freeze you, then what good are you to Jaydür?"

With a subtle nod, she made her way toward the cave entrance.

Blackness enveloped them when Archai closed the stone door behind them. Dripping water sounded like it was coming from all directions at once. Cold bit at the girls' noses, caught off guard from the change of temperature from that outside. They shivered.

"Run your hands along the wall on the right and follow it," Archai instructed, his deep voice more foreboding now than ever. "And be mindful of where you step. There may be a few drops."

"Drops?" Naoni said, her voice tinged with concern.

"Small ones," he assured.

The cave narrowed into a tunnel carved into the walls by time, aided by the small hands of miners. *Dwarves*, Caia thought as she led the way. Her hands touched across a part of the wall that felt scratched by claws or marred by swords. Naoni accidentally stepped on her heels, drawing her from thoughts of strange creatures and bad men.

Quiet moaning sounded through the passages, raising hairs on Caia's neck. It reminded her of a ravine in Nov'Eit surrounded by walls, moist with damp trails drawing from the river. On days when the weather was brutally hot, the winds would come down between the stone, whispering and groaning through the crevices. Caia was convinced that the noise came from such a happening. Indeed, a wind at the right altitude could manage small entryways into caverns like these.

"How does the wind enter such deep reaches?" Naoni asked. Caia thought it strange her friend asked what she was thinking.

"That is not wind," Archai replied in a quieter voice.

That brought the folcavian to a full stop, and Archai bumped into her.

"Well, what it is then?" she demanded.

After a slight pause, Archai replied, "Breathing."

Caia froze in her footsteps and turned, pulling Naoni in front of her.

"No!" Naoni hissed. "I am not taking the lead!"

"Whatever monster may be here, I will not be the first to meet it," Caia replied, struggling with her friend.

"So you sacrifice me? What a swell friend you turned out to be!"

Archai grabbed both girls, moving them against the wall and taking the lead. "Though memory might have failed me over thousands of years, I cannot recall the previous Voices being so faint of heart."

Naoni, always quick to counter, argued, "I am not—" Her words were abruptly cut off by a throaty wheeze blowing dust and debris their way. "I am not faint of heart. I simply want nothing more than to be farthest away from whatever the confounded thing is. So, what is it?" she demanded, squeezing behind Caia.

"Nothing," Archai replied.

"How agitating you are," Naoni snapped in reply. "You're laughing at us. Obviously it is something if you claim the wind is not wind but breath!"

"Well, unless we cross its path, it does not matter what it is, does it?"

The three moved forward, following a curve in the tunnel. While at first the opposite wall had felt as if it was closing in on them, the space now widened. The breathing quieted for a bit and the nerves of the girls settled.

Archai stopped and held his hand out behind him, stopping the girls as well. "The way will soon open into a wide chamber," he whispered. "When the air grows warm, we cling to the right side. Believe me when I tell you, you do not want to take too large of a step to your left. Whatever you may or may not see, do not make a sound. Stay close." With that, he took Caia's hand, then she reached back with her other hand and took Naoni's.

Caia wondered why such a silence would be needed, but it did not take long for her to realize that they neared the creature inhabiting the cave. Visions of large, burly trolls or monstrous, dragon-like man-eaters danced in her mind. What else could be so massive and call for the three to keep such silence? The breathing had returned and was now loud enough that she knew they were just yards away from its source.

To her dismay, Caia's boot bumped a stone, sending it clattering across the cave floor. That earned a tight squeeze of her hand from Archai, but the host of the cave seemed unbothered and they continued on. Archai kept moving forward, stepping carefully across the way, closer to the back of the chamber.

A fiery orange glow lit the room, revealing them to whatever monster lurked nearby.

Archai froze. His face lit up with the strengthening light, and Caia noticed him drop his face to the ground, then turned to face the creature head-on.

A large bulge of something Caia couldn't recognize rose up within the massive chamber. Caia recoiled into the wall behind them as if she would melt into it, realizing there was a massive drop. That's why Archai urged them to keep close to the wall. A fall like that would have killed them.

A human-like face became clear in the light. Eyes blinked tiredly before setting on the three, who stared dumbly in return.

"A trulian giant!" Caia whispered. She turned to Archai and noticed he was neither afraid nor concerned, but frustrated. The giant looked like a man but stood near sixty feet tall. Giants were rarely seen outside of the far islands of the south and never before seen by the elven girls of the wood.

"Sto'Eck," Archai said to the giant. "I apologize for disturbing your slumber."

"No apologies necessary," the giant replied, each word drawn out in mid-yawn. The mere power of his voice shook the foundation of the cave, and stones rained from crevices of the walls. "I always welcome visitors, few as they are."

Archai opened his mouth to speak but was cut off by the giant.

"Much time has passed since the last time I saw a man," he said, turning his head in curiosity. Eyes wide with recognition, Sto'Eck smiled and leaned over with his hands on his knees to see the three better. "So long it has been since I last saw *you*, Sapient."

"Yes," Archai replied. "It has been—"

"What time has passed; do you know?"

"Well, at least—"

"Not that time is something either of us would feel," the giant continued.

Archai sent a narrowed gaze to the girls, wordlessly blaming them for waking the behemoth, while Sto'Eck prattled on. "You in your plane of the immortals, and I in my cave that sees no sun. Time is naught but a sense for those who thrive on sleep and the occasional search for sustenance."

Caia turned an amused smile to Naoni. The giant, in all his mighty size, could not hear Archai. Either that or all his time spent alone made him lonely and longing for conversation.

"Yes, Sto'Eck," Archai tried, raising his voice. "I am pleased to see you as well but I am in a hurry. You see—"

"A hurry? A Sapient in a hurry?" The giant turned his attention to the girls with a smile that revealed blackened teeth, crooked as tombstones. "Who, might I ask, are you escorting through my mountain?"

Archai lifted Caia's hand, impatience clear on his face and in his twitching brows. "This is Caia Foriei, Voice of Apan and Naoni Arduun, Voice of Folc. We are—"

A great clatter resounded through the mountain and more stones rained onto the three. In a breath, Archai spun around Caia and pulled the girls beneath him, sheltering them from the rocks. When all was quiet, he looked up at the giant and Caia peeked over Archai's arm. He stepped aside and grabbed the hilt of his sword as screeching and cackling echoed throughout.

"Where beauty be, there the ugly will follow," Sto'Eck groaned. "I understand. Fear not, my lord and ladies. Such foul creatures have no means of crossing my way. Go now and rest assured in the Sapient's safekeeping."

The last words spoken embedded in Caia's mind as she watched the giant gather stones and block the doorway. He was not fast enough, though, as a handful of goblins squeezed their way through. Sto'Eck just as quickly knocked them off the edge of the path with no real effort. It was time to go.

They traveled fifty yards of darkness before the three saw light. At long last, the warm air from the outside kissed Caia's face as they exited the tunnel. Silence replaced the hooting of goblins, easing her worries enough to allow herself a moment to take in the fresh air.

"Thank the Highest," Naoni said with a sigh. "That was too close."

Before she even finished her thought, Archai trudged through the gravel toward a path that forked off in two directions. One went into woods more lush than those of the Elven Wood, and the second led into another cavern.

Though not too keen on re-entering any sort of mountainous region, Caia obediently followed him toward the latter with Naoni close behind. To their pleasure, the cavern was beautiful. Five broken arches rose above them, nearly touching the top of the caverns. Aged vines and branches intertwined with the arches, making it difficult to tell what was man-made and what belonged to nature. Great white pillars crumbled along either side, bringing to attention the missing rooftop of what was once a great temple. The cave ceiling itself was the temple's true shelter from sunlight and weathering. *No wonder it survived so long*, Caia thought.

Water cascaded into the cavern through several tributaries—five that Caia could see—and streamed into a narrow river draining through another opening in the ground. Flowers and long grass grew among vines along the edges of the stone walls and pillars, basking in the slivers of sunlight spilling through cracks in the cavern ceiling.

"Where does this water flow?" Naoni asked, touching the fast-moving water.

"There are more caverns beneath us," Archai replied.

"It's like a web of caves," Caia whispered more to herself than to the others. "I never knew this existed."

Without a word, Archai motioned toward the face of the temple.

Naoni frowned. "How long until we reach Sanctuary?"

"We're not going to Sanctuary."

Caia and Naoni shot each other startled glances.

"It was a ruse for anyone who may have been spying on us," Archai explained. "But now that we are in the temple, no one can use magic means to watch us."

Realization dawned on Caia and she looked all around her in a new light. They were *in* the Temple of Pandhea, an underground shrine, dedicated to the very creation of Jaydür. Its existence was easily overlooked since it was very difficult to find. Throughout history, only three were known to have discovered the place.

"Dy'Mün is aware the plan was a ruse, yes?" Caia asked, following Archai.

He nodded as he led her and Naoni up old crumbling steps until they stood before a seven-foot stone door. Fine silver lines were etched into it like molten metal, drawn into the tree-like symbol that appeared by Archai's eye when Caia first met him.

Archai touched his palm against the symbol, making the silver shine bright white; then, with a gentle push, the door opened. The air from inside wafted out, smelling of rain and earth.

Archai gestured for the girls to enter.

"Caia!" a voice called out, startling her. She turned in time to be crushed in an embrace by Solin.

"By the Highest! How did you find us?" she asked, clinging to him. "I thought I'd never see you again! After my father…" her words stuck in her throat at the notion of losing Solin as well.

"Get inside," Dy'Mün urged as he came up behind Solin. "We can catch up when we're all safely inside."

The elves and Dy'Mün entered the temple and

Archai followed. Caia could feel his eyes burning into the backs of her and Solin.

The temple was stunning. The walls ran up the height and length of four levels, with colored light spilling in from stained glass windows, illuminating the room in all its splendor.

"Light comes from the windows, but we're underground," Solin's voice echoed as he wandered the temple in wonder. Caia was close by, her hand gripped tightly in his, refusing to let him go after their brief but biting separation.

"As long as there is light in the windows, the Highest bestows his blessing upon the temple," Dy'Mün explained.

Archai stepped lightly behind Solin and Caia, his attention on their hands.

"Your disgust with Solin is not well hidden, Sapient," Naoni whispered behind Caia.

Caia resisted turning around and tried to focus on Solin as he pointed out wonders of the temple.

"I was not aware of any obligation to hide it," he replied.

"I cannot help but feel that their love for one another is what bothers you," Naoni went on.

Archai's nose wrinkled in annoyance at the sentiment. "My belly twists and sours bitterly at the sight of him. The boy is a parasite. He only delays the growth of the Voice of Apan."

At that, Caia couldn't hold herself back. She let

go of Solin's hand and spun around to face Archai. "I can't stand it. One moment, you're kind and understanding, then the next you're firing insults. Look, I understand you don't know love the way people of Jaydür do. But it's as real as you are, and we doubted *you*, didn't we? How is it fair for you to come along and insult what we've built together? Isn't it enough that I'm sacrificing it all?"

"I'm sorry I brought it up now," Naoni cut in with a squint of thought in her smoldering copper eyes. "Let's not get into an argument about this. It's not as if we have any say in the matter, Caia," Naoni went on. "Not unless we're willing to watch the world we know die with us. For the last few days, you've hung on Archai's every word—and rightfully so. Keep hanging on to it. Or are you going to deny peace to all of Jaydür?"

Solin shook his head and stepped forward beside Caia. "None of you know anything. If any of you truly knew Caia, you would see she's been preparing for this day since before we left Nov'Eit—as have I. Why can't we have our last days together without being chided by those who claim to care?" Solin leaned down to Caia and whispered in her ear. "Let us find a way to speak alone, at least once before this ceremony."

Caia nodded, then watched as the man she loved walked deeper into the temple. She took a deep breath and ground her teeth at the thought of him leaving her again. In all their years together, they'd never left each other's company in anger or sadness, yet in the past few days, it was a recurring theme.

Behind her, Archai lifted his hands to the stone door they'd entered through. A blue haze outlined the doorway until smoke curled from the crevices of the brick and earth around it. Caia watched him—the bitter, angry ghost of a man who never knew more than the ageless walls closing in on them. She pitied him, and yet she feared him, for after living for so many years, his mind should have been gilded with wisdom and understanding but instead was filled with a frigid bitterness that only an existence spent loveless could form. Fear of a similar future hovered in Caia's thoughts. Would she become as callous as Archai had shown he could be?

The cracks between the door and the walls Archai enchanted burned, and the stone melted together, forming a more permanent closure. Caia knew the horde was near, but a sense of peace suddenly emanated from Archai, and she felt they were safe for the time being.

"Come," Dy'Mün called back to her. Naoni was already in the next room, where Solin wandered. "There is not much time. The Room of Ceremony is the last in the temple."

The Sapient came up in Caia's peripheral vision, and she didn't look up until he offered her his elbow. She stared dumbly at him and without really thinking about it, took hold.

"None of this is easy," Archai started, facing forward.

Caia, thinking she knew what he was going to say, released her hold, but before she could pull away, he squeezed his arm to his side, catching her hand. "I'm not done yet," he said, passing her a sidelong glance. "You must hear me."

The two passed through a corridor with pillars, gray as the mountain rains, lining each side. Their agedness showed, boasting the many centuries they stood in the darkness. They were old and crumbling, yet sturdy enough that one could feel confident the cave roof would not collapse upon them in the course of another thousand years.

"I do not care what you have to say about my relationship with Solin," she explained. "I don't see why we're drawing out the stresses of this when you know I've already made my decision to let him go."

"I wanted to apologize," he cut in.

Caia froze and a blush rose to her cheeks. "Oh."

Archai smiled widely, catching Caia's attention. She hadn't seen him smile like this in all the days she'd known him. He was a rather attractive man. If only his heart mirrored the beauty of his face, he could have had a chance at finding love after all.

"I know my words may be harsh, but they must be said. Solin will be fine. He will find a way to live on. In all the years *we* will be gone, he will have a family of his own, and you will not have to feel the sting of regret. You do not do it for me or for anyone else, but for him."

"Well now," Caia retorted, "if you're speaking honestly, it would seem like there is a shred of decency left in you after all."

The two entered the final room of the temple where true sunlight spilled through stained glass windows, high in the temple walls. Each window depicted the Elven Willows in their associated color, pouring streams of red, blue, green, and white into the chamber. A raised stone platform stood in the center of the room, and four twisted trees sprouted from the ground, lining the edge. Each tree held an orb of a different color among its branches, matching those colors that were on the door leading into the temple, as well as the colors of the windows. It was clear they represented the four elements of the Voices.

A mirror about twenty feet high and at least eight feet wide hovered in the air behind the four pillars. A steady ripple moved within the glass as if someone were dipping their finger in water.

"This is it," Dy'Mün said, drawing the girls' attention. "We are here. It is only a matter of time now. In the morning, we will begin the ceremony. We are safe—for now. Rest up. I must prepare." The Elder sat before one of the pillars and studied the markings etched along the branches.

Naoni stepped up beside Caia and watched

Dy'Mün for a few moments until it was clear the Elder wasn't going to budge anytime soon. "So," she began, turning to Archai, "how long will this take?"

"It is up to the old man's memory," Archai replied. "The script on the pillars is old; he must remember how to read it. If it were up to me, I would simply tell him, but the mental process that goes into relearning the language is needed for Dy'Mün to keep control throughout the ceremony. Or else things can go terribly wrong."

A stone clattered along the ground to Caia's right, and when she looked, Solin stood by a wooden door at the side. She joined him, but not without first meeting the watchful eyes of Archai, who followed their every move. Naoni, too, watched them displeasingly. "Is it such a good idea for you two to wander off?" she asked through full, pursed lips.

"We're only looking around," Solin replied as he tried to push the door open.

With a scoff, Naoni shook her head and turned her back to the pair. Clearly, she now held the same opinion of the couple that Archai did.

The door was stuck at first, and only after Solin shoved his shoulder against it did it open. Dirt fell from the edges and a cloud of dust tickled their noses and eyes. Stepping inside, the door shut heavily behind her. The room was strangely empty but for a small stone bench along the far wall. The walls themselves were etched with hundreds of old scripts that matched what was on the pillars Dy'Mün read. Caia ran her fingers along the scratched markings, wondering when the last person to touch them was there and who it could have been.

The sudden sense of being watched prickled the back of her neck, and she turned to Solin. She could see he was pained, not in the least bit hidden. He wasn't the type to hide his feelings or hold back his thoughts from her. That was one of the greatest parts of their relationship; she never had to wonder what he was thinking or how he felt. Their connection was something anyone could ever hope for, starting from childhood and remaining intact as they aged and grew to love one another.

"I am not sure what to do, Caia," Solin said, breaking the silence. His words were soft-spoken and his voice croaked slightly on her name. It was like there was some invisible wall holding him back from saying what he had in mind, but he made an obvious effort to force his way through it. "All of my hopes for a future have been dashed."

Caia's lips parted, searching for the right words, but all she could think about was what Archai had said. *He could have a family,* he said, and there would be no regrets.

"Solin," she began, "I don't know what to say. You can find someone." She pieced her words together in an attempt to make the whole situation sound less hopeless and dismal than it felt. "You can start a family and live your life—"

"No," Solin cut in, shaking his head briskly, crossing the distance between them in what seemed like a single step. "I don't want to think about that. Not now. Can I just sit with you without a word? I just—" Solin's eyes glassed over as he gingerly tucked Caia's white hair behind her pointed ear, and a half-smile crept across his lips. "I have been dedicated to you my entire life. I just need a few last minutes with you before you leave me."

With her heart in her throat, Caia nodded and led him to the stone bench, where she pulled his arm around her and rested her cheek on his shoulder. Too long had passed since they sat so close. Too many thoughts went unsaid, and too many fears went uncomforted. She closed her eyes and inhaled his scent as her throat constricted, and the tears in her eyes grew hot. Years of memories flitted through her mind. Every major event and every simple happening, Solin was there. He deserved to have her every attention and every assurance that her heart belonged to him.

It wasn't long before Solin's hand cupped her cheek and he pulled her closer. "What will I do without you, Caia?" he whispered. He turned her face up to his and the tears fell down her cheeks. Her chest shuddered as she struggled for enough air to respond.

Solin leaned his forehead against hers and his breaths began to match hers, telling her he struggled as much as she did.

"I...don't know...if I can...do this," she admitted through short gasps.

"Caia," he managed, taking her face into his hands. Knowing him, he was likely thinking through every possible way of making the pain go away. But there was no answer. Not this time.

"You will do what needs to be done," he replied. "And you'll know that I love you, and nothing can ever change that." With a deep breath of conviction, he pressed his lips to hers. Her heart thumped against her chest, bringing spots to her vision and a fire to her belly.

Caia unthinkingly gripped his shirt in her fists, then ran her hands over his cheeks and down his neck. Such a kiss was the deepest of promises for elves, creating a connection known as the *leg'et inmi,* or "tied of heart." An unseen cord of energy formed between them instantly, a cord so strong it was capable of spanning any distance. Legends told that not even death could sever such a connection. Solin offered his very soul to her, and Caia gave her own in return.

The sound of rushing blood in her ears was all Caia heard until the door crashed against the wall of the cellar and in the blink of an eye, Archai held Solin against the wall with his fingers wrapped around his throat.

Caia screamed and jumped to her feet.

"You will keep your mouth shut, Caia. The single shred of decency I have left is all that stops my fingers from crushing his throat." Archai squeezed his hand, bringing a gargled gasp from Solin. Nostrils flared and eyes wide with rage, Archai slowly drew his sword from its scabbard. "You are so much stupider than I thought, boy."

Solin's eyes rolled back and Caia grabbed Archai by the arm, pulling with all her strength, but the Sapient was far stronger. "Archai, stop! Stop it! Please, let him go!"

Archai thrust Solin across the room, slamming him into the opposite wall. Caia turned to run to him, but Archai snatched her by the arm, dragging her out of the room. "No time for that. You're coming with me."

"Old man," he shouted across the temple, drawing Dy'Mün from his study. "It's time."

Caia pulled against Archai's hold, trying to pry his fingers from around her arm, but his grip was too firm.

"Archai!" she cried. "You're hurting me!"

Dy'Mün rose to his feet, confusion written across his face. "By the Highest! Release her, Archai! She is a *Voice*!"

Archai's anger was so heavy, his hands trembled. "I will not stand aside while that *boy* destroys every chance we have with the Voice of Apan. He will no longer touch her. I forbid it."

Caia shoved against him, hoping he'd loosen his hold on her, but he did not budge.

"You have no right!" she cried. "I demand you to let me go!"

Archai spun and leaned over to meet Caia's gaze at her level. "Do you not understand what you are risking? Do you *want* all of Jaydür to be lost for your single moment of passion?"

Blood scalded Caia's cheeks. "Archai, it was only a kiss—"

"I know what you did!" Archai roared. "I am no fool to the way of the elves!"

"By the Highest, Caia," Dy'Mün interjected. "A kiss?"

Archai swallowed hard, making it obvious how difficult it was to keep himself under control. "I do not look to hurt you, Caia," he started. His voice wavered slightly. "But strengthening your connection with Solin is going to get the rest of our world killed."

"You've bonded yourself?" Dy'Mün asked. "Caia, how could you? Solin!" Dy'Mün eyed Solin severely over Caia's shoulder. "Such a kiss might have sealed a dark fate for all of Jaydür. You both know better than this."

Breaths heaved as Caia looked over her shoulder to find Solin behind them, eyes narrowed and jaw set. His hair was wild and his hand sat gingerly on his left shoulder, which clearly had been hurt by Archai.

"I didn't mean to," she croaked. "I didn't think it

was such a bad thing."

Archai dropped her arm and stepped away in frustration. "*I* will read the inscription and get the ceremony started," he said. "I am done helping this *child* who does not think beyond her own pleasures."

Dy'Mün shook his head and turned to join Archai without another word. That alone was like a knife to her chest. The old man was like a second father to her.

Caia's eyes darted between the two men, then set on Naoni, who stood near the raised platform. She said nothing and instead turned her back to Caia and Solin.

A tear slid down Caia's cheek as she looked back once more to Solin.

"You will stay away from her," Archai called from the platform. "Sit right there."

Eyes watery, Solin dropped to the floor where he stood. The look on his face was beyond mere shock. He looked startled, as if only now realizing what they had done.

Caia never felt like so much of a disappointment. Her heart was split down the middle, half yearning for her beloved who sat yards away from her, and half considering running away forever to a life where she wouldn't be so harshly judged for wanting to love.

Archai's voice suddenly echoed throughout the temple, shaking Caia out of her dark thoughts, though whatever he was saying was unclear, as he spoke in a language she could not understand.

Dy'Mün called from beside the platform. "Come. Naoni, you stand behind the ruby pillar and Caia, you are behind the sapphire. Take hold of the orbs."

The girls followed instructions, waiting patiently for the next when the walls of the temple shook all around them. The dust that filled the crevices of the walls for centuries floated down onto everyone.

"What's happening?" Naoni asked, bouncing glances between Archai and Dy'Mün.

Archai's lips tightened in frustration and he hurried to the largest mirror that rose behind the girls. He touched the glass with the palm of his hand and called out, "Keiren! Locke! Venidh lanol neu ajundha." The girls exchanged nervous glances. He was calling for help.

The glass rippled more quickly and within it, two shapes took form: one of a white panther with a blue gem protruding from its forehead and the other, a white tiger with a ruby protruding from its forehead. "Níha'mehn it Pandhea," voices spoke, coming from the animals within the mirror. "Welcome."

"We are in a hurry," Archai exclaimed. "We must send the Voices to safety."

"They are without the gryphon's eyes. How do you intend to locate them when the time comes?" Though neither of the animals' mouths moved, Caia knew the question came from the white tiger.

Archai pulled two long chains from a pocket at

his waist and hurried to Naoni, where he placed one around her neck. He then went to Caia, placing the second necklace around her neck.

"Archai?" she said, looking up into his eyes with a breaking voice and tear-blurred vision. The situation was becoming more real by the second and terror gripped her now. "I'm sorry," she said weakly.

He took her hand with a look in his eyes of pity or guilt, or maybe a mix of both. "I will find you," he said. "We'll make fewer mistakes then." He turned to the mirror and stepped away from the girls. He nodded and within seconds, the orb grew warm in Caia's hands. She looked to Naoni, who looked just as scared and confused.

The main doors of the temple shuddered as the hooting of goblins carried through the air.

"We must hurry!" Solin cried as windows crashed in, giving way to a string of goblins. Dy'Mün whispered with his staff in hand and pointed the top end toward those that entered. Just like at the battle of Nov'Eit, a light shone from it, disintegrating a handful of creatures. But it was not enough.

A cold burst of air whooshed from the orbs and whirled around the girls, causing them to lose their balance. Electricity crackled and shot out toward the mirror, cracking the glass. Rather than falling, the shards gathered into a ball of white light, which grew and grew until it refilled the mirror frame. Suddenly a current pulled them toward the whiteness.

"What do we do?" Naoni cried. "Archai!"

Archai turned just as he ran his blade through the chest of a goblin and shouted, "Do not go into the portal until it is completely open!" He sliced through another. "When the air turns warm, let go of the orbs and let yourself be pulled in!" Two sinstarians rushed him from different directions. He raised his hand and a smoldering white light flared from it, incinerating one sinstarian as he spun his sword at the other, killing it with a direct swing.

The door finally splintered and cracked, snatching all hope of survival from the girls as a multitude of dark creatures rushed toward them. But the lightning bursts surrounded the girls, and the creatures of the dark halted with shrieks and cackles, seeming afraid to get any closer. One creature, covered in armor from head to toe, climbed the wall onto the ledge of a window and nocked a black arrow, aiming it at Caia. As the creature released the arrow, Caia was shoved aside by Solin and the arrow pierced his shoulder instead. Her hold on the orb was severed and the pull of the portal dragged her toward it on her belly, feet first. She clawed at the ground, desperately grasping for an anchor, partially blinded by lightning bursts and her whipping hair. The necklace from Archai snagged on a ragged stone on the ground, snapping the chain just as her hand wildly grabbed something solid; it was Naoni's ankle, and both girls were dragged in, their screams echoing throughout the temple. Dy'Mün and Archai spun around to help them, but the portal was closed. The girls—and Solin—were gone.

Chapter Five
Going Mad

"What are you so afraid of?" Doctor Evan Corsa asked from the red leather recliner on the other side of the coffee table.

Ella Wiles wiped her clammy palms down the sides of her jeans. She hated when he asked her this question. It wasn't the first time. She understood there was some kind of method to his therapy sessions, but she didn't understand it.

"I'm afraid of hurting her feelings," she finally said. "My mom worries easily, and she's had enough stress since my dad left."

Corsa replied with a quiet *hmm* and tapped his pen on his clipboard. "Last week you were afraid of hurting your sister's feelings."

Ella didn't reply. So what? She didn't like being anyone's cause of distress. "Is that bad?"

"Not at all." Doctor Corsa lifted the first sheet of paper over the clipboard and studied the next. "I do notice a theme to your episodes."

Oh, nice. He was calling her night terrors "episodes" now.

Doctor Corsa uncrossed his legs and sat up straighter in his chair. "When you feel you've disappointed someone or feel there is a chance you may disappoint someone, you have night terrors," he explained. "It doesn't explain why your night terrors are full of fantasy creatures and wars, but that could be your imagination feeding into a subconscious fear. Possibly even your mind trying to tell you your fears are childish."

Ella swallowed hard and furrowed her brow. She hated when he focused on the fantasy aspect of her dreams. The goblin-like creatures and gray-skinned men with snake eyes felt more like memories than simple dreams. Besides them, there were the four people she somehow knew were friends in her dreams. She knew their history and her relationship to them, even if she couldn't quite make out everyone's face. Though one face in particular she *could* see. His face was clear enough that Ella had drawn hundreds of pictures of him since she was a child.

"So, Ella," Corsa continued, "it seems the night terrors are becoming more of a stress reaction, which is fully treatable."

That immediately drew Ella from her thoughts. "I can't have Mom pay for more pills. Not now."

Corsa closed his eyes and waved his hands

dismissively. "I'll give you a sample to test them out. Don't worry, it'll be free. It's a week's worth. If they help you ease the stress, then we'll talk about a payment plan."

No word came from Ella.

"I won't mention anything to your mom, if that will make you feel better," he added. An odd twitch at the corner of his smile gave Ella a sudden sense of suspicion. He was hiding something.

"Isn't that illegal?" she asked, wondering if calling him out was a good idea.

A knot rose and fell in Corsa's neck as he swallowed, like a snake with a gerbil being slowly digested inside. It was gross. A shudder crawled up Ella's spine at the thought. She hated snakes.

"No, no," he started. "Look, if you want to talk to your mother about medications, I am more than open to doing so. But I'm here for *you*, Ella, and I want you to be comfortable with me. There is no reason to worry." A nervous sensation came from him like stink from a dead fish. He was *definitely* hiding something.

No reason to worry? Uh-huh. It was easy to say, but worrying was what Ella did best. Especially where her suspicions were concerned, because she was *always* right about people. But it wasn't worth arguing about now.

Ella took a breath and nodded, then Corsa got up and walked behind his desk. A wooden drawer squealed on metal slides and the drawer slammed shut before Corsa made his way back to her. She looked up to him as he eyed the pill container over the top of his glasses. His salt-and-pepper hair hung just slightly below his brow and into his eyes, making his already dark brown eyes even darker.

"Take one in the evening before bed," he explained. "When you come back next week, you'll tell me your experience with them. Does that sound doable?"

"Yes. Thank you, Doctor Corsa."

With that, he gestured toward the door. "Don't forget to put those in your bag," he reminded, pointing to the pills. His throat did that gross thing again with his anxious swallow.

"Right." Ella slid the orange container into a side pocket of her backpack and walked out of the room. Her mother, who sat near the door, bounced to attention as Doctor Corsa said his goodbyes.

In the car, Ella watched her mother, Stephenie, eyeball the clock as they sped down the highway. She was generally a pretty anxious woman with a case of OCD, if you'd ask anyone, but Stephenie denied it.

"I just like things to work in a certain way, is all," she would reply when anyone pointed out her strange behavior. Like flicking her eyes to the car clock every thirteen seconds.

"So what did he say about your dream?" Stephenie asked, gripping the steering wheel with both of her suntanned hands.

The many faces of the green and gray-skinned men flashed in her mind again. Ella blinked away the image, then looked at her mother out of the corner of her eye. Half of Stephenie's face was covered with her blonde-dyed hair, but her mouth was in full view. Her tongue poked in and out of her mouth, licking her red lips in another show of anxiety. She would claim they were chapped, as was the popular complaint for everyone living in the dry Arizona air.

"Not a whole lot," Ella replied. "He just said I need to control my own stress levels, and the night terrors should go away. I can take care of it."

"Are you stressed?" Stephenie quickly asked, flicking her green eyes to Ella. "Is it being reflected in your grades?"

Ella rolled her eyes and looked out the window. "No, Mom. My grades are fine. Better than ever."

"So what's stressing you out?"

"Nothing. I'm fine. The end of the school year is coming. There are finals." It wasn't a total lie. Finals were around the corner, but Ella was in no way nervous about them. Her grades were all straight A's. She was the best student in every class and had a solid relationship with every teacher. To be honest, she wasn't really stressing out about anything but keeping her family happy. She was the oldest, and she was her twelve-year-old sister's role model. After their dad's accident, Ella felt an extra weight of eyes and expectations on her shoulders. No one ever said anything to make her feel that way, but she felt it nonetheless.

The car rolled up to the school. Ella looked at the clock. *1:45pm*. That meant lunch was over, and she was heading to math class.

"Thanks, Mom. I'll see you after school."

"Wait," Stephenie said with a hand on Ella's arm. "What about the..." Her words faltered. "The *teal-eyed man?*"

Ella tensed and her stomach turned, but she kept her focus on not allowing her emotions to show. Stephenie didn't know how much Ella hated when the teal-eyed man was forced into conversation. He was no one's business but her own.

"Corsa didn't say anything about it," Ella replied, her voice quieter than she intended. "It's not a big deal, Mom. They're dreams. I know."

Stephenie's chest rose with her subtle inhale. "I know, honey." She paused, and Ella felt a pull from her mother's gaze, as if an invisible force were trying to discern anything unspoken in her daughter's eyes. It would have seemed like a silly idea to anyone else, but Ella knew she herself could do it, so it wouldn't be much of a surprise to one day find her mother was able to do so all this time as well.

Ella dropped her gaze to her backpack with a fabricated smile. "I'll see you later, Mom. I gotta get to class."

"Of course," Stephenie replied. "I love you."

"I love you, too." Ella climbed out of the vehicle and watched it drive away before walking into the crowded school halls.

She kept her head down, her red curls acting as a curtain between her and the rest of the world. Gripping her books tightly to her chest, she did her best to ignore the student body.

If she didn't look them in the eyes, no one would realize she had been gone, would they? Then no one would have any questions. Ella had kept her therapy sessions a secret for most of her life, and she intended to keep it that way. The only one who knew about Corsa was her close friend, Rhiannon.

"Hey, Ella." Sean, a quiet guy from second period, smiled at her as they passed each other.

She replied with a "Hey," then dropped her gaze again.

"Ella!" Sandra Ortega called from behind. Ella turned and gave a quick smile to Sandra, her next door neighbor. "You weren't in first period. Mr. Sanderson asked me to give you your work so you don't fall behind. We have a quiz on Monday."

"Thank you so much!" Ella replied, feigning a dramatic thanks as she took the sheets of paper from Sandra. "It was a rough morning. Thought I was getting sick. It's all good, though. Probably something I ate."

Sandra smiled and shrugged. "Glad you're feeling

better. See you around."

Ella entered her classroom and slipped into her seat, carefully laying out her books, pens, and pencils. Algebra class was her refuge—the one place where people were so focused on their work, they had no chance to focus on her. She glanced around at her classmates, watching them prepare for class. She knew just about everyone on *some* level, which made it hard to avoid conversation on days like this one. Though Ella didn't consider herself popular, it was clear that most people liked her for the most part.

A drawn-out sigh whispered by her ear just before a voice spoke.

Nidholmen bahlog aledhrinal…

Ella jerked her head to the side, staring at Sara, the girl sitting beside her. "Excuse me?" she said.

The girl cocked her brow, annoyance flashing in her overly black-shadowed eyes. "I didn't say anything."

"Oh, sorry. I could have sworn—" Biting her lower lip, Ella swallowed back the embarrassment flushing through her. Sara was one of the only people who Ella suspected had similar emotional issues to her own but wasn't as good at hiding it. Sara wore her emotions on her sleeve, and Ella avoided speaking to her in the hopes of dodging the girl's negativity. That was another thing of hers—she could draw truth from the eyes of others, but she could also draw on their bad moods.

Aledhrinal...

There it was again. Ella froze and slowly looked around, her eyes lingering on Sara again before darting around to her fellow classmates. No one even looked up. It was like no one else heard a thing.

Níha'men em...

No one was speaking. No one's lips moved. But Ella *heard* it. The voice was ethereal and fluid.

Ella's palms grew clammy, and she wiped them on her jeans. A knot of panic formed in her throat. Something was wrong.

Ella looked to Sara once more, her heart pounding in her chest.

"What is your problem?" the girl snapped.

"I thought I heard—"

"Stop staring at me!"

Ella jerked her gaze toward her desk, her mind whirling. The words, whatever they were, were so loud! The voice was clear and crisp, as if the speaker was just beside her. Ella rubbed her eyes, forcing herself to breathe evenly. This was a whole other level of crazy. If her mother found out, she'd definitely have Ella tested. Corsa would be an afterthought. Would she have her committed?

With a trembling hand, Ella grabbed her pen, clicking the button to make the point dart out and retreat. A chill danced down her spine, freezing her in her seat. Slowly, she turned her head toward the window. Her eyes widened in horror as she tried in vain to make sense of what she saw. There, just on the other side of the glass, was a man with the most familiar face. Ella firmly held his gaze. Wildly unnatural eyes stared back at her, a crisp teal like the waters of the Caribbean. Long silver hair swayed against his back in a breeze as other strands brushed his sleek cheekbones. A sharp, angular jaw tightened just as Ella's eyes burned badly enough that she had to blink. In that instant, he disappeared.

Ella sat up straight, her gaze darting side to side.

"Miss Wiles," the teacher, Mrs. Norris, called, drawing Ella's attention from the window. "Are you all right? What are you looking at?"

Ella slowly turned her head toward the teacher. Her head trembled with the motion, and her sight blurred with tears. Narrowed eyes with deep looks of concern studied her, not unlike the one she often got from her mother.

"I—" Ella paused, passing a glance at the dozen or so pairs of eyes staring back at her. "I'm just daydreaming. Sorry."

The teacher nodded and began the lesson, but not without keeping an extra keen eye on Ella, who could do no more than keep a straight face and pretend to focus. What was she to do? She couldn't admit to what she was seeing. Her mom would never let her live it down, and neither would Doctor Corsa. Maybe it was a side effect of no sleep.

Why lie to myself, Ella thought. The man was so

clearly there, it hurt her head to think about. But *how*? And why?

Seeing him wasn't the last weird thing that happened throughout the day. Ella touched and tugged her ears as she endured the voices throughout each class. The silver-haired, teal-eyed man no longer made an appearance, but one time was enough to put her on edge. He was *there*.

By the end of the school day, exhaustion took over. The wooden desk was cold against Ella's cheek—a welcome change from the feverish heat that coursed through her. Her eyes held the unfocused knots and lines in the wood as her mind drifted off into a silent, empty peace. No voices, no hallucinations.

Rick Harl, who shared a desk with Ella in last period biology class, practically appeared in the seat beside her. He was tall and lanky, with a pointed nose and a side part in his light brown hair.

"Greetings," he said with his beak in another war book.

Ella gently smiled. "You're such a nerd when you say that." Her voice sounded weak, even to her.

"A nerd is nothing to shake your head at," he retorted. "It's something I pride myself in, thank you very much. Do I mock every girl in this room with a Dorito-tan? Of course not. I may not understand the logic behind it, but if that's what makes them happy, why should I bother?"

"You never have a quick response to anything, do you?" Ella replied, slowly lifting her head from the desk.

The pocket of her blue jeans vibrated, startling Ella with a quiet gasp. Her fingers fumbled with the small phone that was suddenly heavy as a brick. A text message from Rhiannon—her best friend for as far back as she could draw memory—read, *Meet me at the school gate after class. We need to talk.*

Ella's heart skipped a beat. Could she tell Rhiannon about the voices? She placed the phone on the desk, but it slipped off the edge and clattered beside her feet. She leaned down to pick it up with a groan, but another hand snatched it away.

"Hey," she objected, but froze when Eric Birmingham—her eight-year crush—handed her the phone. "Hey, thanks," she said, playing off her initial tone of annoyance with a higher pitch in her voice.

"No problem," Eric replied. His smile sent butterflies swarming in Ella's belly. He was about to move on when he stopped and added, "Happy early birthday, by the way."

Ella beamed, remembering that tomorrow was, in fact, *their* birthday. "Happy early birthday to you, too. And thanks for my phone!"

He didn't even look back. Of course he didn't. He *had* a girlfriend sitting right next to him at the front of the class who was everything Ella was not. Whitney Williams was the gorgeous brunette with dark chocolate eyes and a perfect smile. The girl knew her fashion, her makeup, and had the curves every high school guy drooled over. Next to Ella's tall, slim, semi-flat-chested physique, Whitney looked like some godforsaken goddess.

Speaking of the devil, Whitney's eyes were on Ella just then. Her nose was somewhat wrinkled at the bridge, like she smelled something bad. Ella's eyes bounced to Eric then back to her before turning down to the desk.

Sem tälmena. Ella stiffened at the return of the voice. The tone sounded somewhat different now, and though Ella hadn't the slightest idea what the words meant, they were infused with an indisputable sense of concern.

Ella threw her hands to her head, attracting the curious attention of her neighboring students. "Sorry," she said, tucking her bright red curls behind her ears.

After class, students eyed Ella warily as she made her way to the lockers. It was Friday, so there was more energy raging about. Usually, she hated weekends because she didn't see Eric for a couple of days, but today everything changed. All she wanted was to lock herself in her room and cry.

Someone bumped Ella's backpack with more force than necessary and she looked over her shoulder to see Whitney glaring at her as she walked away arm in arm with Eric. Ella ground her teeth and turned back to her locker. What was with that girl? They never had a problem with each other before. They'd never even *spoken* before. It made no sense for her to be giving Ella attitude suddenly.

"Hey," Rhiannon said as she touched Ella's shoulder from behind. "What's up?"

Ella's feet were suddenly more interesting and stole her gaze as she replied, "Not much." Whatever hope she had in telling Rhiannon about her hallucinations was gone. She was far too ashamed. She started toward the edge of campus, toward home with Rhiannon close beside her.

There was a pause and Ella knew Rhiannon was staring her down like she always did when she knew she was being lied to. Ella glanced up when something caught her attention from the corner of her eye and she did a double take. There, across the street, was someone else she'd seen in her dreams. The gray skin and yellow dreadlocks were two clearly unnatural aspects of her terrors haunting her nearly every night. He wasn't close enough to see the scale-like skin on the left of his face she remembered from the dreams.

"Ella?" Rhiannon asked, and Ella forced herself to look away from the man. She couldn't risk having her only friend thinking badly of her now. Not because of hallucinations.

"It's nothing, Rhi. I'm just—" She paused as Rhiannon's attention was settled on where the man had been. Ella followed her gaze, but the man was gone. "—tired. Rhiannon?"

Rhiannon smiled back at Ella. There was something in her eyes; whatever she had in mind to say to Ella was gone. "All right. It's been a long day. Why don't you head home and take a nap, then?"

Ella watched her friend carefully. A nap was not something Rhiannon had ever suggested before.

Ella quickly made her way home and changed into warmer clothes, trying to think back on when the temperature had ever been like this. The house was freezing! The thermostat was off but read sixty degrees. Arizona was not the place for this kind of cold, especially in April.

"How weird," Ella muttered to herself, then jumped when a loud crash thundered through the walls. She hurried to the window and scrunched her face in confusion. Dark clouds crawled across the skies. But there hadn't been any clouds when she walked home from school.

Ella's gaze drew to a flickering silver streak in the sky that looked somewhat like a strip of foil hanging in the atmosphere. Light danced off it like sunlight glimmering on a river.

What is that?

The same whispery sigh she heard in her classroom swept through the room, raising the hairs on Ella's neck. She turned to her mirror and jumped at the sight of the teal-eyed man standing behind her.

Ella shook her head, her heart pounding. It was official—she'd lost her mind. The psychiatric ward was the next place she'd end up, for sure.

"Why?" she asked out loud, knowing that her mother and sister were downstairs and wouldn't hear her. "Why are you tormenting me? Why do I have to see things—to see *you*—if you aren't real?"

Before Ella could take another breath, a hand covered her mouth and her arms were forced to her sides—held there by the teal-eyed man.

"Ah," he said, his breath hot on her ear. "But I am real."

Chapter Six
Man From the Mirror

The reality of the situation hadn't settled in. Ella froze in place while her mind spun in a tornado of confusion between reality and fantasy. Body heat emanated from the man who forced her in place. His hand was big and smelled like a mix of leather and metal. His voice swirled into her ears and her skin tingled while her hairs rose; every one of her five senses screamed at her.

Impossible.

"Do not worry. I am not here to hurt you," he said. His deep voice sparked a sense of heart-wrenching nostalgia in Ella. "But you know that already, don't you?"

Sweat gathered into beads at her hairline as she stared at the man's reflection in the mirror, his eyes locked on hers as if waiting for her retaliation—a consideration that wasn't far from thought.

"Do you know who I am?" he asked, saying every

word slowly and clearly, as if Ella might not speak English.

She swallowed hard and shook her head. His breath smelled like rain in the fall and strengthened the strange feeling of nostalgia, similar to homesickness, that overwhelmed her senses with the man's presence.

His hold tightened and his heart beat against her back. Panic crept over his face and for some reason, seeing that reaction somewhat calmed Ella. Maybe the man really wasn't a hallucination or a burglar. Or a murderer. Or a rapist, or a kidnapper. Or a freak with some fetish for the fingernails of a redhead.

Ella's head spun.

"No?" he said in a near-whisper. There was honest surprise in his voice.

She shook her head once again.

"Dy'Mün was right."

Ella didn't know what that meant or what to do, but thankfully, as he slipped into thought, his grip on her relaxed. She shrugged her shoulder against him, trying to create some distance between them, but he regained his composure—and his hold.

"Listen, can I speak to you without you screaming? I will not hurt you, I swear it, but I cannot release my hold on you unless you keep quiet."

Ella nodded, wondering if she could really keep her word. When the man let her go, she slowly turned and stepped away, eyeing him with suspicion. Sure, the guy had silver hair and teal eyes, but his clothes were the strangest of all. He looked as if he'd come straight out of a nineties *Hercules* episode with his leather boots, black jerkin, and tunic pants. A sword and scabbard hung by his right hip from a brown belt that circled his waist and crossed his chest.

"You do know me," he said, holding his hands up in surrender. "I've heard you speak my name while you have visions in the night."

"How would you know that?" Ella managed to speak with a solid voice. "You've been in my house before?"

The man shook his head. "No. I am aware of you in other ways. For your own sake. My name is Archai," he said. He tried to find his words, but his apparent frustration made him pause. "You watch me as if I'm some strange monster, but you *do* know me."

Ella didn't know what to say. She couldn't disagree because she did know his face but not from real life. So she stood in silence, unsure of what to do. There was no sense of threat coming from the man. He actually looked as if he wanted to disappear just as much as she wanted him to.

"You're really real, then?" she finally asked.

"Of course I am," he replied curtly.

"I saw you disappear. How do you do that?"

Archai furrowed his brow with his reply. "You are not asking the right questions."

Ella's nose crinkled. What kind of answer was that? She wiped sweat off her forehead with the back of her hand and asked, "Why are you following me? What do you want?"

Archai straightened his back and rested his hand on the hilt of his sword. "I'm here to watch over you."

"What for?"

"To keep you safe from the sinstarians," he quickly responded.

"From what?"

"The sinstarians. The grayskins."

Scenes from Ella's dreams enveloped her every thought. She knew who he was talking about.

"I've been searching for you for years," Archai went on, "and to see them so close already makes us wonder if we made the right decision about sending you here."

"I don't know what you mean. Or what a sinstarian is," Ella admitted, trying to control her panic. "Where did you come from?" *Please say Africa.* She'd been there once and hoped her subconscious formed his face from actual memories of that trip. It would make her feel less crazy.

"Jaydür," he replied.

Ella thought for a moment. "Is that in Africa?"

Archai shook his head. "It is a place farther than you can imagine but close enough to reach within moments."

Well, that didn't make any sense. Ella frowned.

"Listen," Archai continued. "I know this must be strange for you, but let me try something." He reached into his pocket slowly, as if afraid to startle her, and pulled out a necklace. He motioned for her to come closer and she shook her head.

"After all we've been through, your discomfort around me is infuriating." The muscles in his jaw tensed as he clenched his teeth. "Tomorrow is your birthday; am I correct?"

"How do you—"

"And you've been hearing things. Another language, perhaps."

Ella stepped back toward her door. Fear washed over her like a wave on coastal rock. Was this some kind of a sick joke?

"How do you know all that? Are you stalking me?"

The man's eyes narrowed and his fists clenched. "I am not the one you should concern yourself about," he snapped. "I am here to help you while others are looking to kill you. Thankfully they haven't quite realized who you are just yet. But it is only a matter of time now. You are having these experiences for a reason, and the longer we allow them to continue with no process to make you remember Jaydür, the closer the sinstarians will get."

Ella pushed her palms against her ears and squeezed her eyes shut. Now they were talking about murder? "Stop it!" she demanded. "That's enough!"

But the man wouldn't stop. In fact, he started listing words or names that she just didn't understand. "Foriei," he barked. "Atar. Do any of these names mean anything to you? Naoni. Dy'Mün." He paused. "Solin."

Her eyes shot open at the last word when a face suddenly appeared in her mind. Her stomach flipped and words poured into her memory.

A grin spread across Archai's face, weighted with satisfaction. "Solin. You recognize his name. By the Highest, I thought all hope was lost."

The face remained imprinted on Ella's mind as she turned her tearful gaze back to Archai. The vision was so clear, and the emotional tie to the boy was strong. "Who's Solin?" she asked, though the pain in her heart and cold in her stomach told her all she needed to know. She still needed to hear it from someone else's lips.

"He," Archai paused, "*was* your betrothed."

"Was?"

"He's no longer a part of your life. You are of the Terehn. He is not. He—," Archai was about to continue explaining before he stopped and frowned. "How much of him do you recall?"

"This is crazy," Ella whispered as memories flitted across her mind's eye. Memories of enormous white stone mountains and birch trees; a ghostlike pale among sparse green foliage. "I have pictures in my head, but they don't make sense. Places I've never been, all glowing a weird white."

Upon hearing that, Archai held up the necklace once more. "This will help sort those out," he explained, taking Ella's hand and pushing the necklace into her palm. His touch was warm and a sense of recognition flamed up again for a moment before disappearing. A picture of an arrow sticking out of his shoulder came to mind and disappeared just as quickly.

Ella looked at the jewelry in her hand with no more than a fleeting glance. She was afraid Archai would disappear again if she looked away too long. "What am I supposed to do with it?" she asked.

"First, what do you know about *hiraeth*?" Archai asked.

Ella blinked in thought and bit the inside of her cheek. "I don't know what it is."

Archai took a breath and crossed his arms over his chest. His nostrils flared as he said, "It is a feeling of longing; a sense of homesickness. But it's for a place you've never been or an ideal you've never been able to live." He turned his head toward the window again and lowered his voice. "It haunts you, but you do not give it necessary thought, because how can one be homesick for a place they've never been? But when one realizes what hiraeth truly is and takes the necessary steps to fulfill the feeling, there is a union of heart and mind. With such a union, a person opens to possibilities never before considered."

Ella tore her gaze from Archai to the necklace. Hanging off a silver chain was a metal bird-like talon holding a marble of some sort, and within the marble floated a small gray cloud of smoke. Her eyes still hesitantly rose back to Archai. "I think I know what you mean," she replied. And she truly meant it. "There is a birch tree near my school. Every time I see it, I get an ache in my chest, like I'm missing something or forgetting something. As if it *means* something."

The corner of Archai's lips pulled up into a half grin. "A birch tree?" He let out a deep, throaty chuckle. "Birch trees make up the vast majority of Jaydürian forests. And your old professor, Dy'Mün, has routinely used the trees for tea, bread, and beer."

At the mention of the professor, the face of a gray-haired, snaggle-bearded man appeared in Ella's mind. Emotions of familiarity and sadness hovered over her like a dark cloud, giving rise to tears in her eyes, which quickly spilled over. Ella wiped them with the back of her hand and looked at her feet, embarrassed by her show of emotion.

Archai cleared his throat. "You need time to take in all that's happened here. And I now have much to deliberate."

Ella looked at the necklace in her hand, then back at Archai. "But—"

"We will speak again," he briskly added, then...disappeared.

With a gasp, Ella circled her room, searching for any sign of the intruder called Archai, but there was none. It took her a moment to absorb what had happened.

"Oh, God," she said. Air was thick as tar as she heaved painful breaths, and more tears streamed down her cheeks. Her hands trembled uncontrollably. "No, no, no. Come back!" He was really gone but the necklace remained. She looked closely and moved the object hand from hand in an attempt to convince herself it was real.

Exhaustion suddenly came over her, weakening every fiber of her being. Her eyes grew heavy. Her skin bubbled in chills of fatigue. Ella dropped to her side on the bed, and pulled her knees to her chest. Was she in shock? Her heart raced, and though Ella felt parched, she found no strength to get up again. Within seconds, she slipped into the darkness of sleep.

A loud knock resounded from the door and Ella woke with a gasp.

"Ella?" Brittany's voice called from the other side of the door.

The bedroom was darker than she remembered. How long had she been asleep?

Ella hurried and opened the door for her sister. "Did you see anybody?" Ella asked in a panic.

"Where?" Brittany answered. "Mom's downstairs. Are you okay? You look sick."

If she looked anything like how she felt, then she should have been mistaken for a shivering corpse. Her fingertips were freezing and an ache snaked behind her eyes.

Ella pulled her younger sister into her bedroom and closed the door. The shaking wouldn't let up.

"Someone was in the house," Ella tried to explain, though she wasn't sure she should be sharing her hallucinations with anyone. Especially after just waking up.

"Who?" Brittany asked cautiously as she dropped onto the bed. She eyed her older sister. Ella ground her teeth at that response. She knew Doctor Corsa had made it clear everyone was to take her "episodes" with a grain of salt. That bothered Ella immensely.

She sat beside Brittany with her eyes still on the door. Thoughts of Archai danced before her mind's eye. He disappeared...right in front of her.

"I don't know," Ella went on.

You're hallucinating, Ella tried to convince herself, but the necklace in her hand confused her. If Archai was a hallucination, wasn't this as well?

"Britt," Ella said, holding it out to her sister. "Look at this."

Brittany slowly took the necklace. "This is cool.

Where'd you get it?"

"Just look at it," Ella said, eyeing Brittany carefully.

"I *am*," she replied before handing it back. "It's a necklace. So what?"

Okay, so the necklace was real. And that meant Archai was real.

Rubbing her hands down her face, Ella was caught off guard by her sister's next words.

"It's storming out. Did you see? At least, it looks like it's going to. Those clouds came out of nowhere. And it's real cold outside. There's also this thing in the sky that has the whole town standing around, staring up at it. Our street looks like it's part of some kind of alien flick."

So that's why it was so dark.

Ella remembered the strange, foil-like streak in the sky and hurried to the window. Brittany was right. Most of the neighborhood stood outside, craning their necks to get a better look, cameras at the ready.

"Nothing on TV is working but the Emergency Broadcast System beeping and talking about hail," Brittany went on.

"That is *so* weird!" Ella replied.

"And every other channel is blacked out. Mom said something about a solar flare or something like that."

Ella walked out her door and hurried down the stairs. "I'm going outside," she called out just before swinging the front door open to the unusually chilly air. The sun hid behind clouds that moved quicker than Ella had ever seen. Rain had to be close.

She walked down the driveway, joining the neighbors as they peered into the sky with curiosity. The strip in the sky seemed to flutter and lash at the edges like a torn book page in the wind. It almost looked like an opening in the atmosphere.

"It's not aliens, is it?" someone across the street asked no one in particular.

"It's not really moving," someone else added. It was Sandy's mom. "It doesn't look any different than it did this morning. That's a good sign, I think. But maybe everyone should go inside."

Ella looked over her shoulder to her bedroom window. The house seemed so stuffy and stale. Before she could consider what to do next, her feet were moving toward the far end of the street. *A walk might clear my head.*

"Something is going on," she muttered through clenched teeth when she'd almost reached the corner of the road. "I'm not going crazy. I'm not going crazy."

Ella stopped when her cheeks stung as wind rushed against her—but it wasn't like any wind she'd ever felt. It was like Death stood just before her, breathing its soulless afterlife all around her. Her heart beat erratically and her palms sweat. She rubbed droplets from her brow with her sleeve and nearly jumped out of her skin when she realized someone stood less than ten feet from her. It was like a freaky shadow in the corner of her eye that didn't disappear when she looked at it. It was the man with the gray skin. Much closer than he was at her school, Ella could see his left eye was disfigured, twisted into a half-empty void. Yellow dreadlocks spilled over his broad shoulders and down to his lower back. Black cloth wrapped tightly around his body into a shirt, almost like a mummy, but still shaped into clothing. Ella tried not to stare, but he was scary and out of place.

There were neighbors nearby and she wanted to look around—to see if the neighbors saw the man as she did—but an unnatural fear of him pouncing on her if she looked away prodded at her stomach. With a breath hitched in her lungs, she glanced over her shoulder and saw that no one watched her. They were all distracted with the silver streak in the sky. When she turned back, the man was lighting a cigarette.

Another chill came from the east and Ella shivered. Her hair blew into her face, small droplets of water dotting her hair like morning dew on grass. She looked back, doing the mental math to see how long it would take her to get back home, then started walking. She pushed the pace, but one look over her shoulder revealed the gray-skinned man taking slow, deliberate steps. An air of threat hung over her.

"Archai," Ella whispered under her breath. She

fumbled at his name on her lips. It was as if some unseen force made her say it.

With another look over her shoulder, Ella's shoe snagged on a split in the concrete and she tripped, scraping her knees on the sidewalk. Scrambling to her feet, she opted to jog the rest of the way home.

"Archai," Ella said again, drawing out the end of his name into an audible whine of fear for her lack of control over her own voice. She was calling for him, but it wasn't her; something else was making her do it.

Finally home, Ella slammed the front door behind her and locked the deadbolt. She hurried to her room, ignoring her sister's question of whether or not it was raining. Running to the window in her room, she looked out to the street, expecting to see the dreadlocked man or Archai, but no one was there.

A lump formed in Ella's throat and tears filled her eyes. A confusing sensation of fear mingled with a longing for some sense of comfort made her stomach twist. The world suddenly felt like a dream with no walls to keep her visions contained. All sense of reality faded.

Ella tried to center on the necklace she still clutched in her hand, hoping to regain some focus through her tears. Archai's name hung off her lips once more, and instead of resisting, she pushed it out.

"Archai?" Ella said, louder than before, in more of an asking tone.

Silence was all that replied.

A pang of disappointment hit her violently in the chest, and a fresh flood of tears streamed down her cheeks. With her back against the window, she slid to the floor, where she buried her face in her knees.

Relentless sobs came in breathless heaves, and she gripped her chest through her shirt. Her own hands felt foreign to her. Her skin felt like she was covered in plastic wrap. Her fingers curled and flexed with the urge to peel her shirt off so her pores could breathe.

Ella's heart pounded hard and fast, and in that moment, the pain was so great and her very soul felt so lonely that Ella wanted nothing less than death. Nothing could be done to stop the hallucinations from wracking her mind, and the man who had answers was gone.

A breathy, ghostlike whoosh filled the room just before the deep voice of Archai spoke. "I am sorry," he said, bringing Ella to a cold stop. She didn't look up, afraid that if she did, he wouldn't really be there, then her madness would be confirmed. Instead, she dabbed her nose with the back of her hand and sniffed. "Are you really there?" she asked. "Or am I imagining?"

"I am here," Archai replied.

Her stomach lurched at the response and the hairs on her arms rose. His voice was familiar and brought with it the sense of comfort her soul ached for. If heaven had a sound, Archai's voice was most definitely it. He was there, in her room. She wasn't alone in her insanity anymore. Her answers stood within grasp.

Ella opened her eyes but kept her face down.

"I am not to be feared," he assured.

"You're straight out of my dreams and standing in my room," she replied, choking on the last word. "That's terrifying."

"I am not a stranger, and I will not hurt you."

Ella slid her gaze from her feet up the carpet in the direction that Archai's voice came from. Nausea twisted her stomach when she saw his boot beside her desk, not four feet from her.

"Why are you here?" she asked.

"To help you remember," he replied. "This world is not your own."

Something about the way he said that touched her. It was almost like déjà vu but with more meaning.

With a deep, ragged breath, she finally met his teal gaze. "There is another world?" she asked.

Meeting her eyes, a pleased yet cautious expression crossed Archai's face. He slowly took a step forward and offered his hand. Ella focused on it, instinctively knowing that now was the greatest moment in her life. After a short moment of hesitation she took it, and when the warmth of his skin touched hers, the faint sense of madness that clouded her mind all but disappeared. Seeing him and feeling him there in the flesh brought a sense of clarity and anticipation, along with the understanding that she was going to be all right.

Archai pulled her up to her feet and said, "Yes, there is another world."

Chapter Seven
You Have Wings

Rain trickled down the windowpane. It gradually fogged from the breaths rushing through Ella's lips as she sat nervously perched on the edge of the window sill. Archai was very real, and as it was much too difficult to look him in the eyes, she focused on the curtain of shadow that fell over Phoenix outside her windowpane.

"I am more than willing to explain myself when you're comfortable enough," Archai said. "I can sense your uneasiness." He stepped to the far side of the room and propped his sword in the corner. "Memory loss of this scale was not expected," he went on. "I am very much uncertain of how to move forward."

Ella took in a deep breath, still weirded out by the way Archai spoke. "Well," she started, looking up through red, puffy eyes. "I've seen a man appear and disappear before my eyes. I don't know what else could happen that would leave me any more interested in what's going on. Just start talking; I'm listening."

"You've finally given up on doubt, have you?" A smirk pulled at one side of Archai's mouth and there was a flicker of recognition that pained Ella. She knew that smile, but she couldn't remember from where. "It only took you seventeen years. Back in Jaydür, you were not trusting of me. You were so cautious."

Ella closed her eyes as she forced herself to swallow. She was parched but refused to leave the room. Archai needed to stay within sight until she had answers, even if his words were painful to listen to.

He stepped toward her. "We can begin our discussion with that," he said, gesturing to the necklace.

Ella opened her palm and looked at the marble with a nod. "Okay. What is this?"

"I'd like to *show* you, but I'm afraid it will have you screaming."

Ella thought on that for a moment. She'd called him, and he came. If she didn't get answers now, she knew she'd end up in a ball of sobs again and regret everything. At this point, she didn't have much to lose. "Whatever you want to show me, will it hurt?"

That earned her a laugh from Archai, which was a breath of fresh air in the stale atmosphere of the room.

"No," he said, taking a step closer to her. "It will

be shocking, but it is nothing physical."

With a deep breath, Ella stood and offered him the necklace. "Show me."

Archai closed the blinds, then made her stand in the center of the room.

Ella's stomach fluttered at his sudden closeness behind her. How did she know he wasn't going to stick her with a knife or something? She blinked away the thoughts.

Taking the necklace from her hand, Archai tossed it into the air. To Ella's shock, gravity did not pull the necklace down. Instead, the chain and orb remained frozen in midair, at her eye level.

Ella gasped and raised her hand to feel around it for a string or anything else that might be holding it up.

Archai pressed her hand down. "Wait," he said.

A white light shone within the marble and Ella's attention fixated on it. The light expanded outside of the orb and she stepped back against Archai, who held her firmly in place with his hands on her shoulders.

"Watch," he whispered.

Small shadows took form within the light, and the more Ella focused, the clearer they became. One of the forms took on a face that looked strangely like her own, though many of the features were far off. Instead of the red, bouncing curls she knew, the hair on the girl she watched was pure white and pin straight, falling down to her bottom. Blue eyes peered back at her in place of her own light brown.

The girl in the light turned and ran through a forest with a laugh that resonated through Ella's mind like dripping water in a cavern.

"What is this?" she asked in little more than a whisper. The images were doing something to her as they slithered into her brain through her eyes. Parts of her mind she never knew were there gradually came to light, one by one, enlightening everything around her. Colors grew brighter. A natural sense of knowing overcame her mind, telling her exactly where Archai stood without having to look at him. *How* he stood. How many breaths he took in a moment. The images from the orb clung to her mind like threads of a spider web, anchoring onto every corner of her consciousness.

"Memories, Caia," Archai replied. "Memories of your life in Jaydür."

Caia. The name pierced Ella in the gut and her heart rate shot up. She trembled and Archai sensed she was troubled.

"Are you all right?" he asked.

Ella ducked beneath the necklace and turned to face him, breaking her connection with the orb. All sense of knowing dissipated. "What do you want with me? What is going on?"

Archai frowned at her sudden hostility. "Caia, calm down. I am here to help you. Why did you break contact?"

"I know that name," she admitted. Her head grew heavy and her knees buckled beneath her, dropping her to the bed. She was going to faint.

"Of course you do. It is yours."

"My name is Ella Wiles."

"Caia Foriei is your name; I will call you by no other. You will remember, and the sooner you do, the better."

Ella took deep, focused breaths, afraid that she may pass out with Archai in her room. Did he know what she'd just witnessed? Could he see that she had indeed remembered? "What do you want from me?" she asked again.

With slow, deliberate movements, he pulled the chair from her desk and sat across from her, his knees almost touching hers. Ella tried not to flinch as she tossed glances between Archai and his sword in the corner of the room. Memories of the sword flashed countless times in the orb, but she didn't grasp its significance.

"Look at me," he said. Leaning forward, he caught her gaze. "I am here to help. You know this. You can feel it. I can see it in your eyes that you recognized me from the first moment. There is no reason to deny it." He took the necklace from the air and tossed it into the air in front of her, allowing the images to take form once again. "Now, this necklace," he continued, "was made by Elder

Dy'Mün. Your memories were stored inside this orb before you were sent to Earth for safekeeping. Do not lose it."

The images shifted from memory to memory as Archai spoke, as if keeping up with his words. When Dy'Mün was mentioned, the face of an old man formed and Ella knew it was him. Images of a young girl studying books flickered through the light; others also appeared while Archai went on with his story.

"Naoni Arduun was sent as well," he went on.

A girl with dark curls and orangey copper eyes formed beside the white-haired version of herself. Ella recognized her but said nothing. She couldn't tell if it was just her imagination or not.

"Archai," Ella said. "I'm trying to understand. But who am *I* to need safekeeping?"

Archai's face smoothed with disappointment at the question. "Can you truly not grasp your worth?" he said. "Can you not sense the life that you pour into this place?"

Blood filled her cheeks.

Archai stood and ran a hand over his jaw. "I sensed an air of constriction and disparagement on Earth from the moment I entered," he said. "What worth it stole from you. Sending you to such a place was far from wise. You have no sense of importance. No self-respect." Archai clenched his fists and crossed his arms as if holding himself back from lashing out. "Caia, you are a fundamental piece to

Jaydür. You are one of four, and the other three cannot go on without you. You are a symbol of peace; the hope that little children hear in bedtime stories. You are a vein within the world and your element is the blood that gives life to it. You are the Voice of Apan. The Voice of water. And without you, peace, hope, and life is all but gone from Jaydür. Can any of these humans," he scoffed at the word, "claim such value?"

Ella abandoned his gaze before he could finish his speech. Her eyes dropped to her hands, which she fumbled with uncomfortably. How could he say something like that? He didn't know her. Her life was full of ridiculous things like eating glue in the first grade and throwing up in front of her classroom in fifth. The kind of person he was talking about sounded like some kind of goddess. Ella closed her eyes at the thought of Archai's words.

"I won't coddle you, Caia," he went on, giving her a sidelong look. "We've no time for that. A shadow creeps from the east, darkening the waters that once ran so clear in Jaydür. The number of goblins waxes as the faith of the people wanes. Fear is struck into the hearts of the young and old."

Ella's gaze shot up once again. "Goblins?" she asked with a frown. "Wait, what kind of world are we talking about here?"

Just as she asked, the images in the light of the orb changed to that of a horde of green men with hooked noses and pointed ears—walking monsters. The sight churned her stomach and brought bile to the base of her throat, but she held back her instinctual reaction.

Ella was dumbfounded. The goblins stood in ranks like an army before a great field laden with bodies of men, women, children, and livestock. It was the scene from her night terrors.

"And that? That's real?" she asked, gesturing to the scattered bodies.

Archai's eyes were low and dark with concern, when he looked up to her and nodded. "Many died that day."

"Ella?"

Ella jumped up in surprise at the sound of her mother. "Yes?" she called as her thoughts raced. How would her mom react to a stranger in the bedroom?

"We're going out tonight with the Suttons," she replied from the other side of the door. "Be ready to go by six."

Ella relaxed. "Okay. No problem."

She took a breath and sat back down on her bed with a leg underneath her.

"You said 'Voice of ...' something," she continued.

"Of Apan," he replied. "In the Elvish language, it means 'water.'"

"Elvish?"

Archai nodded.

"Goblins, elves," Ella said with furrowed brows. "Those things are fantasy."

"It is taking a considerable amount of self-control for me to overlook your words and not break something right now, Caia," Archai said, his voice dropping into a deeper octave. "Please, just listen. Elves are the highest of men in Jaydür," he explained. "Goblins and sinstarians are the lowest forms of life in the lands, if you were to ask me, and very much real."

Heat rose to Ella's face. "I'm sorry," she murmured, suddenly worried about offending Archai.

"Don't apologize to me," Archai replied. "You do not apologize."

Could she not do anything right? This man was so harsh! "Everyone apologizes sometimes," she said with a frown.

"Ask me what you have on your mind," he cut in. "I can see your thoughts are reeling."

With a nod, Ella wrung her hands and hesitantly looked to Archai. "All right. What is a Voice?" she asked.

It was strange how Archai didn't often move. He rarely even blinked as he sat there, eyes fully locked onto her.

"A Voice is an ageless, celestial being," he quickly explained. "They are keepers of the elements, and your element, as I mentioned before, is water. Water is one of the two most crucial elements—the elements of life—the other most important being fire. This puts you in more danger than the others. You and fire."

Ella couldn't go on without asking, "Celestial? What, like a god?" She almost laughed. "You think I'm a god?"

Archai shook his head. "I *know* what you are. You are of the Terehn, as am I."

"Celestial," she repeated. "Right." A fear of being horrifically pranked prodded at her heart. But she saw enough to know this was no joke. "What is 'Terehn?'"

"In Elvish, it translates as 'time-spirits.' There are eight of us. The Voices, the Sapients—which I am— and the Keepers of the Chambers who live within the Rehnedhen, a spirit world parallel to Jaydür and Earth."

Ella rubbed her forehead as a sharp ache snaked its way to the back of her eyes. *So many strange words.* It was just so much to take in, and she suspected she'd already forgotten half of the names that had been mentioned. If not for witnessing Archai's disappearing act and the memories in the orb, she'd have kicked him out long ago. It still seemed impossible, but she couldn't ignore Archai's words now.

Looking to the window, he let out a long breath and said, "You must rest. As much as I would rather not stop now, it is clear you are mentally exhausted."

"No!" Ella jumped up. "Please. I don't want to be

alone."

The look on Archai's face made Ella drop her gaze and fumble with her hands again.

"Has something happened?" he asked. His tone was calmer. Quieter.

"The voice," she replied. "I haven't heard it since you've been here."

Archai turned toward the window and glimpsed down to the street. "From what I can tell, the voice is the eled'hwen. We saw it within you, days before you were sent here. It seems that once it sensed danger so near, it brought itself to the surface all at once."

"The 'eled'hwen?'"

Archai nodded. "The elven light. It is something like a separate consciousness. Yet it is an extension of yourself at the same time."

Ella bit the inside of her cheek. His awareness of what she was experiencing was…uncomfortable. "How did you know I've been hearing it?"

"I've been watching you, Caia, and the connection we have is something that cannot be explained with words. But whatever has caused it, I'm glad for it." A smile touched his lips. "It seems it is helping you realize that, indeed, I am not a madman."

Ella looked down at her lap with a weak smile of her own just before the creepy guy from down the street came to mind again, as well as the voice. *Tell him*, it said.

"Archai," Ella swallowed nervously. "I've seen one of those guys with the gray skin. Just before you showed up here this time."

Archai's lips parted and he was clearly drawn into thought for a moment before realization crossed his face. He rubbed the inner corners of his eyes. "I was gone for two minutes, and they step up. *Two* minutes."

Ella didn't know what that was supposed to mean. "I went outside for a walk and he stood there watching me. Then he started following me, but I came home."

The moment of silence between the two was interrupted by the sound of the microwave, reminding Ella that her mother and sister were downstairs. "So they know who I am?"

Archai shook his head.

"But the way he was watching me…"

"They may suspect you, but they are not convinced."

"How do you know?"

"Well, you're still here. We'll know when the enemy knows. The whole world will know if you're discovered—and not in a pleasant way." Archai looked up to Ella and frowned. "The expression on your face concerns me, Caia. I must find a way to prove, once and for all, the existence of Jaydür. If the sinstarians have their attention on you, there is absolutely no room for doubt."

He rose to look out the window at the shadows in the street, as if making certain they were not being watched. Whatever he was thinking was intense, and Ella's stomach twinged with anxiety.

"If we needed to be alone without fear of being heard, where could we go?" he asked without turning.

"I'm not sure. We've been fine here, though," she replied. "I mean, how loud do we need to be?"

Something about the way his eyes fell on her made her heart race, and she wondered once again just how safe she was with this man, regardless of what he'd shown her and what she "remembered."

"Let's say, if one would feel the desire to scream, where could we go where it would not be heard?"

Ella rose quickly to her feet and retreated to her door. Archai pursed his lips and reached out to her. "No, please," he began with renewed eagerness. She froze by the door with her hands behind her, grasping the doorknob. He stepped forward with hesitation and spoke through tight lips. "I do not mean to scare you but I sense that doubt remains within. What I can show you—to prove beyond a shadow of a doubt that I am who I claim to be—will frighten you. But that response is inevitable in these circumstances. Until the idea of the impossible melds into your mind, you will have doubt. I can erase that doubt but you need to trust me."

Ella had to swallow hard before she could manage a response.

Trust. She hated that word. It was the bane of her existence in this house. Every argument ever made with family or her therapist ended with it. Every "solution" to her "problems" was trust. Trust. Trust. Trust. She was done with it.

"Are you so sure I would scream?" she asked under her breath. Something within her changed, and Ella could feel it. Resentment and animosity fell away as a strange sense of resoluteness discharged from her like a wave, and the smile forming on Archai's face was proof that he noticed.

Arms crossed over his chest, he considered the girl before him. "Maybe not, after all."

Ella straightened her back and raised her chin, collecting all her uncertainties and shifting to confidence. Whatever this man had to show her, she could handle it. One thing she knew for sure was that holding her tongue was no challenge. "Then show me," she finally said.

Archai dropped his arms and turned his back. "If this is what will win your trust, I will risk it." Drawing his shirt over his head, he revealed two scars in the shape of a V, each at least twelve inches long across his back.

Ella covered her mouth and gasped in shock. "Oh my God! What happened?"

Archai's shoulders heaved with every breath. Ella noticed something strange then. It was as if he was *nervous*.

"Archai?" she said, concerned, but before she could go on, her attention was brought back to the scars.

They moved.

His skin rolled as something burrowed beneath. Ella covered her mouth to quiet herself but wasn't sure she'd be able to keep silent as his skin stretched outward, and something like bone protruded toward her. The skin tore, though no blood dribbled down his back, and with a jerk of Archai's shoulders, great white wings spread from his back.

Ella backed up against the wall, frozen in awe. The air in the room grew thick and a cold sweat beaded her temples. Archai's head was down and as he turned to face her, his eyes looked up through his lashes, seemingly afraid of what he'd see. "Caia, are you all right?" he asked, turning to face her head-on. "You're white as death."

Her gaze dropped to the ground just as her knees lost the strength to hold her up. Archai caught her before she hit the ground and helped her to her bed. Her hands shook on his forearms, cold and sweaty.

"I'm dizzy," she whispered.

"You're in shock," he explained. He knelt at her feet to catch her eyes and smiled. "But you didn't scream."

Moving her hand to his shoulder for support, she flashed a half-smile in return. "You have wings."

Archai didn't manage a response before Ella

collapsed into his arms, just barely conscious. "Rest now," he whispered. "You're going to need it."

"Ella?" Her mother's voice rose up the stairs with her footsteps, and Archai quickly collected the girl into his arms. Ella's head lolled around. "No more worrying about who will find or hear us." His face looking down at her was the last thing Ella saw before she faded into darkness.

Chapter Eight
Believer

A light ache lingered behind Ella's eyes, so she decided to leave them closed for a moment as she came to. Last she remembered, she was in her bedroom with Archai and—she paused, her brow wrinkling in thought as she tried to recall everything.

He sprouted wings.

The image her memory called to mind was beautiful and amazing, her emotions wild, flaming in all directions like a fire in a breeze. The very idea that such things existed excited every aspect of her being. Something within her felt like it had come alive. But all feelings were quickly tossed aside when she finally opened her eyes and realized she was no longer in her bedroom.

Pale sea-green wallpaper shrouded the walls, clashing horribly with the orange, flowery quilts spread across two queen size beds. A covered mirror hung above a white dresser, and the mattress squeaked beneath her as she quickly sat up to meet Archai's gaze from across the room—a hotel room.

For a moment, Ella could do nothing but shake her head in disbelief. As the magnitude of the situation sank in, she jumped to the window and pulled the curtain aside. She knew where she was but couldn't believe she was there. Across the road was the familiar setup of restaurants placed before the towering triangular glass roof of the Arrowhead Mall. A new fear curled within her as she slowly turned to face her abductor.

"You kidnapped me?" she said when she finally found her words.

Archai didn't move from his chair. He simply studied her every move, the massive white wings moving ever so slightly behind him. "Kidnapped? No. I borrowed you from your family, your concerns, and your misplaced sense of safety." He stood up, stretched his wings, and took a water bottle from the mini refrigerator, then offered it to her. "Drink. You're dehydrated."

Ella quickly stepped back as he advanced toward her. He frowned in what looked like honest surprise. "What is it now?" he asked. The soft caution he used toward her before was all but gone. He was different now. Harsher. Unafraid of what she might think or do.

"You took me from my home and brought me to a hotel?" she asked, bleary-eyed. "I don't even know you!"

"Your moods are becoming a sore," he replied, stiffening at her accusations, then countered, "I brought you where I can help you; where I don't have to hold back because of *your* insecurities."

"Insecurities?" she said with a sniff, barely holding back her tears. "Wanting to feel safe is not an insecurity."

Archai rolled his eyes as he tossed the bottle of water onto the bed beside her. "You're safe with me," he declared flatly.

"How do I know that?" she snapped. With his silence, Ella closed her eyes and tried to collect herself. "Okay, I get that there is another world and that people want to hurt me. I've seen proof of that. But now that you've kidnapped me—now that you've taken me from my home against my will—how can I know *you're* not the bad guy?"

It took a moment for Archai to respond, but when he did, he moved swiftly. With the hilt of his sword suddenly in hand, Ella cowered against the window in fear as Archai unsheathed the blade and...dropped it to the floor. Her gaze flickered between his and the sword, which was bright with the reflection of the ceiling light and the white of his wings.

"Pick it up." His demand was quiet but severe. Enough to make the hairs on Ella's neck rise. There was no fault in the hold of Archai's gaze as he waited for her to follow his directions. The flare of impatience in his eyes urged her on as she knelt down and reached for the hilt of the sword. Whispers fluttered around her from all directions as her fingers hovered just above the blue cloth wrapping the grip. There was magic of some sort at work here. She pulled her hand back and looked up at Archai, who simply urged her on with a sage nod of his head.

"Did you hear that?" she asked.

He remained silent, but the dark look in his eyes was answer enough. Her hand hesitated over the blade once more, uncertain what to expect, but when her fingers lingered above the hilt and she heard nothing, she wrapped her fingers around the clothed metal. All at once, a white light flashed across her vision as if drawn by a lightning rod. She blinked and tried to focus her eyes. When the brilliance subsided, she was met with a hooded man whose face was inches from her own. Something tugged on her wrists. She looked down to find chains binding her wrists together, but the hooded man immediately cut right through them with a sword. A sense of panic overcame her; she couldn't control herself. She thought to push the man away but simply stood, watching him. It was then that she realized she was having a vision.

When he stepped back and pulled down his hood, Ella inwardly gasped in surprise.

"You are welcome," Archai said in her vision with an airy voice as he tossed an arrogant grin and glance aside to someone else present. There was smugness in his eyes.

Ella tried to turn her head, but everything blurred around her, causing her vision to shake.

"I suggest we make our way on foot," the ethereal voice went on. "Since we are in no immediate danger. We can hide our tracks as we go."

"Archai?" Ella tried, feeling her arms reach out and meet his steadying grip, but she remained within the vision as the scenery drooped and swirled, like water washing sediment off rock. Suddenly she was surrounded by forest in the last glow of twilight. The air was cool and damp as if it had just finished raining. The smell of pine and smoke filled her nostrils and made her skin prickle with recognition.

"Will I like you better then?" she asked in the same echoic tone. It was her voice but every consonant leaving her lips had a vaguely different sense of pronunciation—like an accent of some sort. "Or will you be just as *coy* as you are now?"

"Whether you like me or not will not matter," Archai responded. Ella looked toward the voice and saw him pass by the trees, running his fingers along the bark, his deep-set teal gaze secured on her.

"I'll always be there. You will be with me for all time. Unless, that is, someone removes *your* eyes."

His cold stare faded as a sense of falling filled her with terror. The ground dragged beneath her, scraping her back, wrists, and arms as a horrid cackling resounded all around. Again her hands were bound and the sense of impending death brought vomit to the base of her throat. The face of the snake-eyed man from her dream appeared before her when Ella was suddenly plucked from the ground. Her vision was blinded yet again with a white light, and she returned to the first vision with Archai's face just before her own.

With a rapid-beating heart and sudden clarity of sight, Ella was back in the hotel room with Archai standing before her.

"If I was the 'bad guy,'" he said, his breath warming her face. "I've had more than one opportunity to kill you."

The sword clattered to the floor and Ella couldn't stop herself from sobbing as she rose up onto her tiptoes and wrapped her arms around Archai's neck, half for the support and half because she simply didn't know what else to do. What she'd just experienced were not just visions. They were memories and she remembered them as if they'd happened just the day before.

"I'm sorry," she cried, shaking uncontrollably. "I'm so sorry. I didn't mean to forget."

It took some time for Ella to calm down, but when she did, she found a place by the window where she sat in silent thought. Archai urged her to take the moment of clarity and meditate on it all. He said this was why he took her from home. With no one to call or check in on her, Ella could collect her thoughts in peace.

Ella looked over her shoulder at Archai, who now lay on the bed, his wings wrapped around him like a cloak, eyes closed. He wasn't asleep. He was planning. She remembered him doing it by the fire on their way to the Temple of Pandhea.

Pandhea.

She remembered the name. She remembered the *idea* of the place. She failed to bring more of the journey there to mind. All she had were the images from some of her dreams, flashes of memories, and now, the ones she'd just acquired from Archai's sword. An idea dawned on her suddenly and she dug into her pocket, pulling out the orb and chain. She wasn't so impressed with it now, considering what she'd seen that day, so without a second thought, she tossed it into the air and watched the memories, taking them in as her own.

The speed with which she recalled things was incredible yet frustrating at the same time. They were *her* memories. Why couldn't she recollect everything all at once now instead of one bit at a time? And how long would it take to gain it all back?

A face passed through the orb and Ella froze, focusing on it. It was a man with hair as dark as a crow. His eyes were like blue fire, and his skin was as white as snow. Only one guy she knew had a face like that.

"Solin."

Ella reached out as hundreds of thousands of moments with Solin crossed the fabric of her mind and interweaved with the scattered few of Eric in this life. *Eric?* She jumped from her seat, knocking the chair down behind her; Archai was on his feet just as quickly, wings spread, ready to take flight.

"What is it?" he demanded.

"Solin," she said through heaves. "Eric. Solin is Eric." She spun to look Archai full on, knowing he didn't quite understand her meaning. She pointed to the frozen image of Solin and cried, "He's here! I know him. I see him five days a week. All my life, I've felt something with him. I connected with him in some way that I never understood, but now it all makes so much sense."

Archai let out a breath of relief. "All right. This is nothing of great severity. So you happen to have contact with the elf boy. That is no great deal. He has nothing to do with any of this."

"Archai," Ella pressed, not sure why he was so calm and unaffected. "Don't you understand? Solin is here and he has no memories. We have to help him."

Archai's brows rose as he sat back down. "No, we don't. The boy has played his part. He's nothing to do with us."

Ella hurried to his side, kneeling beside him,

taking his hand. "He has everything to do with me! He saved my life. I owe it to him to help him remember."

"He is of no concern to the survival of Jaydür," Archai went on, releasing her hand. "And either way, even if we *wanted* him to remember you, there are no memories to bring back," he said, his voice calm but cutting. "They were not preserved in an orb like yours and Naoni's."

Ella's gaze suddenly dropped from his.

"What now?" Archai asked.

The Voice of Folc's name brought up an image of the dark curls and copper eyes of a familiar girl. It *was* Rhiannon. She thought she connected the dots earlier, but now she was certain.

Oh my God. Naoni was here, too.

Ella looked up at Archai, searching his eyes for any trace of knowledge in the matter of the Voice of Folc. He didn't seem to know anything, and Ella decided it would be better that way. She was having a difficult time with this herself, and if Naoni's whereabouts were known, she'd be dragged into all of this as well.

"Nothing," Ella replied.

That didn't fool Archai for a second. "If you know something about Naoni—"

"Then I will tell you," she replied, casting a venomous glance. "Until then, I want Solin helped."

Archai looked up to the heavens in exasperation.

"He cannot *be* helped, Caia." With a hand running down his clenched jaw, he tossed a glance at the girl. "Your mind will not be freed of him, will it? Solin was a pest in Jaydür, and now his unintentional crossing has made him a pest in this world. I suppose hearing the explanation from someone else may be better accepted than it is from me."

Archai turned to the covered mirror above the dresser and pulled off the sheet he had hung over the glass. "Apparently, my words hit you like water on stone. I think it's time we call on Dy'Mün."

A light sparked in Ella's eyes at the mention of the Elder's name. Of course! Why was she bothering with the Sapient when she could go straight to an Elder? Maybe he'd be more willing to help.

"Damn you!" a voice cried out, coming from behind, before, and beside. "You insolent imbecile!"

Ella jumped back in surprise but couldn't withhold her laugh of joy when, within the glass of the mirror, Professor Dy'Mün's face materialized. He was the same as the last time she'd seen him. His face was wrinkled with age and wisdom that could only be seen in a true Elder. His eyes were green and unusually soft, considering that he was shouting his frustrations at Archai.

"You were told to remain within sight and still you cover your mirrors!" The old man went on, his beard and mustache quavering around his thin lips. "One of these days, you're going to find yourself in a sea of trouble with the Elders."

Ella decided it was time to step forward. She flickered her eyelashes, afraid to blink—afraid that the wonders would cease. Not because of the magic at work before her but because of the speed at which memories of the professor were returning to her.

The Elder's eyes crossed to her and he stopped, surprised at the sight of her. "Caia," he said in an almost whisper. "Am I dreaming? Are my eyes fooling me?"

Ella smiled. "Hello, professor. Your eyes are fine. I'm here."

"And she's remembering," Archai added with a small but prideful smile of his own. "Her memories were not wholly lost, Dy'Mün. With a little push," he explained with a shake of his wing, "she's come to understand our situation."

"We've been so lost without you, Caia," Dy'Mün said, his eyes bleary and tearful. "At long last, we can move forward."

"Professor, I am so happy to see you, too," Ella said with a sniff.

"Before we get ahead of ourselves here," Archai cut in. "I need you to explain something to Caia." He stopped until he clearly had Dy'Mün's attention. "Caia is in contact with Solin, but for obvious reasons, he does not remember her."

"You don't say!" Dy'Mün laughed. "How remarkable that they happened upon one another in that world! Do you think Naoni—"

"Caia insists we 'help' him remember."

At that, the Elder frowned and his gaze wavered. Whatever hope there was in receiving help from him quickly dwindled.

"It is unfortunate, the way things have turned out," Dy'Mün said. "But he cannot be helped."

"Professor, you know I can't leave him like this. There must be a way," she pressed.

"There is no way." Archai's tone was cold and uncaring.

"Of course you'd say that!" she cried. "You've hated him since the beginning. Since before the temple!"

Archai exchanged glances with the professor, who didn't seem to notice what the Sapient had recognized. "Great job," Archai said with a grin. "You're remembering on your own."

Ella stopped and thought on his words for a moment. "Yes, I remember a lot from the temple." Her eyes dropped to the floor and she felt more tears stain her skin. She was pleased that she indeed was remembering on her own, but Ella couldn't let this go. "Please," she continued. "I made an oath. I can't just go back on it."

Archai crossed his arms over his chest. "Caia, you're pining after a boy who doesn't know nor care who you are. What if he had died? What would happen to your oath then?"

"It would be absolved, of course. But—"

"So consider him dead."

If Archai would have taken Ella's heart from her chest and wrung it with his own hands, it would be no different from what she felt in that moment. She dropped onto the bed and clenched her fists as her voice lowered with her reply. "I can't consider him dead when he clearly is not dead. He is here. His soul is inside of him."

"A very changed soul," Dy'Mün reasoned. "The Solin you knew from Nov'Eit is not the boy you know here. He's been renewed. Reborn. It's as if he were never a part of Jaydür. After a lifetime living among humans, he doesn't know better. He is unable to regain his past."

Archai's attention flicked to the entrance of the room. Ella trailed his gaze. "It's time to go," Archai cut in.

A deep furrow crept across her brow. "What's wrong?"

"Your mother is worried about you," Archai said.

"I imagine she is," Ella replied. "But she'll survive. I have other things to worry about right now."

"People are looking for you," he added, covering the mirror without so much as a goodbye to Dy'Mün. "With a sinstarian on your heels, the last thing we need is to attract more attention."

Ella checked her pockets, not thinking twice on

how Archai would know something was happening. "I don't have my phone. Should I call her?"

"Yes. She is causing something of a commotion."

Taking the phone from the nightstand between the beds, Ella dialed Stephenie's number. Only one ring made it through.

"Hello?" The panic in her voice was clear.

"Mom," Ella tried as Archai prompted her toward the door. "Hi, mom."

Ella!" her mother cried. "Where are you? Are you all right? Where did you go?"

"I'm fine, Mom. I'm at the mall. I'm sorry. I forgot my phone. I'm on my way home."

"Dear God, Ella," her mother said with a cry. "I've been worried sick. You didn't say a thing! You just disappeared. I'll come get you."

"I'll take you," Archai said, loud enough for her mother to hear.

Stephenie quickly responded, "Who is that?"

Ella lost her words for a moment. How in the world was she going to explain Archai? "Um, I'm with a friend." The explanation was weak, but she was caught off guard. "He's taking me home. We'll be there in a few minutes."

"He?"

"Mom, I'm almost there. We'll talk when I get home. Love you. Bye."

She hung up and ran a hand through her red curls, which, by that point, were completely untamed. "How the heck am I going to introduce you to my mother?"

"As your friend," he suggested. "Like you said. We might as well meet, seeing as I'll be spending a lot of time with you now."

Ella studied her new "friend" for a moment. There was so much about him screaming, "I'm not quite human but I may pass as weird."

"This is not going to work," she said with a whine. "You look more like a college guy than high school. My mom is going to kill me."

Archai cocked an eyebrow and stiffened. "Kill you?"

She waved a hand dismissively. "It's just an expression. She's not going to be pleased with our being together."

"Pleased or not—"

"Yeah, yeah, I get it." By now she knew that Archai had his mind set on a plan and nothing said would change that. Opening the door, she realized something. She turned, almost bumping into Archai. "Um," she started, pointing to his wings. "Those."

"I cannot fly without them," he explained, knowing she meant for him to get rid of them.

"When you fly, you can pull them back out."

He grabbed her shoulders and turned her back to him. "Don't scream."

"What are you…" She gasped in surprise as he pushed her outside, slid his arm around her waist, covered her eyes, and pushed off the ground. Flying *now*? They were going to be seen!

Wind streamed downward against her for at least a full minute before it whipped wildly around. Why were her eyes covered! She wriggled a hand free and pulled on Archai's fingers with a hunger to see like she'd never felt before.

To her dismay, gray clouds shrouded most of her sight, but she figured they'd only last until Archai rose above them. But as they climbed to new heights, the atmosphere grew darker and the clouds thicker. She turned her face to meet Archai's and swallowed hard when she was met with a distracted frown. His gaze was set above them, but she couldn't tell what he was looking at.

It was pointless to keep her eyes open. The air dried them instantly after every blink. Ella finally gave up and turned her face toward Archai's chest. That's when she noticed something—he *really* smelled like rain. Stealing another peek at his face, she felt an ebb and flow of emotions coming from him. Agitation, then uneasiness, sudden determination, then confidence and back again. Were these *his* emotions? A memory flashed in her mind from the ceremony in the Temple of Pandhea. Archai had the same expression on his face and the same sensations coming from him. He was worried about her.

It was difficult to make any movements at the speed they were going, but she found his wrist by her ribcage and squeezed it reassuringly. He looked down at her for the first time, and when they locked eyes, she felt a wave of conviction and resolve crash into her.

They *were* his emotions.

He turned his attention back to their flight and after another two moments, they began their descent. This time Ella's stomach soured with anxiety.

"Are you all right?" Archai asked, stealing a quick glance at her.

Ella nodded and swallowed hard.

What would her mother say when she showed up at the house with the likes of Archai? His eye color was unnatural and his hair was not something typical. His tall, lean build was something like a model in a magazine. He was attractive. But what was he doing with her? That was the main concern Ella had. How would she explain his affiliation to her?

Darkness came over her vision once more and Ella tried to pull Archai's hand away. Landing was abrupt and somewhat jarring, but the instant Ella felt her composure return, she pushed away from him.

"Why are you doing that?" she asked, annoyed. Realizing they stood at her doorstep, she lowered her voice. "What's the point in covering my eyes?"

"To protect you. I used a spell when we left the hotel and when landing so none would see us. If your eyes were to be opened, you'd instantly go blind," he explained matter-of-factly.

"Oh." She had nothing else to say to that. She looked him over again and watched as the feathers of his wings dropped to the ground. Ella didn't know how she'd explain such a mess to her mother; as if reading her thoughts, Archai looked over his shoulder at the ground and with a circular gesture of his hand, they all disappeared.

"Oh, good," she said with wide eyes. This whole magic thing still amazed her. "Now, your sword."

He frowned. "My sword?"

The door opened before Ella could say more and her mother stood with hands on her hips and dark eyes, though her glare immediately softened when she looked at Archai. Her cheeks blushed. Her hands shook as she self-consciously fixed her hair.

"Hello," she managed, more to Archai than to her daughter. She reached out her hand. "I'm Stephenie."

Ella looked up at Archai, who seemed unfazed—if not humored—by the woman's blatant attraction. *How embarrassing,* she thought.

"Mom, this is…" she hesitated. "Mr. Archy. A friend from…"

"From school," Archai said, shaking her hand. "Dillon Archy."

Dillon? Ella tried not to physically react.

Stephenie shook hands with raised eyebrows. "From school? You can't be a student. You're so much more…mature."

Ella's stomach lurched. "He's a student teacher,"

she lied. "A previous student of the school. Oh, and he teaches theater." She figured that would be the easiest explanation for his clothes.

"Oh, I see," she said, eyeing his outfit as if just now noticing it. "Come in," she added. Her gaze returned to his face. "Did anyone ever tell you that your eyes—" she paused for a second. "They're incredible."

"Thank you, ma'am," Archai replied with a smile.

Stephenie led them into the kitchen, where they all took a seat at the table.

"I'm sorry I didn't say anything before I left," Ella began. "I didn't mean for you to worry. It was very in the moment. I guess it didn't cross my mind." Ella frowned. Her mother's attention was clearly not on what Ella was saying as she scurried to the fridge and pulled out some sodas and frozen éclairs, glancing up at Archai every few seconds.

"So, how long have you been student teaching, Mr. Archy?" Stephenie asked, ignoring her daughter's explanation. "It couldn't be very long. You look remarkably well for your age. How old are you? Did you mention your age? Most people tell me I look much younger than I am."

Oh no. If Ella knew one thing about her mother, it was that she prattled when nervous. Or in this case, attracted to the inhuman man at their kitchen table.

"Right," Ella said, standing and taking Archai's hand in a shake. "Thank you, Mr. Archy, for the ride.

I have a dinner to start getting ready for."

"Dinner?" he asked with obvious disinterest but clear intent.

"Yes," she replied curtly.

He turned his attention to her mother. "May I ask where you're going?" He flicked his gaze to the girl with a knowing smile, sensing her irritation growing.

"Ruth's Chris Steak House," she replied. "For Ella's birthday, though it's tomorrow. We always celebrate a day early." Her grin was wider than Ella had ever seen on her mother. She was *definitely* attracted.

Archai laughed in mock surprise. "Then I may see you there! What a coincidence. I have something to pick up from a friend there tonight and I thought I'd stop for dinner."

Stephenie quickly put her hands on Ella's shoulders and gave them a firm squeeze. "Honey, why don't we have Mr. Archy join us for your birthday, seeing as you two spent some time together today?"

"No," Ella snapped. "He's got other more important things to do." Her tone was strong, stubborn, and clear with her meaning.

Archai stood and pushed his hands into his pockets as he stepped back. "I really don't, but I understand Ella's concern. She would feel embarrassed with me there."

Stephenie's eyes turned dark with ire for her

daughter. "Oh! Ella's not that rude! We're leaving at six o'clock. It's the restaurant on Camelback Road. Is that the one you planned on going to?"

"Of course. It's the only one I'm aware of." Archai's grin was enough to make even Ella's stomach flutter, but her annoyance with her mother was enough to keep her mentally grounded.

"All right," he said as he made his way to the door. "I would love to join you," he said, glancing back as he left. "Thank you for the generous invite."

Ella stood with her mother at the doorway, looking out into the driveway. One aspect about the entire idea of Archai joining them for dinner made her sick to her stomach; Rhiannon would be there. There would be no protecting her from all of the craziness once Archai realized she was Naoni. "All right, I'm going to go get dressed," Ella said to her mother.

Stephenie rubbed her eyes and felt her pocket for her cell phone. "I need to make a few calls and let everyone know you're home. Everyone's been worried sick. But Ella, honey, wait."

Ella was halfway up the stairs already. She dropped her head down and made her way back to her mother. She knew it was too easy. In what world would she get away with spending time with a guy like Archai? "Yes?"

Stephenie cleared her throat and crossed her arms, twisting her face into a concerned frown. "This man,

Mr. Archy. He's part of school staff. What are you doing going to the mall with him?"

Ella shook her head. "No, I ran into him there," she lied.

"Right." Stephenie rubbed her left ring finger with her right hand, and Ella's eyes widened with dread. It took one look and some common sense to know what was on her mother's mind.

"I just wanted to make sure nothing more was going on between you two," Stephenie explained. "He's much too old for you."

"And he's much too young for you, Mom." Ella couldn't believe she said it out loud and neither, it seemed, could Stephenie.

"Hey now," she snapped in reply. "I wasn't implying…"

"Mom," Ella gestured to her mother's hands. "Dad died when I was little. I don't remember him much. If you need a guy, I won't hate you for going on dates, looking for someone. But it won't be Mr. Archy."

Blood rushed to Stephenie's cheeks at her daughter's words. Brandon Wiles had died in a car accident when Ella and Brittany were toddlers. Maybe their mother never thought about remarrying or even dating until now. She never brought home a date, nor did she ever hire a babysitter to stay with them. Ella knew it was hard on her mom, but Archai was obviously one hundred percent *not* the man she should waste any time pursuing.

"Ella, be ready in twenty minutes," Stephenie replied, then turned and walked away.

Ella dragged herself upstairs, cringing from the awkwardness of the situation. When she opened her door, she jumped in surprise when she was met with Archai in her bedroom. Again. She quickly shut the door and whispered, "Didn't you just leave?"

His chuckle was like a deep growl from his chest. "I've nowhere to go. You're my charge."

A headache suddenly shot across her forehead. Her fingers pinched the bridge of her nose as she sat on the edge of her bed. "You mean you're going to stay here with me? At all times?"

Archai nodded. "Not inside this room but within reach."

She was tired of trying to make sense out of everything Archai said and did. "Look," she said, starting for her closet. "I have a feeling this is going to be very difficult. You can't always be around. My mom will notice and it'll be weird. She just hounded me for spending time with an older man."

"I am not an older man," he said, leaning back on Ella's desk. He reached for a silver frame with a picture of Ella and Rhiannon, but Ella snatched it from him before he could look any closer.

"How old are you, then?" she asked.

He smiled. "There is no answer to that. I have no age. I just am."

Ella contemplated his words with the picture frame hugged to her chest. The idea was ludicrous. How could someone not have an age? Her speechlessness was a little embarrassing so she perused her closet, tucking the frame between her folded jeans, and found a gray sweater she rarely wore. Arizona weather was hardly permitting of heavier clothes.

"Okay, then," she finally said. "How long have you been around?"

The ring of metal sounded in Ella's room and she peered back out through the door. Archai studied the edge of his blade. His eyes brightened with the light that reflected off the metal, as memories seemed to be playing in his mind. His lips curved, revealing a perfect set of teeth in an arrogant grin. "Something longer than four thousand ages, I would say." Something changed in his eyes suddenly, and in that moment, his mind appeared to travel away from Ella's room. "I've witnessed the rise and ruin of kings and kingdoms for ages. I was present for the birth of language. The very course of the moon and stars has grown dull in my time."

Ella had the distinct feeling this was not the first time Archai had spoken those words.

Silence filled the room once again for a moment as Ella found her reply. "I hardly know what to say to that," she said quietly, fumbling with the pair of leggings she picked out to go with her sweater.

His eyes flicked to her from behind the blade of his sword. "Then that is because there is nothing to say."

Ella nodded and smiled as she closed the door to change in the closet.

Chapter Nine
The Restaurant

The gray sweater Ella had chosen was itchy, reminding her of the real reason she rarely wore it. There wasn't much difference between the oven temperatures of the desert scorching her skin and the uncomfortable scratchiness of the sweater's material. Her skin tingled beneath the threads from the abuse of her fingernails. A deep breath escaped Ella's lips as her mother pulled the car into a space across from the restaurant. Not only was she immensely anxious about the truth of Naoni hitting Archai tonight, but there was a weird vibe coming from Stephenie, and Ella's stomach kept turning every time they made eye contact.

"Oh, honey," Stephenie started just as she was about to open the car door. "The Suttons called about five minutes before we left. They won't be able to make it."

There was a weird inflection in Stephenie's voice

that made Ella clench her teeth. Her mom was lying.

"So it'll just be us and Dillon," Stephenie went on, checking her makeup in the rearview mirror. Her hands slightly trembled. She was nervous.

Ella could hardly take it. On one hand, she was glad Rhiannon was now out of the picture. Her friend could live in the peace of her ignorance for a bit longer. But on the other hand, her mother had literally just canceled her best friend out of their plans so they could be alone with "Mr. Archy." And she was suddenly using his first name!

"How convenient," Ella murmured in response.

The sound from Stephenie's throat as she swallowed her guilt was loud. "What's that supposed to mean?" Stephenie asked.

"You obviously went out of your way to get us alone with Archai—er, Mr. Archy. Why bother lying about it?"

A high-pitched squeak left her mother's lips as if she were about to spill a mouthful of innocent denial, but she slumped her shoulders and dropped her face with defeat instead. "Fine," she replied in a pitiful tone. "You're right. But you know what? I would rather Mrs. Sutton not meet Dillon. I mean, *Mr. Archy.* I'm sorry."

"Are you afraid she'll judge you for wanting to meet a younger man or are you afraid she'll steal him for herself?" Ella replied with a slight laugh. She didn't know what had gotten into her, but a stiff and uncomfortable chill crawled up her back for every moment they sat in the car. Ella couldn't tell if it was an emotional response to her mother or something else.

"Ella, please!" Stephenie groaned. "Can you please give me a chance?"

"With *Dillon?* No, Mom. Find someone else. Anyone else, and I won't have an issue. Anyone but *Dillon* would be fine."

Stephenie opened the car door with a huff and replied, "Well, Ella, you're going to have to deal with it tonight. We're here; he's probably here already. We'll talk about it later. You might want to think through what it is you have against him in the first place. This isn't like you."

Ella looked in the backseat at Brittany, who was stifling her laughs. "You are so screwed," Brittany said with a laugh.

"Oh shut up. At least I'm speaking up."

Ruth's Chris was alight with dinner patrons, most coming in pairs. To Ella's relief, the lights were dimmed enough that it would be difficult to notice everything that was off about Archai, which was a lot.

"We have a reservation for five but only four will be here," Stephenie said to the hostess. The three were led to a table in the middle of the floor, and Ella cringed at the thought that they'd be within sight of basically everyone in the restaurant. They were going to have to eat quickly.

With her eyes on the door, Ella's heartbeat quickened and she started to sweat. The stiff sensation she felt in the car grew stronger. It was a feeling similar to walking in the dark after being warned of snakes on the path. A light buzz floated around the room from the scattered chatter as Ella browsed the menu, but focusing was still hard. She wasn't even hungry. A brief but sharp chill ran down her spine suddenly and she raised her gaze. As if drawn by some sort of power, Ella's eyes drew immediately to another guest's—a man who sat alone in a back booth. That chill was now a frost set behind her breastbone, inching toward her extremities by the second. She flicked her attention to the door but quickly returned it to him when she realized he wouldn't look away. With a cup to his lips, his gaze remained steady. A sense of uneasiness overcame Ella, and she shifted slightly to the right in her seat, blocking her view of the man with a conveniently placed pillar that stood between them. She was practically shivering now with a cold only she seemed to feel.

Chatter all but disappeared when the door opened and Archai walked in. Ella sat up, trying desperately to hide her anxiety, and spread the linen napkin across her lap as she muttered under her breath, "Here we go." He would sense whatever it was that was freaking her out, she was sure of it.

"Look, *Dillon* is here," Brittany giggled as their

mother stood to greet him. Ella didn't move; she could still feel the man's intentions on her, regardless of any visual obstructions.

"Good evening," he said in his usual deep timbre. He shook Stephenie's hand and then Brittany's, and finally placed his other hand on Ella's shoulder. It was blissfully warm and a sudden sense of safety overcame her. She looked up at him with a smile, then wrinkled her brow in surprise. He was wearing gray slacks and a button-down shirt with the sleeves rolled up just beneath his elbows. His hair was pulled back into a bun.

"Looking sharp," Ella said with a smile as he stepped up beside her. "I didn't know you could clean up so well."

"Ella," her mother scolded but quickly turned her frown into a glittering smile. "Mr. Archy, it's good to see you again."

"Likewise," he replied, squeezing Ella's shoulder then grabbing her upper arm, pulling her to her feet. "Could you come with me for a moment, Ella?" He turned to Stephenie. "Please excuse us for a moment, Ms. Wiles." He glanced to Ella, and not to her surprise, his expression was less than excited.

"Oh, a-all right, of course," Ella stuttered, and before Stephenie or Brittany had anything to say about it, they were heading for the door.

All eyes were on them as they hurried out, and the instant the restaurant was behind them, Archai said,

"You're not safe here." He stole a look at the man in the restaurant through the windows. "We cannot linger here for long. There is a spy of some sort sitting just a few tables away," he explained. Hairs rose all over Ella's arms and neck and another chill ran down her spine. "If he suspects you are a Voice, your mother—and everyone else here—won't have worries about *anything* because they'll all be dead."

"You think this guy would do something like that? He doesn't look like a sinstarian."

"He's not. Nor is he the type the sinstarians typically send. But he has bad intentions for you, regardless. Somehow he knew you'd be here and came to study you. It's only a matter of time."

Ella shivered again and rubbed her hands up and down her arms. "They? There's more than one?"

"I've rarely seen a sinstarian alone."

A couple walked out of the restaurant and Ella hugged her arms around herself awkwardly as they passed by. "I sensed him before I even got inside the place. What do you think we should do?"

"Make this quick, then leave."

"How do I do that without coming across suspiciously? With the way we just rushed out of the restaurant, the guy is probably more suspicious now than he was when I first got here."

Archai gathered himself in thought for a moment before he pressed his lips together. "I won't stay. I cannot protect you like this," he explained, gesturing to himself. She understood. He didn't exactly look armed, and sitting at a dinner table with a woman trying to flirt with him did not make his job any easier. But something about the man inside told Ella he wasn't who they feared he was.

"Then go," she posed. "I'll have my birthday dinner with my mom and sister while you stay unseen and keep an eye on the guy. I'll eat fast. I don't want to be here any more than you do. But to go into full panic mode about a situation that probably isn't what we're afraid of will only bring on the *real* trouble more quickly."

To Ella's surprise, Archai nodded in agreement. "You are right. My kind is a trigger for sinstarians and the like, and that man's reaction is not what it would have been had he really been a sinstarian. But whoever he is, he is here for you, and I'd like to know why. I can keep an eye on you better from a distance—a *small* distance."

"Okay," Ella replied with a deep breath. "I was really nervous for a moment there. But I think I was picking up on you."

"Or you simply sensed trouble. For a water element, your sensibilities are stronger than anyone else's. Go inside. Warm up and do not look him in the eyes. I'll be close by." With that, he walked around the building and the sighing whoosh of magic confirmed his departure. Ella hurried inside and took her seat, ignoring the man watching her. The buzz of conversation had returned—what an effect Archai had on people.

"Where's Dillon?" Stephenie asked with a curious but nervous smile. "Is everything all right?"

"Um, Mr. Archy had to leave," Ella replied.

Stephenie perked at the news and frowned, looking toward the door. In fact, she seemed to grow angry rather fast. "What?" she said in surprise. "Why? What did you say to him?"

"Mom! I didn't kick him out from our dinner. His sister just had an accident," she lied. "She'll be fine, but he needs to take her home from the hospital."

Stephenie fumbled with her napkin, chewing her lip, and Brittany tossed glances between her sister and their mother. Their mom was obviously upset. Ella shook her head slightly; Stephenie could not have chosen a worse love interest.

Dinner was quiet but for Brittany's talk of her friends at school and a project she had going for the next week. Ella would usually offer her help, but something told her that time to sit around with a poster board and markers would be sorely lacking. Archai's hidden presence was already making her antsy. She didn't physically feel him, but knowing he was there, hiding and watching, made her feel like she was sitting around and wasting time.

The fishy smell coming from Stephenie's meal made Ella feel nauseous. That was strange, considering that she'd never had any real aversion to it in the past. Her mother was a big fan of seafood, so they had it at home somewhat often, but now, seeing a dead bluefish swimming in white sauce and topped with greens, all she had the desire to eat was saltine crackers and take Pepto Bismol. The waiter placed a plate of sushi in front of her and the assault on her nostrils was too much.

"Excuse me," she said as she stood up. "I'm going to find the restroom." Her mother nodded and Brittany ignored her. Ella's hand rested on her belly and she felt flushed as a cold sweat rose to her face. Did she eat something wrong earlier? The face of the man watching her flared in her mind, and she wondered if he had anything to do with how ill she felt.

A winding trail around the other tables in the restaurant led her to the restroom in the back, where someone exited just as she entered. All of the stalls were empty and Ella felt a sense of release in the solitude. She splashed water on her face and leaned on her elbows as she studied herself in the mirror. She looked tired. She *was* tired, and she should be. It had been a long day.

She laughed at the thought of how much had happened and how involved she'd already become in Archai's agenda. It all sounded crazy, but at the same time, there was a sense of belonging when he was around. When she really thought about it, he understood her more than her mom or her sister.

"How sad," she whispered, then jumped in surprise when her cell phone rang. She pulled it from her pocket and frowned at the unrecognized number. "Hello?"

"Hey there, Wiles!" a bouncy voice answered. "It's Whitney from school."

The nausea immediately returned.

"Whitney Williams?" Ella was surprised and suspicious at the same time. "Where'd you get my number?"

"I got it from a friend who got it from your friend, Rhiannon."

"Oh. That's a lot of work to get my phone number. What's up?"

"Look," Whitney continued, "I'm having a party at the beach this weekend and I'd like you to come."

Suspicious was a painful understatement. "And what would possess you to want me there?" Ella asked flatly. "We've never spoken. And you stared me down today like I'd done something wrong."

Whitney's scoff on the other end was clear. "Look, a friend of mine has a thing for your friend, Rhiannon. If they hit it off, we may have to be friends."

"All right. And who might this friend be?" Ella asked.

"Brad Westerson. He's had an eye on Rhiannon for a few years."

Ella flashed a smile at a woman who walked into

the bathroom, then exited but remained by the door. Brad? Rhiannon had a thing for him last year, but she wasn't the type to ask a guy out. She'd tried to bump into him at the mall a few times, but nothing ever came of it. If what Whitney said was true, Rhiannon would still be thrilled. "So you want us to drive down to a beach? Where?"

"San Diego. "If you guys could make it, that'd be great. I can call Rhiannon, unless you think you'd be better at getting her to come."

Rhiannon would no doubt beg her to go if she was approached by Whitney about Brad. Whitney and Rhiannon were kind of, sort of friends when they were younger, though they were not much more than civil with one another now. Whitney was a bit out of their league since they started high school.

"Well, I have a lot going on right now, and I'm not positive I'll be able to get away, but I'll talk to Rhiannon about it and let you know," Ella said.

"Right!" Whitney exclaimed with excitement. Whether it was real excitement or faked, Ella couldn't tell. "I'll text you the address. See you Saturday!"

The line clicked and Ella pressed her phone to her forehead in dismay. "I didn't even say yes yet," she muttered as she made her way back to the table.

Ella tossed her bag onto her bed and locked the door. Archai would show up any moment, she knew it. In the privacy of the closet, she changed into her pajamas and put her clothes away, then sat by the window, looking out into the darkness. Nothing came of the spy in the restaurant. She avoided his gaze, almost forgot he was there even, and forced her dinner down. Conversation was thin and the ride home was quiet. Stephenie was obviously disappointed that Archai left, but nothing could be done about that. She'd get over it. Brittany was too busy texting while eating, so she might as well have been gone.

What a birthday, she thought with a frown that quickly turned back into a smile. Thinking back on the day, she realized that, in fact, this year was already by far the best. She'd made an amazing friend, Archai, who made her feel like she was someone with more worth than she'd ever allowed herself to feel. In his eyes, she *was* someone.

"Everything went well," Archai said, drawing Ella's attention to her bed, where he sat with his arms crossed and his legs stretched out. He looked her over; Ella knew he was checking for anything worth his concern—it was a familiar thing he did. Memories of a time in Dy'Mün's cottage came to mind, though at the time there was clear danger, as Archai had an arrow stuck in his shoulder. Ella swallowed hard at the memory. She wanted more. How could she regain more memories?

Ella nodded and blushed at his keen attention. "It

was all right. Nothing bad happened. I think the only disappointment was from my mom when you left." She laughed and climbed into bed to sit beside Archai. "Well, I guess there's some disappointment for me too. I'm now expected at some stupid party this weekend. I don't think I'll actually go."

Archai faced her and frowned with curiosity. "Where is it?"

"At the beach. Six hours away. I gotta call my friend before the person who invited me does."

"No, wait," Archai started. "You should go. It is a good idea. You will get away from the spies here. They are sure to be unaware that you are leaving, and they would not follow you that far."

"Really?" Ella replied as she bit her lip. "I honestly thought you would think it's a horrible idea."

Archai was already deep in thought and rubbing the five o'clock shadow growing along his jaw.

"When will I be expected in Jaydür?" Ella asked. "I mean, as a Voice."

Archai's gaze briefly shifted to the mirror, from which a sheet still hung. His voice lowered with his reply. "When I deem it necessary. I have reason to keep you here for a bit longer. I know it might seem counterintuitive, considering how close the enemy is, but believe me when I tell you...now is not the time to go to Jaydür."

Ella looked at the time and let out a long

distressed sigh. She grabbed her phone and started pressing buttons. "I need to set my alarm. There's no way I'm going to wake up at a normal time by myself, and I don't want to sleep in."

"Yes, rest. I will go exchange some words with Dy'Mün."

Ella perked at the thought and quickly glanced at her mirror. "You can contact him here, can't you?" She didn't have much opportunity to speak to him before and wouldn't mind having another chance, but Archai briskly shook his. He licked his lips and his eyes grazed over the floor as he thought about his response.

"When speaking to Dy'Mün," he began, "I cannot risk oversharing what has happened in my time here. He is ignorant of how close the enemy is, as I have kept him somewhat in the dark about the sinstarian. If he were to know it all, the Elders of Jaydür would try to overstep my authority and interfere with my plans. The last thing I need is a trio of old mortal men telling me what is best for the Voices. No, it is better for me to speak with him alone so he cannot ask you anything directly."

"The Elders?" Ella asked. Though the use of the word was familiar, no memories came to mind. "Am I supposed to know who the Elders are?" she asked.

"You know some, from lessons with Dy'Mün and your father, but nothing beyond the fact that Dy'Mün is one of them. They are in power over Jaydür until the Voices come together. But as mortals, they tend to act hastily in situations that do not call for it. Those with an expiry do not know patience, and when you are charged with protecting an entire world, hastiness is never the wisest path."

Ella wished she remembered more about the Elders to better understand the situation. But she didn't. All she knew was that Archai was here for her, and she would put her trust in what she knew.

"My father," she asked instead, curious now that he was mentioned. "How is he?" The white-haired, pale face of her father quickly flashed in her mind. Somehow he did not look older than his thirties, and Ella focused on her memories enough to vaguely remember something about the aging of elves. She was startled to remember that elves reached a point where they were considered adults, and there their age plateaued. They could not die of age alone, but through violence such as beheadings or bleeding out.

"Atar Foriei is well. I do not know what he's been up to all these years, but I've heard mention of Dy'Mün keeping in touch with him. I doubt he knows of your current position. And it's better this way. Your father is," Archai paused as he chose his next words thoughtfully, "an emotionally driven individual, and he would no doubt handle all of this quite badly."

"Will I ever see him again?"

"I'm sure you will. Just not as soon as you might

hope."

Ella nodded while Archai stood up and turned off the lights, then leaned his shoulder against the wall beside the window.

"The sinstarian is out there," Archai said, his voice lowering with concern. "I can feel it."

Ella heard his words, but she was frozen in wonder and slowly rose to her knees, her mouth slightly parted and her eyes wide in disbelief. In the darkness, Archai's hair and skin glowed dimly, like a ghost in the night. Though he wasn't even looking her way, his teal eyes were so bright, all Ella could compare them to was the Northern Lights.

"My God," she whispered, drawing his attention. The moment their eyes met, she dropped to her bottom in surrender. All stubbornness was put aside. All fear and uncertainty was drowned in the magic that radiated from him. This man had every inch of her trust.

"It's the Light of the Highest," Archai explained, knowing why she was suddenly so dumbstruck. "Though you glow brighter than me; most of the Terehn do." He dropped his gaze back to the street and his mood turned solemn. Ella looked down at her skin to see nothing different or changed. Human skin didn't glow, so she didn't understand what he meant by saying she was brighter than him.

"You're one of the Terehn as well," she said aloud to fixate the word in her mind. "So why would anyone be brighter than you?"

Archai took in a sharp breath and turned his back to her. "That will have to wait for another time." He paused before adding, "It is for Caia to know, not for Ella. I'll see you in the morning." With that, a breathy whoosh floated throughout the room and Archai disappeared.

Chapter Ten
Make Them Grovel

It wasn't difficult to get Rhiannon to agree to a road trip. In fact, she was the one who came up with the story they used to be gone for the next two days. As far as their parents knew, the girls were going to a slumber party at a friend's house, where they would be studying and working together on a project due the following Monday. Of course, Stephenie wasn't too quick to believe that, so the two girls took a trip to a craft store where they spent a few dollars on foam balls, paint, and pipe cleaners. Props were enough to convince any mother who tried being strict but wasn't aware enough to follow through on a story to find out if it was a lie.

The sun was high and bright, its rays melting into Ella's pale skin. Everyone was there, filling the beach in all directions, eating, laughing, playing volleyball. Ella cringed and squinted through the bright reflection bouncing off the water.

"Oh God, what am I doing here, Rhi?" she asked her friend, forgetting every good intention she had for the day.

"You're about to change your life, remember?" Rhiannon replied with a blinding grin. "And I'm about to get to know Brad better. Now take off your shirt."

Reflexively, Ella grabbed the hem of her shirt and squeezed it in her hand as if forcing it to stay against her skin. "No, I think I'm good."

"Ella!" Rhiannon scolded. She faced Ella head-on and bore her scrutinizing stare into Ella's innocent gaze, shattering it with no care of its fragility. "You were invited to this shindig by Barbie her-freakin'-self," she reminded. "A beach party has rules and one of those rules is 'bikini wear only.' It's the dress code. Follow it."

With every effort to believe Rhiannon's earlier claim that she had a "great body," Ella pulled off her shirt and adjusted her top. She was so embarrassed. Sure, she understood that there was a dress code for beach parties, but people who went to beach parties were not usually as white as her. Did the rules apply to the tan-inept?

Laughter rose and Ella immediately lowered her head, afraid she was the reason for it. And who wouldn't laugh? She looked ridiculous.

"There's Whitney," Rhiannon pointed out. "Let's make ourselves known, shall we?" Without a second thought, she was on her way to make contact with the girl who had Eric's heart. Ella took a deep breath. Ever since her memories of Solin started coming back, the thought of him hurt more than ever. It took every ounce of focus to remind herself that she was here for Rhiannon, and for their safety.

Ella was glad, though, that Rhiannon was excited, if nothing else. She would have no problem fitting in with Whitney's crowd, so she would enjoy herself. Rhiannon was always neutral ground, as far as anyone could tell. She was beautiful enough to be accepted by those more popular yet smart enough for the nerds. She balanced herself pretty well, though Ella used to wonder what it was that possessed the pretty brunette to become such a loyal friend of hers. Now, with some memories of their past regained, Ella knew.

"Look who decided to show up," Whitney called before they reached the blankets and chairs, where a group of their peers sat in a semi-circle. Eric's head snapped up in curiosity, and Ella could have fried an egg on her cheeks, she blushed so badly. Instinctively crossing her arms over her chest, small as it was, she avoided his eyes with every ounce of self-respect she still had. It wasn't just about Eric anymore. Those eyes were still Solin's, and these were not the circumstances Ella ever wanted for Solin to see her shirtless.

"Well, damn, Ella's got a bod!" Whitney went on

to Ella's horror, bringing much unwanted attention directly to her. "I didn't think pasty people were hiding anything like this!"

Everyone laughed and Ella had never felt so exposed. She had to get away from it all. Horrified and a nervous wreck, she took her friend's wrist. "Hey, I forgot something in the car. Give me the keys." But Rhiannon knew better and rolled her eyes.

"Who's playing volleyball?" Rhiannon asked, taking an empty seat at the edge of the group and motioned for Ella to join her. Not knowing what else to do, she sat down tentatively. Her gaze flitted to Eric's for a moment, and she was immediately nauseous when she saw him staring at her. She looked away but could still feel his eyes on her, and as she was sitting in a bikini, that was the last thing she wanted. She tried telling herself that he was shirtless, too, which put them on equal ground. Unfortunately, all she could hear was her own heartbeat thumping in her ears.

"Rhi, I need to run to the car," she whispered in Rhiannon's ear.

"Seriously, you need to get over it," she whispered in return, though much more harshly. Her eyes flicked between Ella's and Brad Westerson's, who sat across from Whitney with a gorgeous smile and a mess of brown hair. "Stop being so ridiculous and try to have some fun."

"Seriously, though, who's playing?" a girl Ella

knew as Becks Anderson asked. "I'm up for a game."

The group chattered about splitting into teams, but Whitney's personal spotlight was a bright beam still locked on Ella. If anything could get worse this day, it was definitely going to, and soon.

Everyone jumped to their feet, including Rhiannon. "You coming?" she asked. Ella shook her head and held out her hand.

"No, but I need to get something from the car," she said for the third time. "Give me the keys."

Rhiannon let out an annoyed breath and tossed her the keys. "Seriously, Ella, if you're not back in a few minutes, I'm coming to get you. I'm not going to let you ruin this." She glanced at Eric, who didn't seem like he was going to play either, and then closed in on Ella. "And his being here? It's perfect. Try talking to him." With that, she ran to grab a place on the court by Brad while tying her hair up out of the way. Ella looked after her longingly. Why couldn't she be as confident as Rhiannon?

"Aren't you going to play?" Eric asked, to her surprise. The last thing she expected was to be talking with Eric. She turned and met his gaze with a strained smile and shook her head.

"I'm not good with sports. It's a death sentence for me if I get too close," she replied.

He laughed, and she couldn't help but feel relief, though the feeling quickly faded. He laughed just like Solin did in Jaydür. She didn't know what else to say, and she found herself staring at him awkwardly. She needed to get away. "I left something in the car," she lied, getting up to her feet with her shirt in her hands. "I'll be back in a few minutes." He nodded and she turned toward the parking lot. She tried to walk away gracefully and at the same time, invisibly. If only she could disappear the way Archai did.

As if waiting for her thoughts to turn to him, Ella heard the whoosh that accompanied his appearance, and she froze in her steps. She nervously eyed the area, waiting to hear his voice but there was nothing. *I'm just imagining it*, she told herself. He wouldn't show up here. She shook her head to get those thoughts out of her mind and continued to the car, where she tossed her things and searched under her seat for her cell phone. She'd have to go back with something in her hand. Stalling, she dropped into the passenger seat and thumbed around her phone. Voices neared and she tossed up a glance before returning to her ruse. She didn't want to go back. She didn't want to face the judgment of regular beach-goers. It was obvious she didn't belong and she didn't *want* to be there.

Her finger pressed the voicemail button and she leaned her head back on the chair. There was no voicemail for her to listen to, but this was the only way to act like she was on the phone without it ringing in her ear. She watched a line of people just arriving and set her eyes on Eric who, from this distance, seemed like he was watching her. She tried to focus her eyes, but she was too far to tell if he was actually looking at her or someone else. She laughed at herself. Why would he be watching her? Whitney was nearby, gorgeous as always.

Ella watched Rhiannon while she played. She seemed very much in her element—a pretty girl surrounded by other pretty people, laughing and involved in the game. Ella took a deep breath and rubbed her palms on her thighs. Introverted as she was, it was difficult for her to find any connection to other people. Except for Rhiannon. Though, ever since Archai's arrival in her life, Ella knew now it wasn't just introversion. It was no coincidence that Rhiannon was the only person who truly understood her.

After five minutes of sitting in the car and collecting herself, Ella decided she'd better return to the party. After all, what Rhiannon said was right. The school's most popular student had invited her, and to stay hidden away would probably just draw more attention to her anyway. That was the problem with this type of group—they kept an eye on those beneath them, watching them, judging them, and Ella was *way* beneath. If she wanted less attention, she'd have to act like she belonged.

A fleeting question of why any of this mattered flitted through Ella's mind. She could ask Archai, but she felt like she knew what he would say. He would urge her to trust him, and to keep to their plan. And so she would.

The sand sifted through her toes as she made her way back to the ring of chairs. Eric was still there watching the group play, and Ella wondered why he wasn't joining them. She tried to put on a confident face as she neared him when her eyes fell to a marking on his back, just beneath his right shoulder. Her steps slowed and her stomach dropped. Memories of an arrow in his shoulder as they rushed through woods on horseback flashed in her mind, and Ella broke into an immediate sweat.

Eric turned and welcomed her back with a smile before turning back to the game. Her heart felt heavy then, as if it were being pulled toward him by some unseen connection pleading for revival. It was a familiar feeling, though she couldn't quite place it. Now was not a good time for trying to tap into her past life, though. Eric was sitting there, and he was open for communication. It was an opportunity she had to take advantage of. Many nights were spent just dreaming of casual conversation with him. If she was going to have to leave for Jaydür, she would regret her silence forever.

With a clearing of her throat, Ella sat across from Eric. His black hair had grown out longer than he usually kept it. He moved strands from his eyes with his hand or a jerk of his head. Ella tried not to think too hard about speaking; the more she focused on what was to be said, the more she'd stutter or blabber.

"What happened to your back?" she asked. "There, by your shoulder."

"It's just a birthmark," he replied, running a hand over it. "I know it looks like a scar, and I get away with making up stupid stories sometimes just to sound cool." He laughed, which made the heaviness in Ella's heart turn into a flutter. His smile was so familiar, it made her warm all over.

Ella nodded slightly and mirrored his smile. "I have a few of those myself."

Afraid to let an awkward silence fall, Ella turned their conversation. "Why aren't you out there?" she asked, sounding as confident as she'd hoped.

Eric turned to her with another smile, and again her heart grew heavy. "Just not in the mood," he replied. "Anyway, I like watching. You get to know people better by watching how they interact with others."

Ella let out a quiet laugh. "I know what you mean."

"I know you do. You're the biggest people-watcher in our school."

Something in his tone caught Ella's curiosity and she frowned, almost afraid to ask. "What do you mean?"

"C'mon, you've got to know your reputation," he said, turning fully toward her and pulling a knee to his chest. "You stare."

Her heart skipped a beat.

"You stare at *everyone*. It's almost like you have a secret against the world," he went on. "And I don't think anyone would be surprised to find that you do."

Looking down at her hands, Ella thought about his explanation. Is that what people really thought of her? "So people find me weird," she said in conclusion.

Eric's laugh cut off abruptly as her response seemed to sink in. "No, that's not what I—" He stopped, then cocked his brows in concession. "Actually, to be honest, yeah, I guess so. But you knew that already, didn't you?"

There was no looking him in the eyes after that. All Ella wanted to do was sink into the ground and disappear. "Y-yeah, of course," she said quietly. But she hadn't known, really. She always thought she had a good relationship with people. She was rarely picked on. Rarely insulted. She *tried* to call on some memories of being treated in any way like she was *weird*.

Eric pursed his lips in thought, then said, "Look, don't take it too hard. I didn't mean to hurt your feelings. I just figured, there are things you can do to make yourself more accepted by other people, if you really wanted to."

With Eric's confession, a newfound courage suddenly overtook her, and she decided she'd make some confessions herself. "Look," she started, forcing herself to look him in the eyes. "I don't like the beach. I don't like being on display as the pasty, weird girl from school. And I lied. No, I didn't know I was considered 'weird.' I really think it's just Whitney and your group of friends who think that. I know half the school body well enough, and no one gives me any trouble." Ella turned to Whitney as she made her way back to where the two were sitting. The expression on her face made it clear that she knew something was going on.

"Well, don't stop bonding on my account," Whitney said with a grin and a flip of her ponytail. "You two look so serious over here, I just *had* to make sure everything was all right."

The temptation to snap at her was almost too strong, but Ella held back. She wasn't sure how much Whitney had heard. Dropping into a chair beside Eric, Whitney slid her arm around his shoulders, practically marking her territory with the dark, scathing look in her eyes. "Oh my God!" She jumped up. "How rude of me! Let me get you an umbrella before you tan!"

Ella climbed to her feet and brushed sand off her bottom. "No worries. I couldn't tan if I tried," she joked, trying to pretend there was no tension. It was a pretty pitiful joke on Whitney's part anyway. She wondered if her friends actually found her funny.

"Oh, that's great, then. But really, I may need to put on some sunglasses, or maybe you can put a shirt on. Your shade of white is a little hard on the eyes. Or hey, better yet, why don't you walk off that way?" she said, gesturing into the distance and making it clear she heard some of what was said.

And well, that was all it took. "Whitney, what is your problem?" Ella finally asked.

"My problem? I don't have a problem. You have a problem. You've been eyeing my boyfriend for too long now and from what we can all tell, you've been flirting with him for too long now, too."

After realizing that the rest of the group was now watching the situation take life, Ella shook her head but lacked the courage to fight back with all she wanted. The whole thing was embarrassing now. The only one in the group who might be on her side was Rhiannon, but she was still on the volleyball court. "I wasn't flirting," Ella finally replied. "Your boyfriend can attest to that."

Whitney giggled. "'Attest?'"

"Attest. Verify. Confirm. I'm sorry, I forgot my vocabulary is bigger than your chest."

The students ooo'ed and laughed at Ella's response. She knew she shouldn't have said that, but shots were being fired and she refused to let herself be put down without a fight. "Why did you invite me?" she finally asked just as Whitney parted her lips to snap a reply.

It was as if she was waiting for that question. Her mouth pulled into a grin and her eyes widened slightly like a cat focused on its prey. "If it were up to me, you wouldn't be," she said.

"Whit," Eric started, passing glances between his girlfriend and Ella. "C'mon, let her be. We were just talking."

"But I'm a good friend," Whitney went on, ignoring his attempt to placate her. "And my friend wanted *Rhiannon* here, and I knew she wouldn't have the guts to come without you. But while we're here, you may as well learn your place. I think we all have now."

Eric's brows lifted at Whitney's words, then slightly furrowed when he looked back at Ella. "That was—" he started.

"Cold." A familiar voice came from behind and Ella whipped around in surprise to find Archai. Thankfully, he opted for dark jeans and a black t-shirt in place of his usual jerkin and a sword at his side. His hair was pulled up like it was at the restaurant, and the stubble on his chin and jaw was beyond the typical five o'clock shadow she had grown used to seeing him with. "Why are you wasting time with people like this?" he went on. "Should I tell them what you're capable of?"

Blood ran from Ella's face at his question. She grabbed his hand without thinking, turning him away from the group. "What are you doing here?"

"Who are you?" Whitney asked. Her eyes were frozen, half in fear and half in wonder, on the man who held Ella's hand—frozen with the familiar wide-eyed reaction Stephenie had.

Everyone seemed to have a similar reaction, besides Rhiannon. The other students' chests heaved as if scared for their lives while Rhiannon watched from a distance. Ella couldn't quite gauge the expression on her friend's face but mouthed to her that everything was fine.

"Come, Caia," Archai said, pulling Ella by her hand, but she jerked away.

"*What* are you doing here?" she asked again.

"I am doing what I do; I'm looking out for you."

"I'm Whitney." Whitney was suddenly beside the two and inching closer to Archai by the second. "I've never seen you before. Are you with her?" she asked, gesturing to Ella. She bit her bottom lip as she studied him head to toe. Ella was quick to make the connection; some kind of magic in Archai made people either instantaneously drawn to him, or terrified of him. But it wasn't working on Ella.

Archai wrinkled his nose in obvious disgust, then took Ella's hand and pulled her away. Ella didn't say anything as she walked with him.

"Ella!" Eric called after them. "Don't go with him." His hands were trembling with obvious uneasiness at the sight of this strange man taking her away.

Ella threw a glance over her shoulder and secretly pleased with the concern on Eric's face, but she continued on with Archai. She definitely needed a word with him. When they'd gone far enough out of sight, Ella tried to snatch her hand away, but Archai held fast until they reached the sidewalk at the other end of the parking lot.

"You shouldn't let people talk to you like that," he said. His tone was calm, but a touch of bite was just enough to make it clear he was unhappy. "If they knew who you were, they would be groveling at your feet."

"I don't want them to grovel," she replied, and he let go of her hand.

"Caia, on their knees is where people like *that* belong. I will not allow them to speak to you like that."

Ella put a hand to her head as she sat on the curb of the sidewalk. The hot concrete sent pleasant shivers up her spine. California air felt much cleaner, and the heat was more bearable than in Arizona, but Ella just wanted to go home now. Though, of course, there was no hope for comfort there anymore either. This entire situation would follow her the rest of her school days. "If anything, you've now just given them more reason to speak to me like that."

"Then don't let them!" Archai was almost shouting now. "Speak with authority and you shall have it! You are a Voice! Not a worthless human to be played with and poked at."

"Humans are not worthless."

Archai paced back and forth a few feet in front of

her, then abruptly stopped and smiled. "That is exactly what a Voice would say." He dropped down beside her and she looked up at him, already knowing the answer she was going to receive to her question. She decided to ask anyway.

"What are you doing here, Archai?"

"You knew I was here."

She had a feeling he was, but denied it for the sake of her sanity. If she always acknowledged his presence, she'd never feel a moment's peace.

"To be honest, I'm glad you are," she admitted, pulling her knees closer to her chest. "I don't belong with these people and I felt very, very—"

"Out of place," he finished for her.

She bumped him with her shoulder and took a deep breath. "Where'd you get the jeans and t-shirt? You can almost pass as human."

"I have access to anything I could possibly need through the Rehnedhen. I noticed when meeting your mother that my usual choice of clothing draws attention."

"Good choice." Ella looked up at him, squinting against the sunlight. "You look good, Archai."

He smiled and let out a quiet grunt of acknowledgment.

Ella groaned sluggishly before rising back to her feet. Just as she was able to see above the cars, she saw Rhiannon's dark curls bouncing toward them.

"Ella," she called, then hesitated when Archai

stood beside her friend. "Ella, are you okay?"

"Stay here," she ordered Archai. "I'll deal with her." She turned and nodded to Rhiannon, rushing to meet her halfway. She turned her friend so Archai wouldn't get a better glimpse of her and recognize her as anyone familiar—and Ella *knew* he'd find her familiar. "I'm fine. But I think I'm ready to go home."

Rhiannon frowned. "I'm sorry about all this. We can go. But," she turned her attention to Archai, "who is that guy?"

Ella looked back at Archai. "He's a friend of the family. Happened to be around. Crazy coincidence and whatnot but, uh, let me say goodbye and then we'll go. I'll meet you at the car."

That was a lousy excuse, but Rhiannon went to the car and Ella hurried back to Archai. "All right, we're going home. I'll see you there," she told him.

He affirmed what she'd said but narrowed his gaze toward the dark-haired girl walking away. His air of recognition already had anxiety creeping up Ella's back.

"Right," Ella went on. "I'll see you there, then." She took a few steps backwards, then turned and hurried after Rhiannon. With one look back, she found Archai had disappeared, then she jumped into the car.

"Well, that went well," Rhiannon said as she put her car in reverse.

Ella forced a laugh, matching her friend's sarcastic tone. "Yeah, really."

"I'm so sorry, Ella. Really. I didn't know they would be so stupid."

Ella raised a dismissive hand. "Don't worry about it. I don't care."

Rhiannon looked sidelong at her friend. "Of course you care. Eric was involved and one thing I know about you is that when Eric is involved, all you do is care. You don't have to pretend."

"I'll be fine," Ella replied, sinking into her seat and looking out the window. Her mind fell on what Archai said. *Speak with authority and you shall have it.* It worked for him, obviously, but he had magic. He could make anyone lust for him or fear him. It likely wouldn't be the same for her. Not that she would want it to. Authority was not something to be forced but to be willfully accepted by others. The last thing she wanted was to force people to heed her every word out of magic or fear. Ella shook the thought from her mind and watched the clouds go by as the girls made their way back to Arizona.

They drove for two hours before Ella took the wheel. Rhiannon pulled out a book and spent most of the next few hours reading before they traded places again. Both were silent. Ella remained in her thoughts, wondering why the whole situation bothered her so much. Bullies would be bullies, but giving in to their harassment would only feed their desire to bully more. She knew she was giving them the power to continue by being so affected by their attacks. Seeing her reaction, they would only push her more.

The sky grew darker as they neared Phoenix and water pattered gently against the windshield. Ella closed her eyes and eventually drifted off to sleep, but instead of dreaming, she *remembered*.

Shame and the tight, suffocating sense of regret choked Ella as she sat on the floor of an old stone building in her memory-dream. Though she didn't remember ever seeing it herself in this life, she remembered the temple and the reasons behind being there. An indescribable sense of omniscience overcame her. There were five others in the room, and the emotions of each of them stretched out toward her like unwelcome hands. Archai's feelings toward her were the most difficult to process, which made Ella freeze in thought. She passed a look over her shoulder, and Caia gently floated from her body, suddenly standing next to it. She walked with soundless steps toward Solin, whose eyes were on her elven self, wide and frightened. The memory of the kiss that had taken place in the room separate from the main temple room came to mind, and the scene suddenly changed.

Ella's blood burst with warmth as her lips moved with another's. When she opened her eyes, Eric, the human, looked back at her, and she woke with a gasp.

The little Miata bumped lightly along the road in the dimming Arizona light while a quiet tune came from the radio. Rhiannon passed a glance to her friend in the passenger seat. "Hey," she said. "Have a bad dream?"

"Bad?" Ella replied as she put the pieces of her dream together. "I—" she stopped. "I don't remember." But she did remember. She remembered everything. Her obsession with Eric made all the sense in the world—the feeling of nostalgia that overwhelmed her when he would make eye contact or speak the most meaningless of words was there for good reason. They had shared an elven kiss.

Ella placed a hand on her belly. "Pull over," she said.

With one look at her friend, Rhiannon pulled over. Ella jumped out of the car and vomited in the grass on the side of the freeway.

"Are you all right?" Rhiannon asked from inside the car.

Ella nodded and waved dismissively at her friend. But Rhiannon was not just any friend; she was *Naoni*. And Naoni was just as angry with her as Archai and Dy'Mün. Her best friend had turned her back in the moment she made the biggest mistake in all of Jaydür's history. Could Ella blame her?

A chill poured over her heart just thinking about the connection she created with Solin through the kiss—the leg'et ínmi. *That* must have been what she felt in her chest as soon as she made the connection of Eric's birthmark to the day Solin was shot by an arrow and they first met Archai in the woods. It was also the reason behind her lifelong fear of disappointment that put her in therapy sessions with Doctor Corsa. That one moment with Solin in the Temple of Pandhea was a life-altering choice made in a moment of weakness.

A part of Ella tried to forgive herself. After all, Solin was her everything. He stuck with her and comforted her throughout all the years—no one else could claim as much—but another side of her hated herself for it. The leg'et ínmi was something she would carry for the rest of her life.

Ella's vision shook and blurred as her head pounded. She couldn't let Rhiannon think anything was wrong beyond carsickness. She needed to keep control over her body and keep careful attention on her words. But God, the memories hurt.

When her stomach settled, Ella got back into the car and pulled her seatbelt over her shoulder with a quiet, "Sorry."

Rhiannon shook her head. "It's fine. You okay?"

Ella nodded and the two continued on their way.

Moments of silence passed, and Rhiannon eventually took the opportunity to chat again. "So, seriously now," Rhiannon started. "Was this trip *all* bad? Can you tell me what you and Eric talked about? I mean, you guys were alone for a while before

Barbie popped in."

Ella shrugged, trying to focus on the question. Solin was taking over her thoughts. Or was it Eric? Were they still the same person like she was still Caia?

"We did have some time to talk," she managed around the menagerie of memories flitting in and out of her thoughts. "But I'm not convinced the entire conversation wasn't a setup."

"What do you mean? I thought we came because Brad wanted to get to know me. That wasn't set up. He was pretty forward with me."

"You're right," Ella replied, squeezing her eyes shut. The inability to think straight was frustrating. "I'm sorry. I just don't know what to think."

"Well, I saw your lips moving. I even saw you smile. Something happened there with Eric," Rhiannon pointed out.

"I'm not smiling now," Ella said, hoping that Rhiannon would let it go. But of course, she was never one to let things go.

"Yeah, obviously." Rhiannon's response was curt. "So what did he say?"

There was another moment of hesitant silence from Ella as she mulled over the conversation in her mind. Why did it matter what he said? It changed nothing. He wasn't the guy he seemed to be throughout all the years she'd pined after him. But he didn't belong in this world any more than either of the girls did. How could she take anything he said too seriously? If he could remember who he was, he would have her in his arms and on his lips in a heartbeat. Ella's heart fluttered at the thought.

"Ella," Rhiannon pushed.

"He told me that everyone thinks I'm weird," she finally admitted. Her eyes remained on the droplets sliding down the windshield. It wasn't so much what others were thinking that bothered her; it was what *he* thought about her that mattered.

From the corner of her eye, Ella saw Rhiannon's hands grip the steering wheel tighter. She sensed her friend's anger but still didn't look away from the window. She hurt. Her stomach turned and her heart ached.

The sudden presence of that other part of her—the one Archai explained was the essence of the Voice—crawled through her mind, and this time, Ella didn't fight it. She recognized it now as something familiar, and something that belonged. So she gave in to the feeling of another's control. It was comforting. The more she conceded, the more she felt like she was drifting, until she was like the clouds she'd watched earlier—light and aimless. A tear fell down her cheek as she allowed the essence control over her mind more and more.

Then, as if snapping out of a deep sleep, Ella took a long, deep breath and sat up straight in her seat. The dark sensation over her suddenly lightened, and an air of fresh determination filled her as she looked to her friend and said, "I'm just *really* ready to be home, I think."

Rhiannon glanced at her friend, then did a double take, as if she'd noticed something different. She swallowed hard and shifted uncomfortably in her seat. "We're almost there," she said quietly.

Something about the scenery changed for Ella, and a sense of déjà vu came over her; it was a sensation similar to regaining her memories from the orb. The brightening of colors and the natural sense of knowing made more sense to Ella now, when it had previously thrown her into a rage of confusion. This was what she lacked in her memories; though the Voice was present in her mind, it wasn't allowed the proper influence *over* her mind—until now.

With a new perception of the world around her, Ella studied her hands in wonder. There seemed to be a glow like Archai's coming off her skin. She looked up to the road ahead of them as a grin spread across her face. Caia had just hit the surface.

Chapter Eleven
Caia's Awakening

Standing just behind the bedroom door was Archai, eyes wide and bright with anticipation. The moment he made eye contact with the Voice of Apan, he dropped to his knee in reverence. "Caia," he said, unable to keep his head down for more than a few short seconds. He grinned even wider. "I felt something change, and here you are. Your eyes are blue. Your hair is white. You—you are—"

"I am Caia," Caia replied. "Still much of Ella's body, but the human essence is now weaving with my own."

Archai rose to his feet. The air around him vibrated with excited energy but diminished just as quickly as it first sprang to life. "What's wrong?" he asked, the concerned inflection in his voice clear.

"I remember what I did," she replied, dropping her bags by the bed as she plopped onto the edge of the mattress. Her hair brushed her elbows, making

Caia realize just how much shorter she was used to wearing her hair now. "The kiss. The hatred toward me from *everyone*." It was difficult not to raise her voice as anger seeped into her already dour mood.

Archai's shoulders slumped as he shook his head briskly and stepped forward. "No, Caia. Please don't lose focus here. Not now. That was so long ago. It's over. No one has ever hated you. Can you not imagine the thrill everyone will feel when they find out you've awakened?"

Caia chewed her lip as she sat in thought. She rubbed her arms and let out a flustered sigh.

"Come," Archai said, taking her by the hand. She let him pull her to the covered mirror where he pulled down the sheet, and Caia eyed the glass. Her eyes were indeed the unnatural, icy-blue shade of a water elf, and her head was graced with the long snow-white tresses she knew in Jaydür. "You don't have to listen to me," he went on before he lifted his voice in a commanding tone. "Keiren Kai."

The instant the name was spoken, the glass rippled and the white panther from so many years ago materialized in the mirror like a white ghost. Sapphire eyes peered from a white-coated feline face. A voice spoke but the mouth was unmoving. "Terdhen fost trecd, Amna Voka."

Caia muffled her cries of surprise and joy. "Time has passed, Lady Voice," she translated. "I understood that."

If one were to imagine a cat smiling, Keiren had done just that. "It is a relief to see you as *you*, my lady," he went on. "I've been watching you most ardently."

An accent was clear in his words and his form was reminiscent of every memory Caia held of Jaydür. The voice that came from the creature was echoic and ethereal. Keiren sighed as he turned to Archai. "As for you, Archai, you have officially been deemed a complication. You were told *not* to cover the mirrors."

Caia furrowed her brow. Wasn't the purpose of covering the mirrors to not be watched by the enemy?

Archai's eye contact didn't falter. "As you can see, the essence of the Voice is now taking root in Caia. The human, 'Ella,' is no longer the reigning consciousness here."

Keiren sighed in resignation, shaking his head as he replied, "Yes, I can see that. And this is wonderful. But know, Caia, though you've grasped control of your circumstance, this is not the end of your struggles. I foresee...many more to come." Keiren stopped and the fur above his eyes furrowed as if he were in deep thought. His ear twitched, and his attention turned to Archai. "Sapient, why don't you take her to see Meilon?"

An air of confusion and misunderstanding suddenly filled Caia, and her heart rate began to rise. She looked up to Archai and found the same deep concern on his face that came from Keiren.

"What is it?" she asked. "Who's Meilon?"

"Meilon is an oracle," Archai replied. "Not the most pleasant of women in Jaydür."

Caia perked at the reply. "In Jaydür?"

Archai nodded. "Now that you've awakened, it is time to take you home. You are not well-hidden here any longer. Magic is seeping through your skin. We may as well make our way to Meilon when we cross over. Though that would leave Naoni out here somewhere, and she will be at the mercy of chance. If I'm no longer in this world, I won't be able to sense if she's in trouble."

Caia swallowed hard and bit her lip in thought. How angry was Archai going to be when he found out she knew Naoni's whereabouts? "How would they find her?"

Archai crossed his arms and scratched the scruff on his chin. "They will sense her. We can't know when, but it's only a matter of time. She crossed over with her orb and it will take its effect eventually, bringing her essence to the surface."

Caia nodded. If what he said was true, then Naoni could be stalked in that exact moment. "And what if..." She stood up straight and pressed her lips together. "What if I know where she is?"

Fresh urgency lit up in Archai's eyes. "You *do* know! I saw it in you before! Why haven't you said anything?"

"I was afraid of getting her involved. I didn't have my memories. But I understand now. Calling her is not a problem."

"No," Keiren said. "She must be spoken with away from your home. There are two other humans here who will be a burden if they overhear anything."

Archai opened the window and gestured for Caia to follow him. "We will go to the hotel we were before."

Caia looked back at her bedroom door, knowing her human mother and sister would come looking for her soon. But this was more important, and the situation had to be handled. Without a second thought, she grabbed a crocheted slouch-hat to cover her hair, and turned back to Archai where she took his hand. With a flash of light, Caia and Archai were in the air again.

An hour passed before Rhiannon knocked at the door of the hotel room. The sky was darker than ever and rain was a relentless presence for most of the day.

Caia's heart was in her throat as she opened the door and gestured to her friend to enter. Archai was standing on the other side of the room by a green arm chair in the corner, and Rhiannon froze when she saw him. Caia smiled reassuringly. "It's all right," she said as she locked the bolt. "Rhiannon, this is Archai."

"Yeah, I remember him from the beach," Rhiannon said, flicking her attention between her friend and the strange man in the corner. "What's going on? And why is your head being swallowed by an ugly crocheted monstrosity?"

Caia touched her hat with a frown. She knew it wasn't pretty, but it was necessary. Her hair was far from normal. "I'll explain it all. You need to sit, though."

Archai lifted the chair and placed it in the center of the room between the two queen beds, then stretched out his hand. "Hello. It's a pleasure meeting you...though I wish we'd met much sooner." There was a glint of frustration in his eyes that Caia knew was her fault.

Rhiannon took his hand and replied, "The pleasure's all mine." She smiled mischievously at Caia. "So what's going on? How did you find this absurdly attractive man?"

Archai's wide grin was bigger than Caia had ever seen on him before. "I like her," he said. "She's rather unchanged."

Rhiannon glanced between the two. "Ella?"

Caia sat on the bed beside Rhiannon and took her friend's hand, hoping to keep her grounded through what she was about to hear. "Try to open your mind. This is all going to sound crazy, but you need to hear us and push away all skepticism."

"What's crazy is your freaking eyes aren't brown

anymore, have you noticed? And I hope you don't think you're keeping your white hair a secret from me. It changed in the car, I saw it."

"Wait," Caia started, mentally going through the last few hours. She was so distracted with all that was going on, what Rhiannon saw didn't even cross her mind! She felt utterly stupid. "Why didn't you say anything? My hair turns magically white and my eyes are suddenly blue and you say nothing?"

Rhiannon looked into her friend's eyes and let out nervous a laugh, wiping away the sweat from her free palm. She dropped her gaze and rubbed her lips together in a smoothing motion. With a deep inhale, she said, "You know, I've been waiting for this for a long time." She paused, though her lips remained parted. "I know why I'm here." With another short pause, Rhiannon sat up straight, licked her lips again, and said, "Níha'mehn it Pandhea."

Caia's mouth fell open as she gripped her hat and slid it off her head.

Archai's arms dropped to his sides as he stepped forward, eyes wide with surprise. "You know," he said.

"I've had suspicions for a long time, but it really hit home when that guy with the gray skin was by our school. You saw him too," Rhiannon said to Caia. "And then, when I saw you in the parking lot in Cali, loads of memories flashed in my mind. I don't have all the facts, but I do have this." She dug into her pocket and pulled out a necklace identical to Caia's. "I don't know where it came from. I got out of bed one day and it dropped on the floor. I started having all sorts of weird dreams every night after that."

"That's the way the orbs were created to behave," Archai explained. "You were born with it around your neck, but the essence of the Voice made it imperceptible to human senses until you were old enough to cognitively handle the memories that come with it."

Caia's attention bounced between Archai and Rhiannon. Nothing they said was remotely close to her own experience. "Why did she have her necklace and I didn't?" she managed to ask.

"Yours broke when you fell and were pulled into the portal," he replied. "Naoni's didn't."

"Naoni," Rhiannon repeated the name, reaching for its familiarity.

"Yes, you are Naoni. Caia is slowly returning to her natural physical state, as you can see," Archai went on. "Something you will also experience. Naoni's essence seems much more potent in you than Caia's was in her until recently."

"So, what *is* this?" Rhiannon asked as she looked closely at the necklace, engrossed in it.

Archai took a breath of what seemed like relief. "Your memories from Jaydür—your true home."

She swallowed hard and passed a glance to Caia before asking, "What does it do?"

Caia replied this time. "Toss it into the air."

Rhiannon wrinkled her brow but did as she was told. Instantly, the air around her vibrated and a pulse of energy pushed out from the orb. Rhiannon fell backwards, tipping her chair over, and landed on the carpet. She scrambled backwards toward the door. Her eyes darted left and right as if trying to remember where she'd been sitting. Sweat beaded her forehead and her breaths were short and fast.

"It's all right," Caia said, kneeling beside her friend.

Rhiannon looked up and a gasp escaped Caia's lips. She spun to meet Archai's surprised expression.

"How?" Caia asked as she paced back and forth across the room over and over again. She couldn't calm herself with the surprise and anger that surged through her blood. Rhiannon was Naoni—already. "How does she remember *everything* and I don't?" Caia asked, flinging an accusing finger at her friend.

"Calm down," Naoni said from the bathroom, where she studied herself in the mirror. Besides her eyes, there was nothing vastly different about her. She'd apparently always looked like her elven self. It was the energy that surged from her that made all the difference.

"Don't tell me to calm down," Caia snapped. "It feels like I've been working on this *forever*. Archai had to sprout wings for me to consider even listening to him! I've been carrying my orb since I first saw him and nothing—*nothing*—like this happened to me."

Naoni emerged from the bathroom with eyebrows cocked and lips pursed. "But you weren't born with it. Even so, your eyes are blue, your hair is white, and your ears are clearly not human. What more do you want?"

"I want my *memories!*" Caia cried, looking to Archai with pleading eyes, but he only continued to stare at Naoni with a pleased expression on his face. "Archai?" Caia pressed.

The Sapient finally looked to Caia and lifted his brows innocently. "She kept her orb," he replied. "There's not much explanation beyond that. Maybe when we return to Jaydür, memories will flood in."

Caia bit the insides of her cheeks. Her patience thin as paper. "So what about 'Rhiannon?'" Caia asked. "What does she say about your change?"

Naoni frowned. "'Say?'"

"Yes," Caia went on. "Ella wouldn't let the elvish essence come to the surface. Essentially, I, Caia, was forced down and out of mind beneath the human essence's skepticism and confusion."

Naoni looked to Archai, then back to Caia with a shake of her head. "What are you on about?"

Caia dropped onto the edge of the bed and spun to face Archai. "She has no human essence," she cried, as if he were at fault.

Archai leaned forward and allowed his hands to hide the irritation on his face before saying, "Ladies, you're going through much, I know, but how to handle it is beyond me. We need to move forward. There is much to consider. Why don't we just go to Jaydür and work this all out with Dy'Mün?" he suggested.

A coldness came over Caia's heart again as it did when she was with Eric. "No!" she curtly replied to Archai's suggestion. "I'm not ready. I have things to resolve and I need to see my family again."

"And Eric," Naoni added.

Archai passed glances between the girls. "I hope beyond hope your delay has nothing to do with him."

A sudden chill in the air made Caia wrap her arms around herself. Of course, the delay had *a lot* to do with Eric. The leg'et ínmi made her physically ache at the thought of distancing herself so much from him, but she couldn't tell that to Archai; he wouldn't understand. Besides that, her mother had lost her husband, and now she would lose a daughter. Who knew what pain it would cause her? "If we leave now, there's no telling when we'll be back. Don't you want to say goodbye to your parents?" Caia asked Naoni, ignoring Archai's displeasure.

"I plan on leaving a runaway note," the dark-haired elf replied. "I imagine we could do that together. We can come up with something believable and give our families some level of comfort in our disappearance, however small."

"And you're just fine with this? You have no concern about how it might affect them? Or who you'll hurt?"

Naoni's sleek, dark brows furrowed, and the bridge of her nose slightly wrinkled. "Don't presume to know how this might affect me," Naoni curtly replied. "I simply haven't connected to my family here the way you clearly have with yours. That doesn't mean I love them any less, but it does make the needed sacrifice more bearable. I'm glad for that much."

Even Naoni's speech had returned to what it once was. Her facial expressions. Her *everything.* How could Caia be such a failure in every respect?

Archai nodded and stood up. "Naoni's plan is one you can harken to, Caia. Make the note, and let us be gone from this world."

Caia looked evenly at Archai. Nothing about the situation made her ready to just up and leave. "No," she finally said. "I need more time. One more day, at the very least."

Archai looked at Naoni, who shrugged in reply. "I'll take you both home, then. You two can spend the day working out whatever is needed to be free to go by tomorrow night. After I leave you home, Caia, I'll go with Naoni and stay with her until she's filled in on our rules and expectations, but I will have some eyes on you."

That caught Caia's attention. "Whose eyes?"

"Keiren's. If anything happans, he will do what's necessary and I'll be summoned before you can hold your breath."

It was suddenly clear that this was the first time since they'd met that Archai was leaving Caia alone, and that bothered her immensely. There was a quiet pleasure in knowing she could call on him at any moment, if just for the company.

Archai opened the door and gestured for Caia and Naoni to join him. "We must be proactive now, and get things done. The fate of Jaydür is riding on our backs." The girls joined Archai, and with an arm around each of them, he told them to cover their eyes, then took to the air.

Archai's discomfort in leaving Caia became clear in the time he spent laying out rules for while he was gone. This time, he told her to keep the mirror uncovered. She was still somewhat confused about what covering the mirror actually did besides keeping enemy eyes off of her, but she trusted the Sapient.

Now alone in her room and with her eyes on the glass, Caia dropped to the floor and leaned against the wall with the window just above her. The emptiness of the room felt like a void. Like an echo of what she was feeling inside—a cold, unknowing ambience.

The only sounds were her own breathing and the occasional clink of silverware in the kitchen downstairs. She felt so alone.

The sense of isolation made Caia's stomach turn. She rested a hand on her belly and closed her eyes, only to be faced with Archai's pleased expression toward Naoni. The happiness on his face was like nothing Caia had ever seen. He lit up; he'd never looked at her that way. In fact, he was mostly angry or serious when he was with her.

I must be such a disappointment to him.

The thought of disappointing someone so integral to Jaydür and the Voices scared Caia. Naoni's change was quick and her acceptance came easily. That's what was expected. What would happen to Caia if her memories didn't ever fully come back?

Caia pulled her knees up and wrapped her arms around them with a deep, uneven breath. Her heart leapt with anxiety in the continual silence.

"Caia," a whispered voice spoke.

"Yes?" she said, looking around the room.

A bluish white light shone at the edges of the mirror. Caia stood back on her feet, and looked into the glass.

Chapter Twelve
Disappointment

"What is troubling you?" Keiren asked. His form slowly emerged through the rippling of the glass, reminiscent of every memory Caia held of Jaydür. She sat on the edge of the bed and admired Keiren as he spoke. A pleasantly familiar sensation filled her at the sight of him, even though she had just seen him earlier in the day.

Her smile faltered and she hesitated before saying, "It's nothing. There's just a lot going on and I sort of feel like my hands are tied."

There was a glimmer in the cat's eyes, and a fleeting wonder of potential telepathic ability flitted through Caia's mind. How much did he *really* know about her and her thoughts?

"You are doing well, Lady Caia," he said. "You cannot force things to move forward. The Highest Power moves at its own pace and for every delay, there is reason."

Memory of such high respect for the Highest Power rang in her mind like a bell. It was Jaydür's concept of the universe and everything within.

"Perhaps," he went on, "regaining it all would hinder your ability to retain your love for those you lived with in this world, and as such, cause a level of pain you are not ready to deal with."

Caia shook her head. "It's not just that; I feel as though I've disappointed Archai," she explained, rubbing her hand up and down her arm as if to warm herself.

"It seems as though your memories of being an elf have not eliminated such simple worries." A deep chuckle resounded throughout the room, and Caia couldn't decide whether that made her feel better or slighted.

"He's been working with me for what feels like forever," she quickly explained, as if to justify herself. "And then Naoni comes along and earns a smile within five minutes of meeting him."

"Are his smiles so valued by you?"

Caia set her gaze on the wall beside the mirror as she considered Keiren's question. After a few seconds of thought, she lifted her eyes to his with a set jaw and said, "Well, yes. After he's put so much time, effort, and concern into me, he's become someone of value to me."

Keiren's ear twitched as he looked pointedly at her. "I see." Caia sensed the cat had more to say about her values, but he turned their conversation back to Archai. "Archai does not show his emotions the way mortal men of this world do," he said. "You must remember that this man has been alive for thousands of years. His thoughts and feelings are not easily perceived. What you would think of as normal or expected would likely be unthinkable to him. With time, you will come to know him and understand him better."

He was right, Caia knew. She'd really only known Archai for a total of maybe a month—and that included the time spent with him in Jaydür before being sent to Earth. This was something she needed to remember at all times if she was to keep her own emotions under control when it came to him.

Satisfied that Caia was reassured, he gestured to the window. "My lady, I think a walk might be of good use."

Caia looked to the window and her brows popped up in surprise. "By myself?"

"It is not yet nightfall and this separation from Archai may be just what you need to think things through more clearly."

"But," she paused, surprised at what Keiren was suggesting, "Archai wouldn't let me go anywhere alone."

Keiren sighed. "I understand the Sapient's fears, considering what had happened with the last Voices, but he's gone a bit too far. How will you gain independence if you are never left to your own devices? Regardless, you won't be alone," he explained. "I will keep an eye on you."

It took no more than that nudge to get Caia out of her bedroom. She grabbed the gray slouch-hat and covered her white hair, then hurried down the steps, avoiding the kitchen where her mother and sister were. It sounded like they were going over some school papers of Brittany's. Apparently, Brittany was nominated for some math scholarship that required her to go to a college in Washington. Their mother wasn't thrilled about the idea and avoided the topic for almost a year, so it was nice hearing them discuss is now. Caia stopped at the door and listened.

"I guess it's a good reason for a road trip," Stephenie said from the kitchen. "We'll get a better sense of the campus. I'll see if I can take off work."

Caia let out a small smile at the idea. A road trip would be good for them after "Ella's" disappearance.

"I'm going to go for a walk, Mom," Caia called out from the front door.

"All right, hon. Grab a sweater. The weather is all over the place today. It's very weird," Stephenie replied.

"Already did."

The weather *was* weird. There hadn't been a sunny day since before Archai showed up and it wasn't cold or hot—just uncomfortably warm. As Caia reached the end of the driveway, she looked up and froze. A black storm front was creeping in from the east, arching toward Phoenix like a wall of rushing warhorses. She'd never seen such dark clouds and the very sight of them screamed danger. Her walk would have to be shortened considerably. Caia pulled her sweater tighter and looked around. When the street was empty, she took a deep breath and started on her way. She only got a distance of about thirty steps before her walk came to a jarring end.

"Ni nell m-êgul!" Archai's voice rang out from behind her. Caia spun around, only to have her arms firmly gripped. "Can you not heed the simplest of instructions? Are my words so empty?" His eyes were wide and bright with anger.

"Archai," Caia said, wincing. Pain snaked down her arms from the pressure of his fingertips. "Nothing happened! Let me go!"

"What are you doing out here alone?" he went on, releasing pressure just the slightest. Before she could answer, he grabbed her by the wrist and pulled her back toward the house. His eyes flitted left and right, making sure no one saw them, then yanked her against his chest. In the blink of an eye, they were in her bedroom again and she was shoved onto her bed. Archai turned to the bedroom door and held out his hand, palm forward, and whispered something in Elvish. The walls of the room glowed blue and Archai began to shout, "Keiren! You hardheaded louse!"

Caia winced at the volume of his voice, but

something told her that the glowing of the walls was some sort of sound barrier and no one beyond those walls could hear him.

The mirror rippled and the formerly white Keiren stepped through the glass as if it were a wall of water, entering the room in the likeness of a black panther. "You will mind your words when speaking to me, Sapient," Keiren said before Archai could continue his rant. Caia leaned against the headboard as Archai stepped toward the cat.

"You allowed her to leave the home alone!" he accused. "There are creatures everywhere seeking out the Voice! Have you seen the skies?"

"She was not alone," Keiren said. The muscles in his shoulders and neck twitched with his words. "Do you lack all confidence in her, Archai? You know that if there were any danger nearby, her intuition would stop her. If anything, *you* have just drawn more attention to this place by your impulsive use of magic."

"Archai, please calm down," Caia tried, rising slowly to her knees. He didn't even pass her a glance.

"I am her guardian," he continued in a biting tone. "My rules will be obeyed without question, do you understand me, Keiren?"

Keiren turned to Caia and shook his head, seemingly unperturbed by Archai's volume and tone. "My lady, you did nothing wrong. My confidence in you is immeasurable. Do not let his overprotectiveness make you feel any less than you are." And with that, Keiren turned and entered the mirror just as he had come. The glass rippled and only her reflection beside Archai's remained.

Archai spun around and ran a hand through his hair and down his jaw, then turned back toward Caia. He gestured to the mirror, but no words came from his lips. The muscles of his jaw clenched and flexed as he paced the room wordlessly for another moment. When he calmed down enough to find his voice again, he sat on the bed beside Caia, leaning his back against the headboard. He grabbed Caia's hand and took a deep breath.

"I wish I could make you understand," he said, placing her hand palm-up in his own. Caia was thankful that his tone had lost its sting as he looked down at her hand, running his thumb over the inside of her palm. "She," he paused, and a smile touched his lips. "She had a mark here. On both hands. It was the tree of the Terehn. It would glow white at all times. It was how I could tell she was happy, healthy, and full of the eled'hwen. Everything about her was joyful and calm—always calm." His hold on Caia loosened and his eyes distanced, focusing on something only he could see. "I looked away for a moment—that's all it took for them to snatch her— and the next time I saw those trees, they were black and oozing with the poison infused to defile the eled'hwen. Her eyes—those beautiful eyes of sapphire—were nothing but hollow pockets in a skull."

Caia took his hand in hers and slid closer to him, resting her cheek on his shoulder. She couldn't meet his gaze, afraid to see the pain of what he was reliving.

"She was the second discovered, after Poette, and I was the one who discovered her. This is why, Caia," he went on, squeezing her hand reassuringly. "This is why I worry. My mistake is not something I intend to live through again."

"I'm sorry," she managed. "I just needed to breathe. This whole thing with Naoni—"

"Naoni?" he cut in, looking down at Caia. When Caia didn't finish her thought, he asked, "What does this have to do with Naoni?"

The way Archai asked the question made her feel almost silly, but it was a legitimate concern and was likely going to have to be faced eventually. Caia bit her bottom lip and sat back up. "Naoni just jumped right into everything without a problem. Her memories are back. She's become herself without even trying. I feel like a disappointment."

Archai huffed. "Dy'Mün and the Elders are not easy to disappoint."

"Not to Dy'Mün," Caia said with a huff as she knocked her elbow into Archai's arm. "To *you*." With a sigh, she dropped her eyes to her fidgeting hands. "We worked hard for everything I've regained and it just seems so pitiful compared to Naoni."

"You," Archai cut in before she could continue. "You thought you disappointed *me*?"

Caia nodded.

"Oh," was all he said at first. Caia's palms started sweating at the thought that she had put him in an uncomfortable position. Their time together made it clear he didn't handle emotions very well. Caia let out a slow breath when Archai finally spoke up.

"I don't know what to say about your confession. My opinion on any matter has never been considered, unless pertaining to the protection of a Voice or any other charge." He paused for a moment, and Caia got the sense his mind worked through what she'd just said. "Caia, no." He shook his head. "I'm not disappointed. I never even thought to be. Why would I? You are the Voice of Apan. I would have no right, no reason, to ever look down on you in any manner."

Caia's eyes were still on her hands.

"Caia," Archai said sharply, grabbing her attention. When she met his gaze, he continued. "The speed with which you grow as a Voice is not important. What's important is that you survive and endeavor to be the Voice Jaydür calls you to be. I will *never* be disappointed in you." To Caia's surprise, Archai laughed. "I don't even know what else to say. The thought of you being worried about my opinion is unthinkable."

Keiren's words came back to Caia. *What you*

would think of as normal or expected would likely be unthinkable to him. He was right; Archai was utterly clueless about the very notion of disappointment in this matter. That was comforting to her.

Thunder shook the house and Caia quickly turned to the window. The brewing maelstrom of the storm was inching closer, and she wondered how long it would take to pass. Knowing what she was thinking, Archai stood up and offered his hand.

"We've got a bit of time before this storm hits. Why don't you have that walk of yours? I'll take you anywhere you'd like and I'll keep an eye on you as you have some 'alone time.'"

"Really?" Caia couldn't help but smile.

Archai nodded.

Caia bit her lip. "I do have one place in mind."

Chapter Thirteen
The Ash Pixies

Cafe Merci was always a favorite. Anytime Stephenie had any business or shopping to do in Scottsdale, she'd take Caia and Brittany and stop for tea at one of the tables outside. Caia thought on what life would be like for her mother and sister after she left. Brittany would likely move on to college in Washington, taking advantage of the free money in the scholarship she was offered. She'd get married some day and have kids, making Stephenie a grandma. Stephenie wouldn't remain stagnant for long. She'd realize that she was getting older and that she didn't want to live alone forever, then she'd go out and find a man. They both had plenty of life left to live without "Ella." But they wouldn't see it that way at first.

Caia's chest tightened at the thought of how she could make her leave easier for her family. She would do what was necessary to care for Jaydür, but she would do it in a way that her mother and sister wouldn't be left feeling abandoned.

Thunder rumbled, though it sounded more like a groaning old man trying to get out of bed as the storm moved in. It wasn't necessarily a natural sound, and Caia remembered what Archai said to Keiren an hour earlier. *There are creatures everywhere seeking out the Voice! Have you seen the skies?*

Was he trying to say the storm had to do with Jaydürian creatures?

With a sip of her tea, Caia tried to focus on the light taste of lavender in an attempt to calm her mind. It seemed to race almost constantly lately. *Archai would tell me where the danger lies*, she told herself, then looked around, scouting for any sign of her protector. Nothing.

He's good.

Tiny remains of what escaped the teabag floated around her drink as Caia ran the tip of her finger along the edge of the mug. A breeze blew against her, gently blowing back some white strands that had come loose from the beanie.

Closing her eyes, Solin came to mind, soon followed by his human self—Eric. Caia paused on the thought of him, wondering if she would ever see him again. Would she ever make it back to this world? Would she have the freedom to travel back? Everything about his being here in Terra seemed so wrong, and there was no way to make it right. Of all who were involved in Caia and Naoni transforming back to Voices, Solin Rahngwa sacrificed the most. He was the one left without memory. He was without the knowledge of the incredible person he once was.

"I've failed you, Solin," Caia whispered into her mug as she took another sip. The way her words bounced lightly off the ceramic made them feel empty and useless.

Footsteps sounded from behind, and the thought of how simple people had it in this life brought a sigh to Caia's lips. Work or school, home, sleep, eat, and repeat. The weekends come and everyone drops what they're doing and wanders through the streets downtown. Movies. Dinner with friends. Fun. That was going to be Solin's life—Eric's life.

The footsteps behind Caia grew louder and faster, as if the person was rushing, and Caia tossed a curious glance to her left just as the person came up beside her.

"Oh my God, I knew no one else would walk around with such an ugly bag," Whitney—to Caia's horror—said with a laugh. If it wasn't bad enough that Whitney was there, Eric was with her, holding her hand. Caia looked down at her olive-green messenger bag. Ugly? It was just green with brown leather handles.

Whitney froze at the strange sight of Caia's new look. "What did you *do?*" she asked, reaching for Caia's hat, but Caia saw it coming and knocked her hand away.

"Leave it," Caia snapped. Something like surprise twinkled in Whitney's eyes.

"Oh my; you're awful touchy, aren't you?" She tossed her bag onto the table and plopped into the chair directly across. "Sit down, babe," she said to Eric, and he hesitantly complied, pulling out the chair on Caia's left. "Look at her eyes," she went on, and Caia suddenly felt like a monkey in a zoo the way Whitney leaned in to see her more closely. "Those aren't contacts. Are your eyes naturally blue and you've been wearing brown contacts? Why would you hide blue eyes?" She leaned in and grabbed a wisp of the white hair sitting on Caia's shoulder. "And you dyed your hair, oh my God. Can I see it? It makes you super pale, you know. You *want* to be pale?"

"Whitney," Caia responded, flashing half a glance at Eric as she placed her cup firmly onto the table with a thunk. "You are the last person I think about when doing *anything*, so it really doesn't matter to me what you think about my choices. I didn't ask for you to sit with me either, so keep moving. Don't wanna get caught in that storm," she added, gesturing behind her with her thumb. The couple exchanged looks of surprise, but Whitney wouldn't let her off that easy.

"Are you having a midlife crisis? She's having a crisis, babe," she said, turning to Eric, who still remained silent. "Is this because of the beach thing? You know I was just being honest. I'm really a super nice person. That's why I have so many friends. I just think some things need to be said, so I say them."

Another breeze blew toward them from behind Whitney this time, and a tongue of cold air licked through in a way that snatched Caia's attention from her companions at once. She turned in her chair to see the black clouds of the storm front formed into a circular, vortex-like formation. The sun was still visible in the west as it cowered away from the malevolence that was surely coming.

Whitney and Eric followed her gaze.

"What the heck?" Eric finally said, breaking his silence.

Caia slowly rose out of her seat and turned halfway to eye the storm. "I think you should go," she said. A wave of static came through the breeze, making the hairs on Caia's arms rise. A memory of the mirror in the Temple of Pandhea, and the electricity before her crossing, flicked before her mind's eye.

A scream rang out in the distance and the wind suddenly rushed around the table in a whirlwind. One scream turned to many as a black billow rose from beyond the buildings in the distance. A hum carried on the air like the buzz of a bee swarm, but the billow coming toward them was no bee swarm. The billow rose, as thick at the bottom as at the top, like a snake rising to strike.

Whitney grabbed her things and she and Eric

started walking backwards, as if afraid to turn their backs on what they were seeing.

"They found me," Caia said louder than she meant to, and Eric's attention bounced between her and the incoming danger.

"What do you mean?" he asked as the three of them turned and walked faster, checking over their shoulders with every step.

Blood drained from Caia's face when Archai materialized not fifty feet away, in perfect view of Whitney, Eric, and the people around Cafe Merci. Whitney halted in her steps immediately.

"It's time to go," he said, gesturing to Caia to continue on ahead. He turned to Eric and Whitney, who stared at him, awestruck. "If you value your lives, you will say nothing when you are questioned about what happened here."

Caia locked eyes with Eric, knowing the likelihood of seeing him again was little more than a hope. She took a mental picture of his face and her mind played the image of her beloved Solin beside Eric's. *Hair black like a crow, eyes like blue fire, and skin as white as snow.* Tears brimmed her vision and she offered a smile as Archai urged her on. "Assuming they don't kill you both first," he quietly added. Prodding Caia forward, he said "Hurry. We must hide you until the pixies pass."

"Wait, what did you say?" she asked, then turned in a frenzy. Eric and Whitney stood like deer in headlights. Caia motioned to them as nasty memories of little gray pixies with black eyes and long fingernails biting and clawing innocent people played in her mind. She remembered running into a similar-looking swarm as a child with her father, who'd struggled to fend them off with salt. Though her father had protected her, a scar had remained on his right ear from a bite.

Caia hated Whitney intensely, but she couldn't let the ash pixies kill her. That would be a whole new level of evil. "Come with us!" she cried as she grabbed as many salt shakers from the cafe tables as she could. "Pour the salt in your hands and throw them at the pixies," she instructed. Whitney and Eric hardly hesitated before they, too, held a little hill of salt in their palms, then ran to keep up with Caia and Archai.

"Pixies?" Eric asked in a hurry.

"Yes," Caia replied. "Nasty little things."

"What, like fairies?" Eric cried.

Caia shot him a glance before looking up at the black cloud. "You're about to find out."

"We cannot bring them along," Archai said through clenched teeth, his attention on the ash pixies. "Brace yourselves!" The swarm came upon them and Archai's sword and scabbard suddenly materialized onto his body as if a hiding spell had been lifted from him. Drawing the sword, he swung it in an arc, killing at least a dozen of the creatures at once. Their high-pitched shrieks attracted more attention, and the swarm came toward them all the thicker.

Caia threw her salt. The shrieks of pain coming from the pixies as their flesh melted told her the trick worked in this world, but they just kept coming. Eric pried one off his face but the teeth of another sank in so deeply that blood ran down his cheek. Whitney screamed as two pulled her hair and another bit away at her chin.

"Throw the salt!" Caia cried, batting off an attacking pixie with her purse. Ugly or not, it knocked the things pretty far.

Eric grabbed Whitney by the hand when the pixies let go, then went running after Archai, who spun in a half circle and sliced his sword downward, tearing into the atmosphere and creating some sort of rift or doorway. Archai grabbed Eric and Whitney by the backs of their shirts and shoved them through, then followed with Caia in tow.

The sudden silence in the room the rift led them to was like a plug of pressure in Caia's ears.

Caia looked up to Archai, then to the others. "Is everyone all right?" she asked. At the sight of blood on Eric and Whitney's faces, she looked around the cellar for something to clean up with. Luckily, the cellar they were in was a cold cellar that likely belonged to an attached home. Canned goods, paper towels, and other typical home goods sat on shelves around the perimeter. Folded between two cans of tomato soup was a small hand towel, which Caia grabbed and offered to Eric. She tried to smile—to seem friendly—but the humans weren't thrilled with what was happening. Then she realized that comforting them was not on her list of priorities. This seemed like pretty good payback for their treatment of her at the beach.

"The ash pixies," Caia started, turning her back on the two to face Archai. "How did they get here?"

Archai searched the room and found a door that led to the outside. Using some rope and chains, he tied it down and replied, "It was my fault. They must have sensed the magic I used in your room when I was angry earlier. Though I'm sure Naoni's change had something to do with it as well. With so much attention on you these last few days, the sinstarians were bound to pick up any anomalies in this area."

Caia nodded and scanned the place for any cracks or separate doorways. The room was empty but for a couple deep freezers and shelves lined with canned goods and other necessities. The only entrance was the wood and metal door Archai just tied shut.

"But *how* did they get in?" Caia asked. "Did they come from the ground? From a portal?"

"From the gateway in the sky," Archai explained, passing a glance to the two humans who stood awkwardly, clearly still frightened. He pointed upwards and went on, saying, "You've seen and heard about that streak in the sky. That was the beginning. Someone in the Everdark opened the doorway. How they learned to do it, I cannot say."

The very mention of the dark forest in eastern Jaydür made Caia's belly turn over, even though she didn't remember everything she once knew of the Everdark. Not yet, at least.

Archai's attention was on the doorway again as he tightened the rope and chain as best he could.

"And a locking spell on the door would also attract them?" Caia asked as Archai finished.

"That's right. I must avoid the use of magic as much as possible. The sinstarians obviously have a way to sense it."

The buzzing from outside grew loud, and with it was the chittering of the ash pixies' maniacal laughter. The metal door shook vigorously as they tried to get in. Whitney and Eric recoiled from the door until they were at the back wall of the cellar. Caia stood by Archai with her hand on his arm, staring at the light that flickered in the cracks around the door as it was continually yanked on. One of Archai's hands was on the hilt of his sword. The fingers of the other curled and stretched at the ready, just in case the pixies found a way in.

"He has a sword," Caia heard Whitney whisper to Eric. She looked at the two in the back of the cellar. Eric nodded but said nothing in return. "Why does he have a sword?" she went on. "Maybe he came from the Renaissance Festival."

"I have a sword for protection," Archai said without looking at her. "And if I were you, I'd be *quietly* grateful."

"Ella, what's going on?" Eric asked.

She turned and stiffened the moment she met his eyes. His own grew wide with an obvious nervousness and Caia wondered if she was now perceived by regular people the way Archai was perceived—as something unnatural and uncomfortable.

With her eyes locked on his, she slowly reached up and pulled off the hat, revealing her snow-white tresses that fell to her lower back. She was going to be leaving Terra anyway. "I'm not Ella," she said.

Whitney and Eric's eyes widened at the sight of the ears pointing through her hair.

"Where is Ella, then?" Eric went on. "You look like her, sort of. And you sound like her."

Caia bit her lip and shrugged. "She's gone. I'm all that's left."

"So what are you? An alien? A spirit? You possessed her?"

"A Voice," Archai snapped in reply as he turned to face Eric. "And you'll show her some respect." He shook his head and glanced at Caia. "The boy is getting on my nerves just as much as his elvish counterpart did."

"Stop," Caia ordered. "He doesn't even know what any of that means."

"Of course he doesn't because he's a feeble-minded human. 'Alien,'" he scoffed at the word.

"Elvish counterpart?" Eric repeated.

"Ignore him," Caia replied. "I'm from someplace else, so to you, yes, I could be labeled 'alien,'" she explained, sitting on a wooden wine crate. Whitney and Eric followed her lead, finding their own place to sit, though Eric made an intensely obvious point of finding a place not so close to either of the girls.

Whitney spoke. "So what are those things out there?"

"Ash pixies," Caia answered. "From my world. What you would imagine to be faeries, only far from sweet. They'd sooner skin your face than dance in mushroom rings."

Whitney shivered and rubbed her hands down her arms for the warmth of friction. "Faeries? Mushroom rings? I never cared about fairytales. But if it weren't for the nasty little bastards that did this to my face, I'd have a harder time believing it all." Whitney studied Caia from head to toe and continued. "So, Ella was just a disguise."

Caia shook her head. "All of that is so confusing, and I wouldn't even know where to begin with an explanation."

Archai leaned his ear to the door. "Not that it matters. The less they know, Caia, the better," he said. "They need to get home and treat their wounds. A bite from an ash pixie has proven fatal to humans."

Caia swung around to face Archai, her eyes bulging with fresh fear. "What? So, how do they treat them?"

"Milk and cinnamon. The wounds must be covered with the mixture."

Caia scanned the shelves for cinnamon. Milk would obviously not be found in a cellar, but if there was one ingredient to help them, she had to try. "How long do they have?"

"They have another few hours before the venom sets in. But Caia, the longer they remain with us, the more they are in harm's way. Ash pixies are the pleasant end of our problems. Sinstarians will be here soon enough."

"Caia," Eric repeated, tasting the name.

Caia's heart nearly burst at the sound of her name on his lips. It had been years since she'd heard it. Moisture blurred her vision but she blinked it away, hoping no one noticed. She waited to see any change in his face—any sense of realization or sign of him remembering life as Solin, but her heart quickly sank when nothing happened.

Archai's disapproving gaze burned into her back with hard, dark eyes. The leather of his gauntlets cracked as he curled his hands into irritated fists. "It sounds as if the pixies have moved on. They can go," he said, motioning to Eric and Whitney. "We should stay until all signs of the pixies are gone. When it's dark, we'll find a bridge to Jaydür."

Caia tucked some hair behind her ear and chewed her tongue. "I'm leaving? For good?"

"My job is to keep you alive, so, yes, I'm taking you back."

Eric rose to his feet and motioned for his girlfriend to join him, but Whitney was slowly piecing things together. She raised her brows in suspicion. "He's your bodyguard?"

At the sound of her voice, Archai's face twisted into a snarl. He looked as if it took great effort not to grab something and make her a gag. "I said you can go," he said with emphasis on each word.

"No, wait," Whitney replied, bursting with new interest. "No one who's a nobody would need a bodyguard. Eric, Ella's someone important." She spun back to Caia. "Are you, like, royalty or something? Is this a real life *Princess Diaries*?"

"Did you hear nothing Caia has already told you? She's, like, higher than that," Archai said in a mocking tone, leaning down to her level. His eyes were raging with impatience. Caia put herself between him and Whitney and tried to grab his gaze while he added, "And I will not hear another word from you."

"Okay, Archai," Caia tried. "That's enough. If he says you two are free to go, then go." She looked sidelong at Eric. "While you have a chance to get to your loved ones."

Archai cut the rope and chains, then Whitney left

the cellar with Eric in tow. He turned and his lips parted, but before anything else could be said the door was pulled shut and locked up again.

Archai turned to meet an angry Caia. She shook her head and said, "Well, that was really horrid of you."

Archai chuckled darkly. "I don't know what you mean."

Caia's gaze lingered on the door and she let out a long sigh. "Will they be all right?" she asked. She tried to tell herself that his safety was all that mattered. Solin was alive and well, even if he was human. He had a chance to really live without any regret.

"They'll be fine," Archai replied. "Now, rest while you can."

Her eyes burned. Her head ached. Caia had no word for what she was feeling in her heart, though. The real pain of it all would come at night, when she was alone with her thoughts. That's how it always happened when Eric was involved. She'd be somewhat numb to him and to life until the moon rose and night crept over, hiding everything from sight, and all that was left to be seen were her thoughts and her feelings. That was when her true emotions came through and when suffering really took hold.

A hand touched Caia's shoulder and she looked up to meet Archai's softened stare. His brow furrowed with concern—or irritation—she still couldn't tell all of the time. "*You* will be fine," he said with a squeeze. "The sooner you let go, the better."

Caia took a breath and closed her eyes only to see Eric's face again. Frustration was starting to boil over. "I don't think I can rest," she said. "I feel like I need to do something. Sitting here will drive me crazy."

Archai looked to the crates along the far wall. A canvas tarp covered a small mountain of other crates and with a swift swipe, he took it and rolled it up, then threw it on the floor. "Lie down and close your eyes," he said.

Caia frowned. "Is that a demand?"

"A gentle one," he said with a smile.

Caia did as she was told and rested her head on the canvas. "Now what?"

She closed her eyes and twitched at the feeling of his hands on her head. His thumbs rubbed between her eyes and his pinkies placed light pressure on her temples. "Just relax." The pads of his thumbs grew warm and soft and Caia didn't realize when her body grew soft as well. Her arms and legs grew limp, the muscles in her face relaxed, and all thought left her mind.

Chapter Fourteen
The Return

"Brittany," Caia said.

A cool breeze swirled into the cellar like a breath of fresh air. At the sound of her own voice, Caia opened her eyes to find herself on the floor where Archai left her, her head turned slightly to the right with the canvas supporting her neck like a collar. She pulled herself up and looked around to find the door open and Archai halfway outside. A memory of Dy'Mün's cottage cellar flashed in her mind, and with it came the emotions of fear and uncertainty she felt that day when Archai left them to find the goblins that shot him through his shoulder.

"How long have I been asleep?" she asked, drawing herself out of the memory as she rubbed her eyes and smoothed out her hair. "The last thing I remember is lying down."

Archai came back down and caught her gaze. "You slept through the night."

"What?" she cried, searching her pockets for her phone. It wasn't there. "The whole night? What time is it? My mom is going to freak out! Where is my phone? Where is my bag?"

"Your mother is no longer a concern. Consider yourself gone from this world—unattached."

"What? You can't be serious." With his silent nod, a burning sensation filled her sinuses, and her chest ached at the thought of never seeing her mother and sister again. "That's it, then? Did you take my things?"

"I did not take anything. And I'm sorry that it pains you, but this is only one of many situations in your life that are going to change. You must learn to adapt. It is not just ash pixies out there, Caia. This world is no longer safe."

Caia paused as she remembered everything that happened the previous day. The world would know now about the pixies, but could they have discovered where they came from? "It must be chaotic out there today," she said quietly. "The news channels are probably having a field day."

"From what I can tell, the people of Terra have gone indoors. Scarcely did I see a person walk by."

Caia nodded and stood up. She couldn't believe she'd slept on the floor without any issue. "What did you do to me?" she asked, remembering Archai's hands on her face. Her stomach soured with anxiety again, still unable to see her bag or phone anywhere.

Stephenie and Brittany must have had a long night, what with her gone and the pixies showing up in the world. With a shake of her head, Caia tried to refocus her thoughts. She would think everything through later. If what Archai said was true, staying away from her family would keep them safer.

"An old Dwarven trick," he replied with a smile. "Usually used by the women to lull their husbands to sleep when they did not want to be kept awake themselves. I am surprised it worked so quickly. You must have been exhausted."

Caia nodded and concern crossed her face. "Did you sleep?"

Archai shook his head. "I've been keeping watch."

"For the whole night? And I was just lying here, limp and probably snoring?"

"You don't snore."

"It's kind of sad that you can say that with such confidence when my own mother can't." She rubbed the crumbly sleep from her eyes and added, "So what do we do now?"

Archai was suddenly serious again. "We cross. The pixies have gone north, so we'll need to find a place toward the south."

"What sort of place?"

Archai offered Caia his hand and helped her out of the cellar, where she was met with surprising darkness.

"Any unpopulated territory, so we can draw the

pixies back without risking more lives."

A short gasp of surprise slipped from Caia's lips. Archai followed her gaze and placed a hand on her shoulder.

"The sky is gone," she whispered.

A black, dome-shaped cloud hung above the city. The center of it was the darkest and most foreboding, though the entirety of the formation eclipsed the light of the sun with a barrier of shadow. The curved walls of the cloud varied between gray and white, spanning as far as normal human sight could reach. There was no blue to be seen. There was no wind to be felt, besides a hot breath of air from the center of the formation pushing downward onto the city.

"That is the Everdark's Cloak," Archai said, answering the question she knew was clear on her face. His grim tone raised even more concern within Caia.

Lightning flashed in different parts of the cloud, sometimes to the left, sometimes to the right, and other times everywhere at once. No bird was in the sky, and no sound could be heard besides distant thunder.

"Did you see this coming?" she asked with her eyes frozen above.

"If I had, I would have taken you the day I came here. This is going to cause a whole new level of problems if we don't figure out a way to close that doorway."

Caia nodded and slowly made her way around the building toward the first intersection within sight. The entire street was taped off and policemen surrounded the area in full body armor.

"How do we do that?" she asked. "How did this happen in the first place? Knowing how it came to be might lead us to a solution to close it."

"Hey!" a voice shouted. It was one of the policemen. "You're not supposed to be here!"

Caia opened her mouth to say something but a woman in an officer's uniform came running up from the other side. "Were you here during the attack?" the woman asked. "Did you see what happened here yesterday?"

"Well, yes, but—" Caia started, looking up to Archai, whose attention was on the sudden crowd of people. His jaw tensed. "We were hiding in a cellar."

"So you saw those things that attacked?" the woman went on.

Fingers wrapped lightly around her arm. "We should not be here," Archai said, hushed.

"Were you bitten? Should we call an ambulance? Others have suffered paralyzing effects from a bite."

Caia snapped her attention to the woman. "Paralyzing?"

"Yes, local hospitals are filled with the victims bitten by these things. Paralysis, cardiac arrest. You're a lucky pair."

Stark realization filled Caia's eyes and she spun,

gripping Archai's sleeve. "Were you telling the truth when you told Whitney and Eric about the milk and cinnamon?"

"Yes," Archai replied.

Caia turned back to the policewoman. "A mixture of cinnamon and milk. Smother it onto the bites. It will stop the venom."

The woman exchanged curious glances with the other officer who stepped up beside her. "How do you know that? Do you know what those creatures were?"

"Caia, we have to go now! Et eled!" The Elvish words rumbled from Archai's throat like a growl. He grabbed Caia around the waist, covered her eyes, and pushed off the ground. A force of air beat down on them as they cut through the wind.

Caia screamed as she clung to Archai's arms, her legs dangling freely in the air. He suddenly dove down and her stomach lurched as she let out a high-pitched squeal.

"Archai! Put me down!"

Instead, she felt him draw her closer to himself and tighten his hold. "We are still too close to the affected area. We can be ambushed before we even see them coming."

The people below screamed. Some in surprise, some in fear—likely not knowing at first what was actually flying above them.

"But everyone sees us flying right now!" she shouted. "They all see your wings!"

"What does that matter? They've just been introduced to ash pixies. What's a winged man in comparison?"

How could he say that? "You're kind of a big deal, if you ask me!" she cried in return.

"The ash pixies have made this world aware they're not alone. There's no point in holding back. Now, we keep the Voices alive and we take you back home to Jaydür."

After what felt like an hour in the air, Archai finally set Caia down in the middle of a desert. He held her by her elbows until her knees stopped wobbling.

"I need you to stay here—quietly," he said in a whisper. "Not a word, understand?"

Caia nodded and looked around. They were alone and far from people, so why the sudden emphasis on silence? Thunder rolled, bringing Caia's attention to the sky again where the very sight brought palpitations to her heart. There was still no break in the clouds—no sign of the sun—even though they flew miles away from the epicenter in Scottsdale. The only light coming from the sky was from the almost constant flashes of lightning within the massive formation.

"Archai?" she whispered, though she wasn't entirely sure why she was whispering, unless the cacti had suddenly sprouted ears. Caia looked up at a saguaro and frowned. A vague memory of sentient trees in Jaydür flashed to mind.

Footsteps sounded behind her and she spun to meet Archai, who appeared out of nowhere again.

"Where did you go?" she asked.

"I had to be sure we weren't followed," he explained, pulling a chain out from under his shirt— something Caia never noticed before. He plucked a ring off the end of it and twisted it onto his finger.

"What's that for?" she asked, and just as the question left her lips, Archai slashed the empty space in front of them, tearing through an unseen veil separating this world from the next. The air had ragged edges that flapped like a book's pages in the wind—just like the streak that was in the sky. A light broke through from behind the edges and a grass-covered landscape flickered into view as if it were behind a curtain of water.

Slack jawed and wide-eyed, Caia took Archai's hand without turning from the tear before her. She brought the ring to her face and peered at what looked like a silver shark tooth sticking out from the top. "What *is* this?" she asked.

"An üsan," Archai replied then pointed to the tear. "And that is Jaydür."

The ring suddenly held little wonder for Caia in comparison to what was hovering before her. An entirely different world hung within reach. All she had to do was step forward and through the tear. "Where will this take us?"

"Right in the middle of Dealuri Grounds. That's about one hundred and fifty miles away from any major villages. There is not much cover of darkness there, so the pixies cannot thrive. They'll be gone and absorbed into the ground within days."

"We're going to kill them?" Caia asked with a look somewhere between concern and confusion.

"Over the years," Archai began, his eyes scanning the skies in the distance, "the ash pixies have left their territories, crossing into villages and homesteads. The Elders considered allowing hunting groups to enter the Everdark for population control, but they did not feel it was something they could rightly do without the Voices being present, for fear of causing too great a dent in populations. Now that you and Naoni will be back, there is a greater chance that balance will work itself out. Taking this swarm out of here will not, in my opinion, harm the population still in the Everdark."

A buzz sounded in the distance, and Caia's heart leapt as she grasped what was happening. The pixies were drawn to the magic in the üsan that Archai used to create a tear.

Something inside of her resisted Archai's plan. Caia put a hand to her chest and she shook her head. "No," she said. "We can't just kill them. Something is wrong."

L.F. OAKE

Archai hesitantly bounced his attention between her and the coming swarm. "Caia, we're a bit close to being overwhelmed by those things. Tell me why this plan won't work."

"Um," Caia's eyes darted left and right as she searched her mind for a legitimate response. But all she had was a feeling. "I...I don't know. I just feel like it's a bad idea. Can't we send them into the Everdark?"

Archai lifted his brows with a frown. "I am not taking a Voice into the Everdark."

"I don't like the little bastards either, but I don't feel good about killing them off. I don't know how to explain it."

Archai ran a hand down the side of his face and grit his teeth. The buzzing grew louder, and with it came a warm breeze blowing against them. Throwing his head back with a groan of resignation, Archai turned to the tear. He slipped his fingers through the rippling atmosphere and seemingly grasped one of the sides by a flapping edge. With the atmosphere gripped in his hands, he lunged his body against the tear. The opening flickered with a blue and white light and was somehow suddenly twenty yards ahead of them.

"Go," Archai said, nudging her toward the tear. "Run!"

Caia looked ahead and without much hesitation, she sped toward the tear.

289

Chapter Fifteen
Welcome Home

Forest suddenly surrounded Caia as she ran. She passed an enormous tree leading out to a field and directly into the path of a horse and its rider. With a scream, she froze as the horse whinnied and rose up onto its hind legs. She stepped back, and though she dodged the horse's kick, she also fell onto the muddy ground.

Her gaze shifted in every direction, taking in the change of scenery as a large, husky man dismounted his horse and held out his hand. "Forgive me, my lady!" he begged.

Caia stared for a moment before scanning the immediate area for Archai, then hesitantly took the man's hand. He wore a plate of armor across his chest and shoulders and had long, disheveled dark hair that he tied back.

"My lady, are you injured?" he continued.

"Darcon, what is it?" another voice said behind

the large man.

"My lord, I did not see her," the man answered as he turned away, revealing the second man. "She jumped out of the woods. I had no time to stop."

The second man looked curiously at Caia. He was a tall, slender man with hair like a golden sunset cascading down to the middle of his back. "Oh," he said, gazing down at her.

The moment his eyes met hers, Caia sensed a feeling of wonder come from him. Whether it was the realization that she wasn't a typical Jaydürian or the confusion of why a girl appeared out of nowhere and was soiled with mud, she couldn't tell.

"Are you all right?" he asked, stepping up beside Darcon.

"I'm fine," Caia replied. "Thank you." She looked over her shoulder, hoping to see Archai come up from behind, but he was nowhere in sight.

"Are you with someone?" the blonde man asked.

Caia froze, wondering how Archai could handle a pixie's bite. "Ash pixies—" she started before realizing she stood in an area much like Archai intended on sending the creatures to die. The sun was high and hot.

The blonde man and Darcon exchanged glances.

"There are no pixies in this territory," Darcon explained. "If there were, they would not survive for long."

"I'm sorry," she replied with a nervous laugh. "I'm

a bit out of sorts. Am I in the Dealuri Grounds?"

Darcon and the blonde man laughed, their brows raised and their eyes wide as if they'd heard a funny joke. "About a hundred miles west of there," the blonde man replied. "You're on the lands of the Asëa royal family—my land."

Caia's face lit up with understanding. This was Prince Leithen! She immediately faced the ground in a bow of respect, glad she remembered how! "I am *so* sorry, my lord! I didn't realize I had—" She paused, thinking carefully on her next words. Were Jaydürians aware of portals and other worlds? "I've been traveling all through the night, your highness. I am slightly turned around."

As she finished speaking, a blonde-haired woman in a red cloak rode up on her horse beside the prince. Behind her, some distance away, was what looked like a small castle surrounded by tree hedges.

"Leithen, darling, who is this, all covered in mud?" the woman in the red cloak asked with a deep furrow of her brow. "And why are you ruining your boots for her?"

A blush colored the prince's cheeks. Shame dripped from his tone as he replied, "By the Highest, Emerwen. Where is your propriety?"

The woman tossed her head without so much as another look at Caia. "Do you not see how she is dressed? She is a foreigner and probably a beggar as well. Leave her."

If it weren't for her nasty attitude, the dark-green shade of the woman's eyes would have been hard to ignore. They were like nothing Caia had ever seen before. Not in her last seventeen years among humans, at least.

"Caia," a voice called from behind.

She turned without hesitation. "Archai! There you are! I was worried something happened!"

"Not now," he replied while kneeling before Leithen. "My lord, I thank you for being of assistance to my guest."

Leithen nodded and smiled. "It was my pleasure. I am sorry we nearly trampled her. From where do you and your guest hail?"

Archai stood as he replied. "She is from the far region of the Willow of Apan, and she traveled here as a student of Professor Dy'Mün. I am simply a friend of the professor's, showing her the sights."

"I see. I presumed it was somewhere distant when I observed the strange clothing." Leithen glanced back at Caia as he spoke. He smiled. "You must visit us again, my lady, if you are settled so near."

"Leithen," Emerwen said. "I am beginning to feel weary. Must we stay in this dreadful heat?"

"The heat will soon pass," Leithen replied without looking back. "Rain season is near."

"Well, now," Archai began, placing his hand on Caia's shoulders. "We must be on our way, or the professor will worry."

Though Leithen smiled, disappointment seeped from him. "We would not wish such a thing," he replied. "Professor Dy'Mün is highly regarded in these parts."

Archai bowed his head as he and Caia turned to be on their way.

"Wait," Leithen called after the pair. "You have not given me your name, my lady. It would be rude of me to leave you without asking when there is every possibility of our running into each other again."

"Oh," Caia began, glancing between Archai and Leithen. "Um, Caia. My name is Caia."

"Caia," Leithen whispered. He took her hand in his and lightly kissed the backs of her fingers. "It has been a pleasure."

"Yes," she replied with a scarlet face. "Thank you."

The man smiled and bowed his head as Archai took Caia's hand. They walked arm in arm as they disappeared from Leithen's sight into the woods. Caia looked back to make sure they were out of view when she asked. "What happened to the pixies?"

"I opened another doorway," he replied. There was something different about him. His shoulders were more squared. He stood up straighter. His chin was held high. "They have been rerouted to the Everdark."

"Oh," Caia replied. "That's not terrible, right?"

Though Archai did not relax, he looked sidelong

at her. "Right."

The field they walked through ended in a line of trees that marked an entrance to a path through a forest. Foliage was thick, covering the ground with grass, flowers, and boulders along the way. Trees grew in various sizes, spanning from three feet in diameter to possibly eight feet in diameter or more. The Arizona brown and yellow hues were nowhere to be seen. The dry desert air was gone, replaced with the clean scent of rain and wet grass. Caia swallowed hard as the realization only then began to settle—this was Jaydür, an entire separate world, and it felt like it.

A small mud and stone cottage with a thatched roof hid beyond a denser crop of trees, not ten yards from a large pond where a hefty boulder sat on the edge. Three horses grazed by the water. A dark wooden door opened, revealing Professor Dy'Mün with a frustrated expression on his face. "I would ask you what happened," he began, "but I've learned to turn to the Keepers for answers instead."

Archai looked to the side in a glance of impatience.

"Why you've chosen to become such an inconvenience to the Elders, I will never know, but I expect now that you are *here*, it will come to an appropriate end," Dy'Mün went on.

"Ash pixies were drawn through the gateway to Terra," Archai replied, clearly ignoring Dy'Mün's complaint. "The humans of that world suffered losses.

This is an entirely new problem we must worry about."

"Where are they now?" Dy'Mün asked.

"I created a secondary doorway to the Everdark."

Shadow seemed to creep over Dy'Mün's eyes at the response. He frowned and flattened his lips, then gestured for Caia and Archai to follow him. Upon entering the cottage, the distinct scent of cedar and wet grass made Caia's hair stand on end as memories played through her mind like a View-Master. The bumps in the wooden planks that made up the floor had the same smooth ridges it did when she was ten years old, spending summers at the cottage and learning what she could while her father was on caravans. That was twenty-four years ago. The thought turned Caia's stomach and she shook her head to push it out of her mind.

The small square table against the wall at the left looked warm with rays of sunshine that spilled through the leaves and branches of birch trees outside the window. A long bench stretched parallel with the table and two small stools were on both ends. The door to her right was cracked open, and Caia remembered the struggle she always had in getting the thing to stay shut when she was dressing. She would prop her bow up against the wood to hold it closed.

"Isn't that right, Caia?" Dy'Mün's voice tore through the myriad of memories.

"I'm sorry," she replied. "What?"

"I was pointing out that Archai isn't the best at keeping his charges fed," he explained. "Are you hungry?"

Caia looked at Archai, who settled down onto one of the stools at the table. He looked slightly more relaxed than he did when they were first walking toward the cottage. "Well," she finally said, moving to sit on the long bench, "I don't think I'm really hungry, but I can eat something for the sake of eating. I'm still somewhat in shock, I think."

Dy'Mün retrieved two small bundles wrapped in cloth and set them on the table before Caia and Archai. "I'll fetch you some tea," he said, then turned to a small cupboard on the wall behind them.

Archai unwrapped the bundles without a word, revealing a loaf of bread beside a handful of thin, smoked slivers of meat in one bundle and dried cheese in the other.

"I know it's not much compared to what you must have had in Terra," Dy'Mün said as he set down two tin mugs of hot tea, "but you and I spent many years sitting at this table sharing this same meal."

Caia grinned, her mouth watering as she tore off a piece of bread and cheese. "Don't apologize, professor. I remember. My nose especially remembers," she laughed.

The velvety, slightly sour taste of the cheese combined with the rustic, dry, and unsweetened bread was incredible on Caia's taste buds. The moment the cheese touched her tongue, her head exploded with more memories from Terra and from Jaydür. "The closest thing Terra has to this bread is called ciabatta," she said. "This is so much more flavorful, though! And what meat is this? Wait, don't tell me." She took a bite of a sliver and moved it over her tongue, tasting the peppery seasonings. "This is deer."

"You're right," Dy'Mün replied with a chuckle. "Judging by your excitement, it's a bit more difficult to gauge when your last meal *really* was. Archai, have you been neglecting our new Voice?"

"She knows enough to eat when she's hungry," Archai replied before taking a bite of the venison. One of the horses outside whinnied, catching his attention for a second before he returned his eyes to the food.

Caia smiled at the Sapient. "I don't think I've ever actually seen *you* eat," she pointed out. "Or drink, for that matter."

Archai flicked his attention to her with one side of his mouth slightly pulled into a smile, but he said nothing to her in response. Instead, he aimed his words at Dy'Mün. "Keiren suggested I take Caia to see Meilon. I can only assume he saw something in our Voice to warrant such a visit. What do you think?"

Dy'Mün sat down on the chair across from Archai and diagonal from Caia. "I think, if the Keeper made a suggestion, you ought to take heed." Dy'Mün took a sip of tea from his own mug and set his gaze on Caia. The corners of his green eyes wrinkled and his white mustache and beard lifted slightly with a smile. "I did not properly welcome you home," he said. He placed an old, time-worn hand over her own. "It's just—it's as if you never left! Though I know time has passed, I did not feel much. Many years were spent searching for you and planning for how we would handle the return of the Voices. But so much has happened to change our initial plans." He took meat, cheese, and bread for himself, then looked up at Archai. "I do think a visit to Meilon may do the girl some good. Maybe she will tell us something we do not yet know. Maybe she won't. Either way, speaking with an oracle is an experience Caia would benefit from, and you can ride through the market on the way back. Let her walk among her people."

Archai nodded and took another bite of his food. "She'll need to change her clothes."

Dy'Mün's wild brows popped up in response. "Oh yes! I have a trunk full of your things in the cellar, Caia. You can see it after you eat. Your father had me store them here, as he assumed I would be the first to see you when you returned. Right he was."

"Can I go now?" Caia asked, half on her feet already. "I've eaten enough, I think. I'm honestly just excited to get going as soon as Archai is ready."

Archai grunted. "I was ready before we arrived."

Caia arched a brow at him and smiled smugly. "Really, professor, I would love to gather my things. I don't have much of an appetite."

"All right, all right," Dy'Mün said with a laugh. "You can eat when you return. The cellar door will be easier to access from the outside. Step outside, then turn right. You'll see it at the halfway point around the cottage. Your trunk is the only red one."

Without another word, Caia leapt to her feet and hurried out the door. A cool, comfortable breeze hit her face the moment she stepped out, and it was *glorious.* The air smelled fresh and felt warm against her skin. After so many dark and cold days in Arizona, it was a welcome change.

The cellar doors were heavy, but Caia managed to lift one of them, spilling light into the dark room. There were many trunks pushed up against the walls, but the red one quickly caught Caia's eye. "Bingo," she said to herself. Opening the trunk, Caia fought tears at the sight of her bow sitting atop a folded tunic shirt and pants. They must have found it after she was taken by the horde in Nov'Eit so long ago. Worn brown boots rested beneath the clothes, along with a belt and quiver. A handful of arrows were at the bottom.

Without much concern about her surroundings, Caia changed from her jeans and t-shirt into the green top and pants. She tightened a brown belt and scabbard around her waist, then pulled green bracers over her forearms. With an excited intake of breath, she placed her other clothes into the chest, then picked up the last item of clothing—a brown, leather, sleeveless vest. Or was it a tank top? Caia couldn't tell, but she pulled it on anyway.

Everything fit as it always did.

"You seem rather pleased with life," Archai's voice spoke from behind just as Caia found long socks rolled inside of her boots. He was crouched at the entrance of the cellar, looking down. He suddenly wore a blue and brown tunic shirt and brown tunic pants rather than his usual black jerkin.

She couldn't help but smile in return. "Shouldn't I be? This is what you wanted, isn't it? For me to remember and to come back home."

Archai looked up as if scanning the area. "You're right. I did want this. We needed this," he said. "But knowing you, you're going to suddenly remember that you've left your mother and sister—not to mention Naoni—back in Terra, without a word. I would rather you have this stark realization now than later, when we're no doubt going to be caught in some stressful or life-threatening situation."

Caia froze with one boot half laced. "What are we planning on getting into?" she asked with a good-natured scoff.

"I have no plans beyond taking you to see Meilon, allowing you to see some sights, then returning you here. But you haven't had the best of luck since I found you in Terra."

Caia sucked on her bottom lip and finished lacing her boot. She rose to her feet and scratched an itch on her nose. "I didn't forget about my mom or sister. Or Naoni. I still intend on returning home to deal with it all, but—"

"This is home," Archai cut in. "*I* will fetch Naoni tonight, after we return here. But your mother and sister no longer hold any significance in any matter."

Archai's words stung, and Caia struggled not to snap back in response. It wouldn't help, and it wouldn't change his mind.

She swallowed hard and tightened the quiver around her waist. Taking the bow in hand, Caia gripped and relaxed her hand around the wood. "Maybe to you, but I'm not done with them yet. We don't have to talk about it right now. I don't want to spend time overthinking it." She slung the bow over a shoulder, then walked toward Archai at the cellar entrance. "I'll deal with it all as we go. As for now, Dy'Mün expects us to go to this oracle and then into town. I would like to go now, if that's all right with you." She slowly refilled her lungs, not realizing that she'd forgotten to breathe during her response. Why she felt so nervous speaking bluntly to Archai, she didn't know.

Archai closed the cellar door behind them, then gestured toward two of the horses grazing nearby. "After you," he said.

Chapter Sixteen
The Oracle

The sun hung high and hot, but Caia faced it, basking in the embrace of warmth with closed eyes as her horse walked behind Archai's. Rays of light streamed between the branches, spilling red through her eyelids.

"The air here feels like magic," she said through a smile. "I'd bet you anything, if you would snag any human from Terra and bring them here, they'd never leave. Just because of the air." Caia took a deep breath and finally opened her eyes. Archai looked on ahead, seemingly ignoring her. "Don't you feel it?" she asked.

"I feel many things," he replied. "But air is not something I notice beyond my own breathing of it."

Caia slumped in the saddle and watched the back of Archai's head. His silver hair hung neatly to his shoulder blades. The gentle clopping of the hooves and chirping of birds was all that she heard other than the light *clink* of metal on metal from his sword on his back. Caia didn't realize until that moment that he'd moved the scabbard from his side.

Strangely enough, Archai was stiff again, as he was when they first crossed over into Jaydür. It didn't make such sense, considering his bright-eyed excitement when she first came home from the beach trip transformed.

"What is it?" Archai asked without provocation.

"What's what?"

"Your thoughts are racing."

Caia looked ahead and lifted her shoulders. "If you can hear my thoughts, you would know what I'm thinking."

"I was never able to *hear* your thoughts," he replied. "I sense, I consider, then I deduce."

"Right. Well, it's nothing to worry about," Caia replied, noticing that the trees around their path ahead thickened. Memories had slowed in their return since the two left Dy'Mün's cottage, and she couldn't quite figure out where they were anymore. But the day was still long before them; Caia intended to make every moment worth it, no matter how Archai acted. "What can you tell me about Meilon?"

A crow cawed nearby, and Caia looked up to her right where it sat perched on a branch, watching the travelers pass through.

"She is a born-seer," Archai replied. He seemed uninterested in the crow, even when it flew from tree to tree, following them as they moved. "Sold to a human king for six copper coins, her gift was used to spy on enemies through the lands. She tried to escape amid an attack on the city but came across an ash wraith. With one touch, Meilon's memories were lost, and she's now only a fragment of what she used to be. Occasionally, she'll be drawn into a violent vision and lose control over herself, so she had herself chained to the wall so as not to hurt anyone."

"Oh my god!" Caia replied, her mouth hanging open. The crow squawked again. "Six coppers? Who sells their kid, period?"

"Life here is not like life on Terra," Archai replied, finally passing her the briefest of glances. "People struggle, and they do what they deem necessary to survive."

Caia peered through the trees around them, thinking on Archai's mention of ash wraiths. She held no memory of the creatures and wondered if there were any nearby.

"Don't worry," Archai said. "I assure you, Meilon is the closest thing to a wraith you will find here. She came here for a reason. It's safe."

Caia nodded then asked, "So, she's human?"

"Was. She is now part wraith and doomed to desolate agelessness."

Caia took in a deep breath and wrinkled her nose at the crow continually cawing above them. "I don't think that thing has stopped yakking at us through your entire explanation," she said. "Is that normal?" she asked Archai, gesturing to the crow.

He glanced at her, then looked at the bird. "That belongs to Meilon."

"Is it...angry?"

"How am I to know? I'm a Sapient, not a bird handler."

The dirt pathway before them narrowed just before coming to an abrupt end. Caia looked around curiously as her horse instinctively followed Archai's off the dirt and into the tall grasses of the forest, ending the rhythmic sound of the hooves. The trees gradually grew more gnarled and twisted as they continued on, until no white birch was within sight. Caia gasped with surprise when the crow landed on the horn of the saddle between her legs and cocked its head at her.

"Hello," she said, tense from the uncertainty of what to do. She looked up to find Archai still ignoring her. "You're a pretty bird," she said, slowly raising her hand to attempt touching its feathered head. The bird snapped at her hand and Caia recoiled before it flew away. She scanned the skies, spotting it on a high branch, and let out a nervous laugh. "That was weird."

"It's a bird," Archai replied.

"Well, you know what? Birds in Terra don't stalk you and land close enough to touch. They're a bit more aware of the danger of humans."

What came from Archai sounded like something between a laugh and a grunt, but with his back facing Caia, she couldn't tell which it was. "Humans are not the same here, nor will we be near any of them until we reach the market. This is Leithen's territory."

Caia fought a humored smile at the mention of Leithen. He seemed very kind and *very* interested in knowing her better, which was funny to her. She had her fair share of interested guys at school, but Eric—Solin—was all she ever wanted. Caia dropped her head and closed her eyes. Eric's words from that day at the beach stung once more. She never thought herself "weird" amongst her peers, nor did any of them really act like she was considered as such. But she could admit her behavior over the few days before Archai made his appearance in her life earned the label.

Caia shook her head before falling into another void of memories she knew she couldn't bring back. "Who was the woman with him?" she asked instead, recalling the blonde woman in the cloak with Leithen. "She was extremely rude."

"Lady Emerwen is the daughter of the man who owns the Port of Farn, west of Aquinia." Archai looked in the direction of Aquinia as if visualizing what he explained. "As the daughter of a rich man, she is one of the many ladies searching to be named Leithen's princess. Likewise, as a rich woman, she is prone to pride and a nasty temper."

The forest floor was obscured in shadow now. The sun was nowhere to be seen through the dense foliage of the trees. The trunks were dark, as were the leaves, leaving Caia feeling as if they were treading through the night rather than midday. Shadows swirled through twisted bark, making it seem like faces peered out at them.

"Is there anything in particular about the prince I should know?" Caia asked, seeking a distraction. A sense of unease filled her senses, clouding her thoughts with expectations of cries or screams or *something* abnormal. Whatever magic was here, it was not something Caia wanted to be around.

Archai's response was snappier than she expected, which drew Caia out of her negative daze. "Leithen is searching for someone," he said. "Do not let him think it is you."

"Searching for what?" Caia asked.

"It's not worth wasting our breath about. He is a prince; you are a Voice. You two will have political concerns to deal with soon enough."

Political? "Is he an enemy?"

"He is our greatest ally," Archai replied. He finally glanced at Caia before continuing, as if making sure she was paying attention. "Do not misunderstand me. As kind and friendly as you may think you come across to him, the prince may see you as a maiden of…interest. He does not know who you are, and he does not need to know just yet. Until then, all communication with him will be avoided. Understood?"

Caia laughed, unable to hold it back, and Archai did not seem pleased.

"What kind of girl do you think I am?" she laughed, gesturing to herself. "I just met the man! I collided with his soldier, and Leithen politely introduced himself and apologized."

"I am not suggesting anything, Caia. I am simply trying to warn you."

With a slight shake of her head, Caia looked up into the canopy. She hadn't realized the crow had left them. Now that she really paid attention, she noticed there were no birds or other creatures in the area at all. Then, from around a large tree trunk, a green ball of light floated through the branches. Caia watched it until the light faded. To the left, maybe ten feet away, another glowed and floated deeper into the woods.

"What are—"

"They're seeds," Archai answered before she finished asking. "Essences that have not clung to anything capable of nourishing life. Some say they are what is left of Meilon, as the orbs seem to go hand in hand with wraiths."

The sudden caw of the crow sounded again, this time from in front of the two. Caia spotted it perching on top of a badly shingled roof, which sheltered what looked like a shack that was aching to collapse. A green light like that of the floating balls shone through the cracks of the wooden panels, making the shack nothing if not foreboding.

"Tell me we're not going there," she whispered.

"All right," Archai replied. "We're not going there."

Caia allowed a sense of relief to overcome her until the two rode up to the shack and Archai dismounted.

"You said we weren't going here!" she hissed.

"Is that not what you asked me to tell you?"

Quickly dismounting, Caia stepped closer to Archai and grabbed hold of his arm. His muscle twitched under her touch, something that would usually make her wonder what she'd done wrong, but at this point, she didn't care. She took a small step back, remaining partially hidden by his body as he made his way to the door. Looking down at her, Archai frowned at her fearful stare, then placed a hand over hers. Oddly, that small motion did help ease her nerves.

Without looking up, she opened her mouth to say something when the door opened and the sound of chains echoed within the shack.

"Enter," a raspy voice called. The tone was thick and made Caia's body fill with goosebumps.

Archai reached his free arm forward and pushed the door the rest of the way open, then stepped inside the shack.

"I see," the voice said weakly. "I see."

Caia looked to Archai and mouthed "What?" in confusion, then looked back to the darkness. She was startled when a woman stepped out of the shadows and into a green stream of light that suddenly lit up the shack, coming from a hole in the ceiling.

The woman was extremely thin and pale—sickly looking. She wore a black gown, and many gold bracelets adorned her wrists and arms. A black headdress sat upon her head, draping over her shoulders and veiling her thin, sparse hair. If time had a mistress, Meilon would be it.

She was barefoot, revealing not only her feet, black from filth, but large shackles around her ankles. Caia couldn't help but stare.

Archai stepped forward and spoke. "Meilon, I am Archai, Guardian Sa—"

"Sapient of the Rehnedhen," Meilon interrupted, her voice cold and foreboding. "I know." The woman inhaled deeply and let out a raspy sigh.

Clearing his throat, Archai confidently continued, making Caia feel more at ease. "I am accompanying Caia Foriei, the Voice of Apan. We were sent by Keiren, a Keeper of the Chambers of the Voices."

"Yes," Meilon continued, her timbre ghostly. "The Voice's cries are clear to me. Her past and future, I now see." Meilon was silent and held out her hand to Caia. Caia's eyes widened and she looked to Archai, who nodded while prying her fingers from around his arm. With a knot in her throat, she took the oracle's hand and stepped closer to her. The moment she took a step forward, Meilon pulled her into the green light and there, Caia came face to face with the oracle.

She didn't know if she was expected to do something, but it was near impossible to do more than stare into the oracle's eyes which were completely white, outside of the small black pupils in their centers. A sensation like that of vertigo came over Caia, and she wanted to lift a hand to her head, but felt frozen in place. After a moment of silence, Meilon held Caia's cheeks in her frigid, bony hands. She cocked her head to the side as she spoke through blood-red lips.

"I see," Meilon whispered as a tear streamed down her cheek. "I see a love perfectly bloomed, promises made, then swiftly entombed." As Meilon spoke, Caia could feel her heartbeat grow faster and stronger. She felt naked with someone inside her mind.

"A past slowly rises through the ever-flowing mist, as she asks, 'what can and cannot exist?' Far more questions than answers will be, for the all-seeing Voice will cease to be free." The oracle stood in silence for a moment before her eyes widened and she continued, "What is this? I see darkness veiling light; yet another coming plight."

Archai quickly stepped forward. "Plight? What new plight? There's been nothing but plight."

Meilon turned her blind eyes to the Sapient with

her reply. "Listen carefully to my words or lost you shall be. You will be her eyes when the Voice will not see."

Archai's face twisted into a pained expression as he looked to Caia. Something like terror radiating from him. "The esgal'hehn?" he whispered. "No, that cannot be. Not Caia."

The oracle stepped closer to Archai and quietly answered, "Will it or not, these all-seeing eyes will fade into darkness as the Voice will arise." She turned around and placed her left hand on her head and sighed. "Sapient, I see the beginning of your journey as one. The test for you is nearly over and done. You must go, with your quest proceed; I have spoken what I see and all that you need. May the Highest Power bless you both on your journey."

As the oracle finished her words, the stream of green light faded, and Meilon disappeared into the darkness from which she'd emerged, leaving Caia and Archai standing alone in the room. Without a word, Archai suddenly turned and walked out of the shack. He looked up to the dark canopy, then took his horse's reins. Caia frowned.

"Archai," she started, then took her horse and followed him. "Archai, wait. What just happened? I didn't understand everything in there."

"Which part did you not understand?" he asked.

"Well, I can tell you that I did understand the part about love. But then she started talking about plight and sight and then you said some word I didn't even understand."

"Esgal'hehn," he replied in a monotone voice.

"Esgal what?"

"Esgal'hehn. It is a process through which you gain large amounts of information and increase the use of four of your senses. It is something that is only supposed to happen to born-seers, knowing who they are and what their task is in life. We did not know you are a born-seer."

Caia thought on that for a moment. She didn't seem to know it any more than anyone else did. "But the Voices are all considered seers, aren't they?"

"Yes, but this is different. The visions the Voices would see were through their mirrors within the Chambers in the Rehnedhen. That is why they are useless without their eyes. A Voice would channel those mirrors on occasion, but none of them would suffer true visions of the mind."

Caia took a deep breath and tried to find her words. Archai's stress about the revelation was clear, but she didn't quite understand it herself. "What exactly *is* the esgal'hehn, though? What's going to happen?"

Archai clenched his teeth and bore his gaze into hers. "There is no easy way to explain this," he said with a quieter voice. "You lose your sight."

Caia swallowed her next question and let his words sink in. Archai mounted his horse and held the reins of her own steady so she could mount. She pressed her lips into a tight line and followed suit. "Can we fix it?" she finally asked.

Archai nodded. "It passes…eventually. The problem here is that the phase of the esgal'hehn can take years."

Caia was staggered. "Blind for years? When will it happen?"

"None can know. We will see what Dy'Mün has to say about it, though Keiren's request for you to see Meilon in the first place makes sense now. He saw something in you, and I needed to know what it was. Without hearing it coming from Meilon's lips, I may not have believed it."

With a nod, Caia's eyes fell to the reins in her hands. Her palms were suddenly damp and her heart thumped hard and fast. She had many more questions that needed answers, but even in Archai's momentary silence, she could sense his frustration and confusion. He needed to work through his own understanding of the situation before she bombarded him with the need for more information. Tomorrow would be a better day for it.

Archai's horse bumped against Caia's right leg, and Archai reached over to place a hand over hers on the horn. "I will help you through it," he said. His brow was furrowed, but his eyes were bright and intense. "You will not undergo it alone."

The smile that tugged at Caia's lips was

impossible to resist. She bit her lip and nodded again, then followed Archai out of the dark forest.

Chapter Seventeen
Into Town

The market sat upon gently sloping grassy fields as far as the eye could see. Tall flags waved in the air through the subtle breeze that blew every so often, and more crows dotted the roofs of the buildings. Chatter resounded throughout the open air as people traded and sold their wares.

Caia's horse walked beside Archai's; they were met with a slew of curious eyes. The younger folks of the town seemed somewhat kinder and offered smiles and waves. The older people were not as friendly. An air of frustration wafted from many of the merchants like an ocean's wave rolling over a shore.

"Seems as though there is some unrest in the market today," Archai muttered just loud enough for Caia to hear. She nodded in agreement, glad to know she was not the only one who picked up on the negativity.

"What do you think happened?" she asked.

Archai furrowed his brow and leaned his elbow on the horn on his saddle in thought. "It could be anything. Maybe we just missed a fight. Or it's possible today is simply a slow day for sales." Archai narrowed his eyes in thought and dismounted his horse. Caia did the same.

A small boy, no more than eight years old, ran up to the pair, blonde hair bouncing in front of his dark brown eyes. "I'll take yer horses and water them over there at the stables, if you like!"

Caia looked up at Archai with questioning eyes. She heard coins clinking as he reached into a purse hanging by his belt and produced a handful of copper coins. The boy's entire face lit up. He hesitated for a moment, shifting his chocolate eyes between Archai and Caia, then quickly pocketed the money. "Thank you, my lord! Thank you muchly!" Taking the horses' reins, the boy started toward the stable.

Caia bit her lip with a smile. "Well, that was very sweet of you."

Archai didn't respond. Nor did he smile or show any other kind of emotion, which didn't surprise Caia in the least.

"All right," he started quickly, as if trying to avoid any other compliment Caia might have had. "We will make our way through this market swiftly, then take you back. The whole point of this trip is to give you a taste of Jaydür, so taste."

Caia pursed her lips as she walked away toward a

blacksmith's stand. The back of the stand had swords, knives, and other blades hanging on display. She watched as a large man in a black apron hammered hot metal into the desired shape. As she watched, he glanced at her, then refocused on his work. In an instant, his eyes were on her once more. "Hello, my lady," the man began as he wiped sweat from his brow. "Can I help you with something?"

"Oh, no," she replied with a beaming smile, admiring his accent. "I'm just looking. I've never actually seen a blacksmith at work. It looks like a long process."

The man laughed. "It is, but when one works at it his entire life, he grows used to it."

"I can understand that."

"Caia," Archai interrupted. "Come this way."

Caia nodded, then looked back to the blacksmith. "Goodbye."

The man bowed his head and returned to his work. As Caia walked away, he looked up once more with a half-smile.

"What was that?" Archai asked with an irritated tone.

"What? I was just being friendly," Caia innocently replied.

"Right. Next time, I would avoid using the words, 'I'm just looking.' That would typically get you spat at. Not the best way for a Voice to blend in with the people."

Caia wrinkled her nose in disgust and continued beside Archai through the market. Every so often, she would stop at a small stand selling trinkets or clothing, completely enthralled with the atmosphere. It was impossible to stop smiling at everything her gaze fell upon. Silver and copper jewelry. Foods and drinks of all kinds. Herbs for cooking and medicine. People were kind for the most part, though someone would occasionally remind Caia of the unrest she felt when she and Archai first arrived, so she made an effort to smile widely and speak kindly to anyone she interacted with. Even so, she kept her words to a minimum, afraid Archai would have something else to criticize her about.

It took Archai a long while to show any hint of a smile during their time wandering, but eventually he let go. When Caia came across a table laden with dolls made of hay and twine, she brought one to her face to have a closer look at how the doll was fashioned. Archai laughed softly and Caia saw his head shake from the corner of her eye.

"You scurry about like a child," he muttered.

Caia wrinkled her forehead and tossed him a glance. "I speak to the people, and you tell me I'm doing it wrong. I quietly look around, and somehow I'm doing that wrong, too. What exactly should I be doing?" she asked.

"I did not say you were doing it wrong," he replied defensively. "I am simply entertained by your bumbling."

Patience was slowly wearing away in Caia. Archai was showing a whole different side to him than he did in Terra. She breathed deeply and walked ahead, this time watching the people. A woman swatted the hand of a boy around ten who reached for a piece of fruit in her basket. A man carried a bundle of candles from a cart to a table, where he spread them out and trimmed the wicks. One thing Caia noticed above all else was the way no person had wandering eyes. Each was focused on his or her work, living their lives in the way they knew best. Children played with stones and strings, wooden balls and tops. One little boy, not five years old, walked with his mother while carrying a lamb half his size in his arms. Caia resisted smiling. Archai had made it clear she was being silly, and that was not the way she wanted to be perceived. Instead, she turned and tried to gauge her next direction, but all thrill seemed to be lost.

"I think I'm ready to go back to Dy'Mün now," she admitted without looking at Archai.

"Now?" he replied, looking around as if trying to see what the problem was. "We've hardly been here. Dy'Mün will send us back."

Caia covered her face and laughed incredulously. "You, Archai, are being difficult." Lowering her hands, she licked her lips and took a breath. "All right. Fine. You go find somewhere to sit, and I'll wander."

"What makes you think such a thing would be all right? You're not to leave my sight."

"Then follow me at a distance and let me *try* to enjoy myself without criticizing everything I do," she finally snipped.

Archai turned his face downward and pressed his lips into a tight line. "I've upset you."

"You've *confused* me," she retorted. "From the moment we arrived, you've been short with me and never gave me any sense as to why or what happened."

Archai looked ahead and nodded in understanding. The wrinkle in his brow seemed constant lately. There was something he wasn't telling her.

"What is it, Archai?" she asked, quieter now. She wondered how long he had been holding things back. Long enough to build up into mood swings, that much was clear.

Archai cleared his throat and gestured for her to move on ahead of him. "Nothing to worry about. You go ahead and I'll keep an eye on you from a safe distance away."

Wind picked up suddenly, blowing Archai's hair across his face and brightening the teal of his eyes. A merchant nearby shouted as his wares became disheveled, attracting Archai's attention.

"Archai, please don't lie to me," Caia finally

managed to say. She crossed an arm over her chest and tucked some free strands of hair behind her ear.

"Forgive me. I am not at liberty to discuss my stresses."

"What?" Caia said with a scoff. "Since when were you not free to discuss things with me?"

Archai's eyes darted from left to right, as if keeping watch for someone who might be listening, and a flicker of truth sparked in Caia's mind. She joined in his skimming of the market, paying close attention to the people buying and selling their wares.

With a step closer to Archai, she finally asked, "Are we being followed?"

"Caia, trust me when I tell you all is well, and we are fine. Spend some more time here in the market and then we'll go back to Dy'Mün."

Frustrated with his unwillingness to talk about it, Caia nodded and made her way back into the market. Natural and comfortable interaction was more difficult with the idea of being followed, though. If Archai was nervous about something, then it was something she felt she needed to be concerned about as well. He was too serious and too collected a man to be ignored in such a state.

Caia looked over her left shoulder as she handled a bundle of herbs wrapped in twine. Archai stood fifty feet away, back straight, chin lifted, and hand on the pommel of his sword. His eyes took in all that was around him.

"It's to keep the ghosts of the Screaming Crags at bay." An old raspy voice coming from a small woman tying the herbs drew Caia from her watchful gaze. "Sage and lavender. Even if you choose to not burn it, it smells light and fresh in the bedroom."

"Oh, I see," Caia replied, bringing the bundle to her nose. It did smell wonderful. "This is awfully beautiful. How much?"

The woman cupped Caia's hands over the smudge stick and grinned a wide, gummy smile. She seemed thrilled, as if her work had never been complimented before.

"Three copper pieces," the woman replied.

Caia stood on her tippy toes to catch Archai's attention, and when he made eye contact, she gestured for him to come to her. He stepped lightly in long strides, his blue and brown tunic bright in the sunlight.

"I want this," she said, showing him the bundle in her hand.

There was no change in expression. No question. No judgment. Just the words, "How much?"

The small woman considered the size of Archai beside Caia and slowly lifted her eyebrows.

"She said three coppers," Caia replied, then leaned in to whisper, "but I'd like to give her more. Do you have a silver piece?"

Archai looked at the elderly woman, then turned his head to meet Caia's eyes. "Have you been threatened or are you just being generous?"

Caia winced. "Too much?"

Archai leaned in closer so the woman wouldn't overhear him. "Nothing is 'too much' for a Voice. But for future reference, one hundred coppers are equal to a single silver, and a hundred silvers make a gold piece."

A nervous laugh escaped Caia and she lifted her shoulders in an innocent shrug. She didn't know what to suggest. "How much would be enough but not too much, then?"

Archai was about to reply when the woman cut in. "You are her protector, aren't you? I can see it in the way you two speak. I can also see by the way you speak and move that this is a new partnership. Your bodies move against one another rather than together, though you are of similar mind and spirit. But you," she pointed to Archai and took one step forward, "you are protecting her from something unseen. I have something more for you." The old woman turned around and retrieved a small bag from the ground by her feet. She reached into the bag and pulled out a small wrapped packet. Slipping her hand back into the bag, she drew out a silver chain with a small ball of silver hanging from it. With a flick of her finger, the ball opened and the woman pinched some lavender from the smudge stick, placed it into the ball and closed it. "This may come in handy one day," she said. "It is not *just* lavender and sage. It grew near an aquinian well, therefore it is blessed by the Voice of Apan."

Caia's face flushed and she tried to smile. With a glance to Archai, she saw his features grow soft as he took the necklace into his hand. In that single moment, his grief was clearer than ever before. "Thank you," Caia said to the woman, then took a silver from Archai's other hand. "For you and your generosity," she added.

The woman lit up much like the small boy with the horses had, and she clutched the coin to her chest. "My lady, this will keep my grandchildren fed for weeks! Thank you!"

Caia turned to Archai, who gazed forlornly at the silver ball, and gently took it from his hand. Without a word, she rose onto her toes and clasped the necklace around his neck. She placed a hand on his cheek and smiled, then turned, nodded to the woman, and continued her walk through the market.

Chapter Eighteen
The Moon Faery

Evening fell quickly after Caia and Archai returned to Dy'Mün's cottage. Purples and oranges swirled at one end of the sky while a black starlit pool filled the other. No clouds hung in the air, promising a clear view of the night sky. The white bark of birch trees stood high, like pale shadows watching over the cottage, protecting her while Archai went to fetch Naoni from Terra. They kept Caia's attention as she sat against the trees outside.

Professor Dy'Mün merrily hummed as he stepped out of the cottage with a pipe in his hand. The spicy smell of supper seeped out of the front door and chimney, reminding Caia of the time spent at the dinner table with Archai and Dy'Mün. It was relaxing and comfortable, reminiscent of her days with her father and the professor.

"How did you and Archai fare during your days in Terra?" Dy'Mün asked. Straightening his robes, he lowered himself onto the grass across from Caia and lit his pipe.

Caia watched as the flame took to the pipe tobacco and a wisp of smoke drifted away. "Not bad," she replied. "He was kind. He was patient."

A ring of smoke puffed from Dy'Mün's lips with his grunt of approval. "Good, good," he replied. "I can see you two have taken well to one another. This is good. I am curious to see how Naoni takes to him as well."

"I don't imagine there will be any issues between them," Caia replied. "She seems on top of things. More so than I ever was. Or still am, for that matter."

An owl screeched in the distance, and a flock of night birds flew out of a nearby tree, making leaves shake loudly. Caia wasn't startled but looked above to see the birds fly together through the pink-tinted sky.

"Don't be so hard on yourself," Dy'Mün replied. He tapped his pipe and let out a grunt, his brow furrowed in thought. "It's very curious how differently you two have approached this entire ordeal. Very curious, indeed. I look forward to watching you both as you rise to your calling. It will be quite an experience for all of us involved."

Caia nodded and gently smiled. She took comfort in the thought that some of those she cared about would stay with her as she took on the position of the great Voice.

"What about the other two Voices?" Caia asked.

She had been meaning to ask the question for some time but never quite remembered it when a good time finally arose. "Where are they?"

"There are some things that cannot be spoken aloud, dear Caia," Dy'Mün replied. "For we risk listening ears, waiting for the right bit of information to make their catch. You will meet with your sisters when the time is right. They are far from here, and they are safe."

Caia remembered Archai's denial to share information with her, and she wondered aloud, "How, exactly, would the enemy hear us?"

"The answer to that is something we Elders are trying to find," he answered with a sigh. "Whereas the Elders keep eyes and ears on the world through mirrors, we are unknowledgeable in any other means of spying. But just because we don't know about them does not mean they do not exist."

Caia nodded. "So we're being cautious, but there is no reason to believe they *are* actually capable of watching or listening to us."

"Correct. I admit, we may be a bit *overly* cautious, but the other two Elders agreed to utilize every eye and ear available to us to keep track of any magic coming and going within a two-hundred-mile radius, and I accepted. We will not speak of the other Voices, but do not hesitate to ask any other questions. You are in a safe place to learn."

Caia pursed her lips in thought. Archai hadn't

been willing to divulge something to her for fear of being heard. But the Voices were the only topic off limits, and they were not within reach. Her attention fell to her feet in the grass. Did that mean Archai was avoiding the listening ears of the enemy? Or those of the Elders?

A soft ringing like that of a Tibetan singing bowl came from the cottage, and Caia looked to Dy'Mün for some understanding.

"Oh!" Dy'Mün exclaimed as he rose to his feet. "They've returned!"

Caia jumped up and hurried toward the cottage where Archai stood, alone, in the center of the room. She froze, her smile fading and turning into a confused frown. There was no wild-haired, copper-eyed fire elf with him.

"Where is the Voice of Folc?" Dy'Mün asked with his hands on his hips. His wild gray brows were lifted high, his emerald eyes wide.

Archai dropped down onto a seat at the table and licked his lips. "I left her."

Taken aback, Caia glanced at Dy'Mün. "What? Why?"

Dy'Mün's mouth opened and closed, but no sound came from him besides a high-pitched groan of confusion. He gripped the sides of his head and clarified, "You left her?"

Archai lifted a hand saying, "Don't worry, Dy'Mün. I discussed it with Keeper Lockesithe. We were of one mind when we realized all signs of the sinstarians left with the ash pixies."

Dy'Mün's mouth shut with a snap. He gathered his robes and turned to the kitchen where he put his hands to work, making tea.

"Professor, you already have water boiled for tea," Caia pointed out.

"Caia, please step outside while I discuss this with the Sapient," Dy'Mün said through tight lips.

"Why can't I—"

"Now!" he shouted. The tightening fists at his side were enough to tell Caia he *needed* her to listen. She would get answers out of Archai afterwards. She was a Voice! They couldn't continue keeping secrets from her.

She didn't give a verbal response but stepped backwards out of the cottage and closed the door.

"Caia," Archai called after her. She pushed the door open a crack and peeked back inside with wide eyes. He pointed to the bedroom. "Sit in there. I'm not comfortable with you outside alone."

"She'll be all right outside, Archai," Dy'Mün snipped. "Stop being so overbearing! I've fortified the area. She has nearly half a mile of room to wander without concern." He turned and shooed her off.

Caia left the door open a crack, stepped away from the cottage onto the cobblestone, then made her way to the large stone by the water. The sky was nearly black, though her line of vision was still quite clear. As a human, she hadn't had the sight she did as an elf.

A grasshopper jumped from beside her foot as she stepped onto the large stone and lifted herself up. The rough surface was still warm from a long day in the hot sun.

"...cannot go about making these decisions without the Elders." Dy'Mün's suddenly loud voice carried through the walls and windows of the cottage, and Caia turned her ear toward them to hear them better.

"The Keepers and I do not need your permission to make judgment calls concerning the Voices," Archai retorted. "We handled it well enough before you three even came into the picture."

"We are here for a *reason*, and it is not your place to omit us."

"You are not being 'omitted,' old man. I'm explaining the details now. We left her because she's safer there. You remember what Meilon said; the esgal'hehn is coming, and the likelihood of Caia obtaining her elemental abilities before then is high. She will not be capable of controlling it while the process takes hold, and she will draw Glim'Ruk's attention."

A sudden silence compelled Caia to look toward the cottage. She strained to work out the rest of what Archai said. Considering she was part of the problem, she had a right to know, didn't she? Caia straightened her legs on the stone and leaned forward until she saw Archai's somber face. Whatever was just said, Dy'Mün was not thrilled, as could be deduced from his hands rising to cover his face.

The stress from the men inside the cottage was strong, and Caia turned to the water to try to mentally distance herself from it. She would get her answers from Archai before bed. She took a deep breath and listened to the quiet lapping of water on the rock. "Patience, Caia," she whispered to herself.

The grasshopper from below suddenly landed just beside Caia's knee, and she watched its antennae twist and turn. It rubbed its leg on its back, and a spark jumped from the motion. Caia jolted in surprise. She watched it carefully, leaning in to get a better look. With another rub on its back, another blue spark jumped.

"What in the world?" Caia said with a nervous laugh. "You're not a normal grasshopper, are you?" She held out a hand, placing it palm up next to the green insect.

The entirety of the grasshopper exploded into a giant spark like a soundless, tiny firework blast, and in its place stood a silver-skinned, blue-haired faery. She was no more than four inches tall.

"You're not wrong," the faery said. Her body shuddered like she had the chills, then she hovered in the air to meet Caia at eye level. The faery looked over her shoulder—though because of the bright blue glow as her wings fluttered, it was difficult to tell for sure—and said, "I'll eavesdrop for you if you help me leave. I've been trapped by this cottage for days."

"Hello," Caia said, awestruck by the sudden reminder of the existence of fae. "How did you get trapped here?"

The faery pointed a tiny finger toward the cottage. "The old man put a magic barrier around this place. I don't know what he's hiding from, but it must be something terrible."

Caia stood up and looked around. Crickets began their night song, echoing in the darkness of the forest. "How far back is the barrier?" she asked. How suspicious should she feel toward anyone or anything? Caia worried she didn't hold enough memory of Jaydür to make a proper judgment call.

"It's not far to fly," the faery replied. "But do you even have power over the magic? The old man was the one who put it up. Not *you.*"

That was true. But she and Archai traveled far beyond the cottage without any sign of a barrier. Caia looked toward the cottage again. The thatch roof was dark now, and silhouettes of straw hung over the top of the window. Through the glass, she could see the men moving, but they still spoke too quietly to hear. They were deep into their discussion, and the severity of it was quite clear. Maybe this was an opportunity to test her knowledge. Maybe as a Voice, Caia had power over the barrier. Dy'Mün *did* say the forest was safe for nearly half a mile into the woods. Did he mean safe from enemies and from wild animals as well?

"Are there bears in this wood?" Caia asked.

The laughter that came from the blue faery was small and high-pitched but no less condescending. "Bears? Here? No," she replied. "Are you new? How did you get here if not through the barrier?"

Caia's lips parted. There was no way to know how much was safe to say to a faery. She gripped and flexed her hands in frustration at her lack of memories of the race. "I was brought in by a friend during the day, *through* the barrier. I don't know what wanders around at night."

The slowly rising blue brow of the faery spoke a thousand unconvinced words.

Caia stepped down from the stone and walked to the cottage, where she pushed open the door. Archai and Dy'Mün quickly looked up at her.

"What is it?" Dy'Mün asked.

"Are there any wild animals in the forest around here?"

"You're not going into the forest, so why does it matter?" Archai retorted with a new rude tone. Something in his eyes spoke warning and anger and distress all at once, and Caia was taken aback. His posture was rigid; his jaw was set. A snarl pinched at the bridge of his nose and his upper lip, and Caia felt her face fall in surprise.

"By the Highest," Dy'Mün groaned and slapped the table with his hand. "You *must* get a hold of yourself, you fool. Did you ever once speak to Draì in such a tone?" He turned back to Caia with a deep sigh. "No, there are no wild animals to worry about here. You are free to roam, just don't get yourself all turned around."

"At the very least, have Keiren accompany her," Archai interjected. "For my piece of mind."

Before Caia could respond, the high-pitched ring hummed throughout the cottage, and Keiren entered from the bedroom door. He was in his white form, rather than the black he donned when crossing into Terra. The blue sapphire in his forehead seemed even brighter in person than while in the mirror.

"It is past time I was called to do something around here," the calm, ethereal voice of the Keeper spoke. "Do you know how tedious it is to listen to you two squawk and squabble in your discontentment?" He walked past the men—neither of whom had anything to say in response—and out the door behind Caia. "Come, my lady. We have things to discuss and a small problem to solve."

"What problem?" Archai asked.

"Nothing for you to concern yourself about."

Caia fought a smile at the sight of Archai accepting Keiren's word and easing back into his seat. The Sapient had never taken comfort in anyone but himself up until now. A fleeting thought of how long they'd worked together in the Rehnedhen crossed Caia's mind as she turned and followed Keiren.

When the door clicked shut, Caia found Keiren sitting at the large stone, his tail curled over his feet, and the blue faery standing beside him. No surprise seemed to be on either of their faces.

"So you're going to be a Voice," the faery chirped through a large grin. "I suppose that makes some more sense now."

Caia met Keiren's eyes and nodded in reply. "And you know this because he told you?"

Blue light burst around the faery again as she leapt into the air and hovered in front of Keiren. "I know this because he's *here*! Though I don't even know what he is. But you've got a Sapient over there, too, and where there's a Sapient, a Voice is feet away."

Caia wrinkled her brow in thought. She couldn't remember if Sapients were recognized by the average Jaydürian. A part of her thought they were only known by those affiliated with the Voices, but she couldn't be sure.

"And this is a perfect opportunity to test some of your strength, Caia," Keiren said. "Let us walk."

Archai and Dy'Mün resumed their stiff discussion, though Archai lifted his eyes to the window once. Caia met his gaze for a second before following Keiren into the woods.

A pale glowing light emanated from the Keeper,

reminding Caia of the night Archai stood in her bedroom with a similar glow. It was dimmer, but a glow nonetheless. Then, from the corner of her eye, her own glow caught her attention. She stopped, studying her hands and arms. She didn't feel any different, but the light coming from her was clear. "Why?" she asked. "Why do we glow?"

"Because we carry the eled'hwen within us," Keiren replied. "All the Voices, Keepers, and Sapients do. The brighter we shine, the more focused we are on our paths."

With a frown, Caia wondered about Archai. He said most of the Terehn glowed brighter than him for a reason, but again, he was not willing to share why. Not then, at least. Maybe it was a conversation he would be more open to these days. Then again, he was not himself, especially now. It ate Caia up inside, not knowing what he and Dy'Mün were discussing and why Naoni was not there with her now. She understood it had something to do with the esgal'hehn, but she needed more information.

"How interesting that you know nothing of yourself," the faery said with a giggle. Her own glow was gone as she sat on Keiren's head above his sapphire, as if it were a seat keeping her from sliding down. "I met a Voice once. She was very different from you."

Realization hit Caia suddenly. "You're one of the fae from the rumors," she said. "Now I understand why you recognized a Sapient—you were acquainted with the Voice of Mae'Ehr so long ago. Archai told me she was discovered in Wood Ruins, and that she often walked the world."

Nahtaia nodded. "She did. She was adventurous. She was also much happier than you seem to be."

"I'm not *un*happy," Caia retorted. "I'm simply working things out. I'm missing large pieces of my memory."

"How did you manage such a thing? Did you fall and hit your head?"

The faery's tone was becoming something of a chore to understand. One moment she seemed sweet and bubbly, while the next she seemed cold and condescending.

"I was forced into a parallel dimension while being attacked by grayskins," Caia snipped in reply. That ought to teach her. Who did this miniscule person think she was? "How did you meet a Voice anyway?" Caia continued, hoping to turn the topic away from her memory.

At that, the blue faery looked down at her hands and lifted her shoulders in a shrug. "I don't know what I did to deserve her time, but—" She paused and took a breath before continuing. "She helped me and my friends. Then she told me I would be called upon by the Voices, though I wouldn't know it at the time." The faery looked up to the canopy and pulled her knees to her chest. "I can't say *this* is what I expected, but it's definitely one of the reasons I quickly accepted who you were."

Caia chewed her lip in thought. She was helping the faery, not the other way around. "You have no idea why you were chosen?"

The faery shook her head. "None. I'm not the only moon faery in this realm. Though I do have a gift no other faery does—it's called distortion."

Caia lifted her eyebrows. "A gift? Like magic?"

"It is magic, yes. Distortion is the ability to change the shape and size of anything. I can be human. I can be an ogre. Or I can make you a mouse." The faery giggled at her own comment. "Maybe not *you,* what with you being a Voice, but most anyone can be turned by my magic."

"And why do you have such a gift?"

The faery's tiny shoulders lifted. "I would like to know myself."

The concept was interesting—one of the smallest of the races in Jaydür having such a great power. But like many other things in Jaydür, that concept didn't make much sense. Angering a faery like Nahtaia could lead to disaster on a monstrous scale. It was a wonder the Voices allowed someone like her to wander on her own. Then again, maybe that was the reason behind interacting with her—to give the faery a sense of purpose that might lead her in the way of doing good, rather than evil.

"We're coming up on the barrier," Keiren pointed

out with a flick of his tail. "Caia, I'd like you to hold your hand out, palm forward."

Without hesitation, Caia did as she was told.

Keiren stopped and sat down, tucking his back paws underneath him. "With your outstretched hand at eye level, I want you to look beyond your hand at the forest before you."

Again, Caia followed the instructions given. She looked at the trees. There was nothing particularly interesting. Then she spread out her fingers and the air in front of her hand shimmered. Taking two steps forward, Caia's hand pushed up against a mostly invisible wall. It felt cold and slippery, like wet glass, and was translucent enough to see through. "This wasn't here earlier, when I was with Archai," she said. "At least, I didn't notice it. This is amazing," she whispered. Terra had nothing of the sort, but a memory of Dy'Mün's magic flickered in her mind like a dying ember trying to burst back to life.

"Yes. Amazing, mesmerizing, shiny," the faery chittered. "How do I get to the other side?"

"I—" Caia shook her head and looked to Keiren, who didn't budge from his place. "I suppose I could try myself." As she spoke, Caia focused on the wall of magic and applied a bit of pressure to it. Though the shimmer of the barrier remained, her hand pushed through it with little resistance. Caia couldn't hold back her titter of delight, a sentiment quickly shared by the faery, who hovered by her hand.

"Finally!" the faery cried. "I've been trapped here long enough. How do I get through?"

Caia pulled her hand back and held it out with her palm up. The faery seemed to realize what she was doing, so she landed on Caia's palm, extinguishing her light. Turning back to the barrier, Caia moved her hand toward it, pushing immediately through. When the faery was on the other side, she took flight and hovered in place.

The faery's eyes rapidly swept from left to right, as if searching for something. "I don't see you anymore, Voice," the faery said. "But I imagine you can hear me just as well. Thank you for your help! I shouldn't be difficult to find when you need help from me and *my* kind. My name is Nahtaia, and you won't be forgotten!"

Returning to the cabin was a much less positive experience. Archai charged through the door, slamming the wood against the stone of the cottage, and stalked into the woods. Dy'Mün soon stood on the threshold, watching the Sapient go.

Keiren nudged Caia in the elbow, and she rested her hand on his head. "I wonder what's happening," she whispered.

"You are returning to Terra," Keiren replied in his unearthly timbre.

"What?" she said, her voice much louder now.

"When?"

Keiren sat and licked his paw before rubbing it across the right side of his face. "Tomorrow morning."

Though her heart sank slightly at the news, a part of Caia was happy with the idea of seeing her mother and sister again. For all she knew, it would be the last chance she had before she was brought back to Jaydür for the next reason. "Well," she started with a sigh, "I told him before that I can't just leave my mom and sister like this. They've likely already sent out a search party or put my face on the missing children wall in every Walmart by now. My mom's been through a lot. I can't let her think she's lost her daughter, too. Whether Archai likes it or not, I have loose ends to tie."

As Caia took a step toward the cottage, Keiren added, "Archai won't be going with you."

Caia froze in her steps. Her belly turned, and her stomach soured with immediate anxiety. Without turning, she asked, "What do you mean? He wouldn't leave me there alone."

The massive white feline stepped up beside her. "It is not his decision. Otherwise, do you really think he would be so angry? He is not a man of emotions. He is a man of a calling, and his calling is being interfered with."

No words came to Caia's lips. Her mind raced through all different scenarios she could cause to make him go with her, but nothing stuck. Realizing this, Caia filled with anger and frustration. "So let me think," she started. "I'm going back to Terra without Archai. He's angry he can't come with me, but he has no choice in the matter. Why? Am I going back with a purpose?"

"You are going back because you are a Voice, about to undergo a process that can get everyone killed. And until that process begins, Terra is safer than Jaydür. The esgal'hehn is painstaking enough for a born-seer, but as a Voice, your mind will be opened in unimaginable ways. You won't be able to control your abilities, and you will draw Glim'Ruk straight to you. It is a risk we cannot take." The pair made their way to the door where they stopped before walking in. The windows glowed a soothing orange from the fire inside the home. "You will remain in Terra until it is clear the esgal'hehn has taken hold, then we will deal with it the best we can—with all the other Voices far from you."

Caia turned and let out a long breath. Clenching her teeth, she scanned the woods Archai had just stalked into but didn't see any sign of him. "Is there nothing I can do to help?" she asked.

"Let us go inside and speak with Dy'Mün," Keiren replied. His tone was still cool and confident, as if they weren't just talking about the life and death situation Caia was the cause of.

With a slight nod, she opened the door and

stepped inside. Dy'Mün sat on a small stool beside the fireplace where he stoked the fire.

"Come on in, and have a seat by the fire," the wizard said without turning. "You may as well sit and ask me the myriad of questions you have hanging on your tongue." His anger was clear in his voice, yet he didn't show it as aggressively as Archai.

"Keiren answered some," Caia replied. "I want to help."

Dy'Mün grunted. "Then you will do as you are told."

"Which wouldn't be so difficult if I could understand the situation more," she went on. "I understand the esgal'hehn is feared—"

"It is not feared," Dy'Mün cut in. "It is revered. The phase is a stage in the metamorphosis of a great seer. The old understanding of the world and everything within it is stripped by the very darkness that will surround you. You can be used either as a tool for extraordinary growth and restoration of a dying world, or as a weapon for mass destruction and suffering. Neither of the Voices before you were born-seers."

Caia sat on the floor at Dy'Mün's feet. Her eyes drew to the flames flickering inside the firebox. The shadows cast on the walls made Caia think of dangerous, dark men coming after her with hate and malice. The very idea made her skin crawl. "So what can I expect from it? Are there symptoms before it happens?"

Dy'Mün shook his head, eyeing Keiren as the cat settled down beside Caia. "There is no way to tell when it will come. It could be tomorrow, or it could be fifty years from now."

"Fifty years?" Caia rose to her knees in a panic. Dy'Mün immediately gestured for her to calm down. "What am I going to do for—"

"I didn't say it *will* take fifty years, Caia!" Dy'Mün countered. "I am simply trying to help you understand our lack of knowledge on the subject. We do not know what to expect. What we do know is that Terra is safe. All gateways to the world have been closed. No sinstarians or pixies or anything else with malevolent intent is there, so you and Naoni will still be safe there."

"But you must be there with no trace of magic in you," Keiren finally added. "That means no magic, no memory orbs, no—"

"No Sapient to depend on," Dy'Mün cut in. The look in his green eyes alone told Caia more than his lips did. "That's right. Archai will stay back and be put to better service."

"'Better service?'" Caia repeated with a scoff. "He's been nothing but helpful and comforting. To what better service can you put a Sapient, a man who was *created* to help the Voices?"

With her blood heated already, Caia eyed the door as if mentally calling for Archai to come and argue for her side.

"He will continue to look after the Temple of Pandhea for the Elders until he is called upon for something else. That is what he did for half a century after the Voices were lost."

Caia rolled her eyes and her next words seeped with sarcasm. "Oh wonderful! Shove him back into an empty, underground temple while the Voice he awakened is sitting around waiting to go *blind*." The thought froze her in her place, stopping her reaction. "Will he even know what's happening if the esgal'hehn occurs in, say, the next year?"

Dy'Mün sighed deeply and pressed his lips into a tight line. "He will be called upon when he is needed. He will be informed of what he needs to know to continue his calling."

"The calling you Elders are ripping from his hands?"

"The calling that is not meant to place so much power into the hands of a Sapient!" Dy'Mün barked. "You do not see it. You place so much trust in him, and he guides you in whatever direction he would have you go."

The words coming out of Dy'Mün's mouth were unbelievable. He couldn't truly mean what he said. He trusted Archai with his life; she remembered that much. Caia searched the wizard's eyes, and she couldn't find a trace of truth in him. Whatever he was saying, he did not mean.

"Your words are as poisonous as the men who urge you to speak them," she managed in a small voice. "You know Archai better than that, and I won't have you talk about him this way."

Something in his eyes changed, and Dy'Mün's face softened. If she hadn't been so angry, she might have thought he hid a smile pulling at his lips. "You will be sent back to Terra tomorrow. Archai will return to his post, and we Elders will find the answers we seek about the esgal'hehn. Until then, I expect you will heed the advice we offer. Now, go prepare yourself for the night." Dy'Mün gestured to the bedroom. "You will sleep in the bedroom. There is a candle by the bed. Leave it lit for the night."

Caia cocked a brow at his last request, spoke a quiet "good night" to the wizard and Keeper, then made for the bedroom where she lit the candle beside the bed and closed the door behind her. Leaning her back against the door, Caia squeezed her eyes shut. A sudden onset of emotion twisted her gut. What would she do in Terra? She couldn't go back to her regular routine of school, homework, and dishes at home. She wasn't Ella Wiles anymore. She was Caia Foriei. Sure she was a bit of a fragmented version of Caia from seventeen years ago, but she was more elf than human now, and she intended on remaining so.

A white linen shirt lay folded on the bed beside a pair of pants made from similar fabric. Assuming they were meant for her, Caia changed, placing her shirt, leggings, and boots beside one another on the floor, then climbed into bed. She leaned over to blow out the candle when she remembered Dy'Mün's request to leave it lit. She turned with a huff when the flickering flame caught her eye in the mirror standing against the door.

Without a second thought and a little bit of spite, Caia took the blanket off the bed and tossed it over the mirror, hoping it blinded the Elders from seeing her. *Let them complain*, she thought to herself, then climbed into bed and tried to sleep.

Chapter Nineteen
Backtrack

The bedroom door creaked slightly, drawing Caia from the half-sleep she spent an hour fighting for. Footsteps neared the bed, and she turned to find Archai leaning over to blow out the candle.

"Dy'Mün told me to leave it lit," she said with a croak in her voice as she rolled over to face him.

Archai frowned. "Odd. He just asked me to blow it out."

Caia watched his face when realization dawned on both of them. Dy'Mün intended for them to speak tonight. Archai turned and eyed the mirror standing against the far wall with the blanket concealing it, his teal eyes glowing in the candlelight. "Aren't you cold?" he asked before looking back at her.

"I'm all right," she replied, pushing herself up into a sitting position. "I'd rather be cold than have them watching me. Covering the mirrors does block them from seeing me, right?"

"Here in Jaydür, they have other ways to watch you. But I'm sure you've made your point, if hiding from them is what you're trying to do."

Archai shifted his weight to one leg before clearing his throat and sitting on the edge of the bed beside Caia. She leaned her back against the wall and curled her feet under her. Chewing the inside of her cheek, she watched his hair move as he leaned his elbows onto his knees and dropped his face to the floor. Neither of them said anything for a while, which was fine with Caia. She loved how she never felt like she was required to say something or entertain him, nor did he need to do any of that for her. They were content in the silence.

Archai's back rose and fell gently with his even breathing, and Caia tried to reach out to better understand what he was feeling, but all that came to her was a sense of acceptance and emptiness, like a cold wind blowing on the backs of those grieving at a funeral.

With a hard swallow, Caia placed a hand on Archai's shoulder. Without a word, he pushed himself farther onto the bed, pressing his back against the wall like Caia so that they sat shoulder against shoulder. His eyes remained downcast, but their color stayed bright. His furrowed brows only made the teal stand out more.

"I should not have left her," he murmured.

Caia cocked her head slightly. "Naoni?"

He nodded. "If I had just brought her home, we wouldn't be in this situation. The Elders would not have known any different."

"I don't understand," Caia admitted. She was hesitant to say more, afraid he would only be more upset by her lack of knowledge of the situation. "Who are they to tell you what is right or what is wrong? *You* are placed to help the Voices, not them."

"Yes, but the Elders *replace* the Voices until the Voices are returned to power. I'm a protector of those in power. This is the way the world works, whether I like it or not." He sighed and shook his head.

"So what really happened with Naoni?"

"Terra is quiet. I left Naoni because I perceived her safer there than in Jaydür. Knowing you have yet to undergo the esgal'hehn, I had to make a judgment call. The sinstarians are no longer in Terra, and though Dy'Mün has a barrier around this place," he gestured to the cottage, "it has cracks that *can* be breached. The likelihood is small, but the possibility is there. We do not have the proper magic to hide a Voice, let alone two of them in the middle of nowhere because this is not where you belong. The magic that truly protects you is found in the Rehnedhen."

"So take me there. Take me to the Chamber of Apan."

"We cannot allow you to enter that realm until you are fully established as a Voice, and we cannot allow you to progress as a Voice with the—"

"Threat of the esgal'hehn hanging over me," Caia finished with a groan. "I'm beginning to hate that word. I don't get it. So what if I go blind and have visions as a Voice? They're just visions."

Archai faced her, but she didn't meet his gaze. "Meilon chained herself to a dark, dank wall for fear of hurting those around her when swallowed into visions. Can you imagine the damage you might inflict with the abilities of a Voice—a being with power in two different dimensions—when drawn into violent visions of war and darkness? That is a question we do not want answered."

Caia glanced at him, though she returned her attention to her lap. She had never compared herself to Meilon. The oracle was not of sound mind, and Caia hated to think of herself as being anything like that. She hated to consider the possibility of ever *becoming* something like that.

"Either way, if you are in Terra, you will have time to regather yourself. Resolve remaining issues. We're not yet sure how long you will be there, but I hope you take advantage of what time you do have. Let go of what needs to go. And don't let anyone take advantage of you or talk you down. Don't be stupid either, and stay in well-populated, well-lit areas. Also—"

"I got it, Archai," Caia laughed and placed a halting hand on his. "It's okay."

He put his other hand over hers and nodded.

"Keiren will be watching you. I trust him more than the Elders."

Leaning her head on the wall behind her, Caia bit her tongue. She had a thousand insults for the Elders in that moment, but Archai's guarded caution when it came to them did birth a hint of concern within herself. He knew them better than she did. "Will I really not be able to talk to you? At all?"

He shook his head. "There will be no communication allowed. I will be in the Temple of Pandhea. Physically and mentally. My focus will have to be there."

The idea confused Caia to no end. From what she could remember, the temple was just an empty ruin.

"What, exactly, are you doing when you're at the temple?" she asked. "Yes, it's ancient. Yes, it's beautiful, but whatever I remember about it isn't worth protecting."

"There are spirits there," Archai explained. "On a different plane, but very much present."

That caught Caia's attention. "What spirits?"

"The Temple of Pandhea is the resting place of all Elders. It is the place even Dy'Mün will go when he passes. There are urns there called *vechs* that the spirits are attached to. If the urn is broken or removed, the spirit attached to it is released and will no longer rest. When the Elders took power after the deaths of the Voices, they placed me over the temple to keep wanderers from defiling it."

The yawn Caia fought was not missed by Archai, but she didn't want to sleep. She wanted to stay and talk to him as long as possible. There was still a lot to learn and it felt like her source of answers and understanding was about to be snatched away from her. But more than that, Archai was very much considered a friend. Being torn from him reminded Caia of the day she lost Solin, and there was nothing about that day she wanted to relive.

"You need rest," Archai said, scooting off the bed. "Push away all doubts and concerns of the Elders. Turn your energy to the esgal'hehn. Prepare yourself for it. We will make this work out, one way or another. I will see you come morning."

Caia nodded as he leaned down and blew out the candle, shrouding the room in a darkness she found quite comfortable. When his footsteps retreated and the door closed, she lay back down and stared up at the ceiling. She tried to do as he said—to push it all away—but she had a lifetime of things to consider and, as Archai put it, issues to resolve. Without knowing how much time she'd be spending in Terra, it was hard to know what to expect or even how to plan. And those were the concerns besides the esgal'hehn, but she wasn't ready to focus on that yet. She was returning tomorrow, only two days after Jaydürian ash pixies attacked a major city in the United States of America—and there were witnesses besides Eric and Whitney. Those two weren't going to let that go, which brought out a whole other level of terror in her. The world would handle the truth however it could. But now, Eric knew who she was. The whole thing was a mess, but Caia had to push forward.

Sleep finally came over Caia like a brief storm, bringing with it strange dreams of running, hiding, and floating in water. Darkness framed her vision in the dreams, and throughout them all, she struggled to see as much of the picture as possible before it enveloped the entire scene, waking Caia with a start.

Bright morning rays shone through the window in the bedroom. Dust floated through the beams, gleaming in tiny bursts of light while birds chirped their songs so loudly, Caia wondered how she didn't wake sooner. Her legs were curled against her chest in an attempt to keep the morning chill at bay. All at once, Caia remembered what the day had in store for her, and the last thing she wanted to do was move.

Murmurs came from the main room of the cottage, and a faint smell of smoking wood seeped into the room despite the closed door.

"You cannot blame them," Dy'Mün said. She could hear him even though his voice was quiet and his tone was short. The realization immediately made Caia sick to her stomach. She had a good conversation with Archai before she slept; she hoped she wouldn't wake to more anger and frustration before she left.

Archai didn't respond, and Dy'Mün went on. "You are aiding the Elders in keeping Jaydür under control. Only you're doing it on a spiritual level."

"Do not think me a fool," Archai finally snapped. "My thoughts cannot be manipulated like a child's."

Caia slowly rose from the bed and put her ear against the door just as Dy'Mün grunted with disdain. "Why must you be so suspicious? This is the way the Highest intended us to handle things if something were to happen to the Voices. We are simply doing what we are meant to."

The clank of dishes against wood sounded, startling Caia.

"Will you *please* gain control of yourself?" Dy'Mün said with a *hmph*. "You'll wake the girl, and she doesn't need to see you so sour again before she goes."

Wood scraped against the floor and footsteps receded. With a slow sigh, Caia slowly opened the door and met Dy'Mün's apologetic expression. He said nothing about Archai. Instead, he motioned to the table. "Good morning. Breakfast is ready when you are. Make sure you wear the clothing you came with before you get going."

Caia nodded. "I put them in the trunk, down in the cellar," she said, then made her way toward the front door. A slight chill was in the morning air, and the birds were just as rowdy. Caia skimmed the area for Archai before hurrying around the cottage to the cellar barefoot, with her arms crossed over her chest. There was no way to know where he always disappeared to, whether he was actually in the area or if he disappeared to the Rehnedhen.

The ground was cold, and Caia focused on not stepping on rocks or sharp pebbles until she reached the cellar. Quickly snatching her clothes, she thought about just changing there, but remembered how Archai appeared at the door the last time she was down there. The last thing she wanted was to be caught half-clothed.

She hugged the clothes to her chest, made her way back to the room she slept in, then closed the door to change. The yellow t-shirt and jeans she owned suddenly seemed odd and uncomfortable to Caia. The style didn't make sense to her anymore, standing in a world where nice clothes were often difficult to come by. "To think," she thought to herself, "graphic tees are running rampant in Terra."

After changing, Caia turned to the mirror. The blanket dropped heavily from the glass onto the floor, one corner in her hand. She studied her white hair and blue eyes and wondered what her mother was going to say when she saw her. She'd been missing for days now, and with her return, she would be completely changed. She wouldn't be able to hide things any longer. She was seen with Archai by two witnesses who could testify that he had the ability to disappear and essentially teleport. Of course, they wouldn't be able to prove it without him there. But it was possible she would be faced with unwelcome questions from the entire world—not just her mother. News channels were likely still talking about the pixies and the victims of their bite.

Caia took a deep breath and closed her eyes while her heart went wild. There was no preparing for this, and it was pointless to let anxiety tear her apart. She didn't have the time or the strength to deal with fear of what might or might not happen. She would handle things as they came.

The scent of food and fire drifted into the bedroom as Caia opened the door. Warmth swirled around her as she made her way to the table and offered a "good morning" to Dy'Mün.

"It is rather a good morning, isn't it?" the wizard replied. "A pity you cannot spend the day doing something more lucrative."

"I'm about to face a world that is very much unprepared to know about the existence of another; I think that's plenty lucrative," Caia retorted as Dy'Mün placed a plate of eggs and meat in front of her.

Dy'Mün didn't reply and Caia went ahead and ate her breakfast. To her own surprise, fear and uncertainty tugged at her conscience with every bite. Not about herself or her return, but about her coming separation from Archai. It wasn't long ago that he left her under the watchful eyes of Keiren to speak with

Naoni, and the sheer loneliness and emptiness affected Caia down to her bones.

Caia blinked away her reverie with an exhale, as if her fears would blow away with her breath, then cleared her throat when she realized her food was already gone. "I must have been hungrier than I thought," she murmured, then stood with her empty dishes. Dy'Mün stepped before her with a hand on her shoulder, and urged her back to her seat before kneeling down beside her.

"I am sorry that things turned out the way they did," he said, taking her hand. "But understand, this is not an end. You are preparing yourself for something bigger than any of us imagined. *We* are preparing ourselves for the same. Everything will work out in the end."

Caia nodded, though his soft-spoken words hardly touched her the way he intended them to. Dy'Mün couldn't possibly understand what she was going through, and Caia didn't feel it necessary to try having that conversation with him. His entire view was skewed as an Elder. He didn't understand how much they were taking away by not allowing Archai to go with her. Their minds were solely on tradition and doing what they felt was best.

"Thank you, professor," she said, holding her tongue from sharing her thoughts. "I hope this will not take long."

Dy'Mün stood up and gestured to the door. "It

will take as long as the Highest wills it. Archai waits for you outside. Be safe."

Caia gently clung to the old man for a moment in a hug that ended with a strange sensation; a distinct sense of knowing overcame her. Images of walking through the woods and fields played in her mind, and she found it difficult to describe—even to herself— the *closeness* of the visions. It was as if she were seeing memories of things coming tomorrow, rather than yesterday. Caia almost felt confident enough to tell Dy'Mün that she would be back sooner than they expected.

Almost.

The moment Caia stepped out of the cottage, she spotted Archai with the horses at the ready. With the obvious return of his stiff, sour mood, she wasn't sure how to approach speaking to him, so though she made eye contact, she said nothing as she mounted her horse. He mounted his own, then started forward and she followed him.

Cool air brought with it darker clouds in the distant skies. Though the sky directly above the cottage was still bright and sunny, the end of the day promised storms with a gray tint in the distance. An inkling of jealousy tugged at Caia with the thought. Memories of summer storms at Dy'Mün's cottage were one thing Caia recalled as clear as day. The earthy smell that came with them had always urged her to open all the doors and windows of the place for the entire span of the day, until the rains began and pitter-pattered on the window sills. A fleeting thought of the strange weather in Arizona came to mind, and Caia wondered if it calmed with her leave.

Archai's horse jerked its head to the left before he tugged the reins to stay on the path. Oddly enough, Caia's horse did the same. They continued forward for a moment before the horses fought them again.

Archai muttered under his breath, and though Caia couldn't quite make it out, she knew it was in Elvish. That brought something to mind that she never quite thought to question until now.

"What are you, exactly?" she asked. "You're not an elf, but you speak Elvish. But you're not a human or a hybrid either. So what are you?"

"As I am of no age, I am also of no race," he replied.

"Oh. Well, that's…cryptic."

Archai gave her the side-eye as his horse huffed and whinnied.

"What's wrong with the horses?" she went on, changing the subject. His short response told her he wasn't interested in the topic.

"It is a blend of factors. Elven horses are creatures of nature and of balance. They are extremely sensitive to coming changes. That would include the storm you see in the sky heading in our direction, and the fact that they are about to lose the closest thing they have to a Voice of Apan—again."

Well, that made enough sense for her. She leaned down and patted her horse on the neck. "It'll be all right. I won't be gone long," she said, forcing a reassuring tone.

Archai turned his head to fully face her with a glimmer of curiosity in his eyes. "What are you sensing?" he asked, which made Caia smile. He showed no suspicion. No sign of disbelief. He trusted her.

"It's hard to describe, but I saw myself walking around woods and fields. They felt like memories, but there was a distinct sense they hadn't happened yet. If that makes any sense."

Archai stared for a few seconds more before turning to face the pathway again. The air around him slowly changed from stiff and professional to loose but composed, almost as if he forgot he was putting on a show for watchful eyes. "It does," he said.

The pair left the woods and came to the fields Caia recognized as the place she met Prince Leithen, Darcon, and Emerwen, but with a quick scan of the horizon, she saw no sign of any other riders. The yellow grasses and flowers twinkled with morning dew and the strong scent of rain suddenly met Caia's nostrils. It was a clean, fresh scent that made her skin bubble with goosebumps. Suddenly, a blue ball of light floated in the distance, growing larger as it came closer.

Caia was quick to recognize the light when it was

close enough that fluttering wings came into view.

"It's you!" Caia said with a laugh. She looked at Archai, who dismounted and took the reins. Caia did the same, then held out her hand. "What was your name again?"

"Nahtaia," the blue faery replied as she landed on Caia's palm. "It's good to see you again, Caia."

"It's wonderful to see you, too! But—" Caia paused as she tried to work out her thoughts. "What are you doing here?"

"Follow me," Archai said, cutting into the conversation, and Caia did as he asked.

"I'm here to help," Nahtaia answered with a mischievous grin.

Caia furrowed her brow but couldn't help smiling. "How so?"

"I will explain in a moment," Archai said. "Let us get where we need to be first."

The grass was tall, wetting Caia's knees. Archai eventually stopped and lifted his hand, which held the üsan ring. "I will create a rift that you will use to cross. The moon faery will join you, but not before using her magic to create the illusion of your human self over your Elven form. You will go home, and you will claim loss of memory. No talk of pixies. No talk of the place we were when the pixies attacked."

Caia opened her mouth to say something when he slashed at the air and created a rift. "This will lead someplace near your home," he explained. "I cannot create a gateway in the same place twice, and even so, we came here through a gate deep in a desert I do not want you blindly wandering. Find your way home, and then play your part. The faery will stay with you." His scrutinizing gaze settled on Nahtaia, and his eyes narrowed as he spoke. "You, *Nahtaia*, will refrain from using any magic outside of the illusion placed over Caia. If you are found to use anything beyond that, you will be punished most severely. Magic is sensitive in Terra, and anything more than a simple spell of illusion can be sensed if the sinstarians decide to return there. Even this much is a risk. Be responsible."

Nahtaia nodded and grinned once more at Caia. "I understand. I'm ready."

Caia stared at the rift and tried to understand what she was looking at. If she were to wager a guess, she would say it looked like her school, near the lockers just inside the gates.

"All right," she quietly replied, then looked to Nahtaia. "So how do you change me?"

Nahtaia let out a loud chortle and bounced her attention between Caia and Archai. "You're changed. We need to go now."

Caia pulled a strand of hair to her face, and between her fingers were Ella's red curls.

Archai gestured to the gateway, and Caia froze with her eyes on the tear between worlds. He was urging her through the rift *now*. Her heart skipped a beat, then raced. Was she really going through without one last talk with Archai? Nothing could be promised in stepping through the rift—not Archai, not answers. Not even the esgal'hehn. Besides the visions, there was nothing to say she would be seeing anyone here in the next decade, outside of Nahtaia.

Caia's feet froze to the ground. She shook her head and said, "Archai, wait. I don't know if I—"

"Stop," Archai demanded. "We're not making this an emotional journey that will haunt your time in Terra. Find your confidence; there is no time for emotion. You told me you saw visions of your return—think on those. I will hold you to them."

Caia nodded with a swallow, and turned to face him full on. It was hard to tell what was the best way to approach a goodbye with him—whether a hug or a handshake was proper, or something he would mock her for later. She searched his eyes, trying to pick up any train of thought or sense of emotion, but that cold, empty sensation was all that remained.

As if he was reading *her* thoughts, Archai stepped forward and took her hand. That gesture alone washed away a heap of anxiety. With his eyes trained on hers, Archai lifted her fingers to his lips and kissed them. Holding them at his mouth for a moment, his breath touching them with the warmth she had only witnessed in him a handful of times, he led her toward the tear.

"There is nothing more to say," he spoke softly,

"besides be careful, stay safe, and I will see you again. This is not the end." His words, blended with the intensity of his teal eyes, poured a sense of warmth over her like an embrace.

Tears threatened, but Caia forced them back. Her words were like a ball of rubber bands on the back of her tongue—heavy, but unable to untangle and spit out. A nod was all she could manage. Nahtaia fluttered beside her and landed on her shoulder.

With only one step between her and Terra, she held Archai's gaze as she said, "I guess this is it. Goodbye, Archai." She stepped through the tear with Nahtaia in tow. Archai stood behind a curtain of translucent atmosphere for seconds before the tear closed up, leaving no sign it was ever there.

Chapter Twenty
Fake It

Home was not far. Caia was right in thinking she knew the location the tear brought her to; she stood ten feet from the gate behind her school locker. No one was around, but the sound of a heavy metal door opening then clicking shut alerted Caia to the fact that there were people on campus.

The sun was hot and glaring on her back, which elicited a groan from Nahtaia.

"Ugh," the faery started. "The air here is *disgusting!*"

Caia smiled and turned toward home. "I don't know how I'm going to do this," she said, her face twisting with concern. "I'm supposed to play the amnesia card, but I have no apparent reason for amnesia."

"Fake an injury," Nahtaia chirped into her ear.

"Right, but how?"

A car sped by and Nahtaia squeaked with

displeasure.

"It's okay," Caia said. "It's just a car. Humans use them to get from one place to another in shorter time."

"Like wings," Nahtaia added.

"Sure. Like wings."

Caia stopped and looked behind her at the road that stretched way beyond the school campus. She needed a head injury or something to be a "cause" of amnesia. She almost entertained the thought of throwing herself in front of a car, but that could end disastrously. Then she turned to Nahtaia.

"Could you hit me hard enough to leave a mark?" she asked the faery.

Nahtaia tugged on Caia's earlobe. "Do you hear yourself?"

"Yes," Caia laughed in reply. "I need something to blame amnesia on. A head injury would do it. It doesn't have to be severe. It just has to be enough to leave a mark. Can you think of anything?"

"Are you sure you don't already suffer from this disease?"

Caia stopped, wondering what Nahtaia was getting at.

"Touch your head," Nahtaia commanded, and Caia gasped at the sight of blood on her hands. "It's not real, but no one will know any better."

"You're incredible," Caia replied, trying to hold back her laughter. She needed to play the victim now.

Caia touched her head, as if placing pressure on the would-be wound. "Stay out of sight," she whispered, then gasped at the sudden human-sized girl who walked beside her as if helping her along the road.

"Where's your sense of adventure?" Nahtaia giggled. "If I'm going to be here, I'm going to *be* here."

The bright blue eyes were definitely the faery's, but coupled with the black and blonde dreadlocked hair as well as light-brown skin formed a combination that Caia had never seen. "You look utterly exotic," Caia pointed out, studying the faery from head to toe. "You stand out."

"From what the Elder told me," Nahtaia replied, "this world is full of diversity. This can't be *that* different."

"It is diverse," Caia continued. "And yet, half of us just try to blend in and look like everyone else."

Nahtaia scoffed and let out a groan. "How utterly *boring.* I think this world would do well to accept the Jaydürian fae as inhabitants. We'll show you how incredible *different* really is."

Caia grinned, then covered her mouth in an attempt to hide it. She was supposed to act injured. "I wonder if I'll ever be unsurprised by you," Caia said. "I'm glad you came with me."

Nahtaia's teeth gleamed behind plump lips in her reciprocated smile.

A car slowed down, and Nahtaia nudged Caia with her elbow. "Someone is coming. Time to play."

The car door flew open and a woman rushed out. "Oh my God! Are you all right? Let me take you to a hospital."

Caia briskly shook her head. "I'm almost home. I just live up the road."

"What happened?" the woman asked, turning to Nahtaia.

"A car hit her," Nahtaia explained, her tone as convincing as any true witness. "Then he just drove off!"

The woman looked up the road as if to see the perpetrator's car, then gestured to her own. "Let me drive you home," she offered. "Which house is it?"

Caia let herself be led by Nahtaia and the woman to the car, then directed the woman to her home. It wasn't two minutes later that Caia stood in front of the house's door, and the woman pushed it open.

"Hello?" the woman called. "Your daughter is hurt!"

Stephenie hurried from around the corner and screamed at the sight of Caia. "Ella! Oh my God, what happened! Where have you been? Brittany! Grab a towel!" Stephenie placed pressure on Caia's head and brought her to the kitchen, where she had her sit at the table. "Ella, it's been two days. Where have you been?"

"She was hit by a car," Nahtaia explained. "The

driver ran off."

Brittany hurried into the room with a towel, her eyes bugging out at the sight of her sister. She eyed everyone in the room, taking an extra few seconds to gaze awkwardly at Nahtaia. "What's going on?" she asked. "Ella, where were you? We thought you were dead somewhere!"

"She's been missing?" the woman who drove the car asked. "I saw her on the side of the road by the high school and brought her straight over."

"Thank you so much," Stephenie said, pressing the towel to her daughter's head. "And thank *you*," she added, looking to Nahtaia. "Do you know Ella? Have you been with her all this time?"

Nahtaia shook her head. "My name is Nahtaia. I saw Ella get hit and I ran to help."

Stephenie nodded and continued wiping at Caia's head. "The gash doesn't look too bad," she said. "It's just a bleeder because of where it is, but I don't think you'll need stitches or anything. But honey," Stephenie went on, taking Caia's face into her hands. "Where have you been the last two days? We have the whole country looking for you."

Caia stared at her mother, blinking with her mouth gaping open. "What do you mean?" she asked, glancing to Brittany. "I've been at school."

Stephenie frowned. "Honey, I mean for the last two days. Not the last ten minutes."

"Yeah," Caia insisted. "At school and at home.

Like usual."

Stephenie looked at Brittany, then to the others in the room before leaning down to meet Caia at eye level. "Ella, you have been gone for *two days.* Two days, Ella! Where have you been?"

Caia looked down to the floor, feigning surprise and confusion. "I-I don't remember."

Caia folded the hospital gown and placed it on the bed she'd spent the last two days in. Test after test, doctors poked and prodded her for any sign of anomaly that could be grounds for amnesia, but they found nothing. She was healthy as anyone could hope to be and as *human* as anyone could hope to be, thanks to Nahtaia. The faery had spent the two days hidden within the hospital room, making sure the illusion kept up with their story. Occasionally, she would take on the form of the girl who helped her just after the accident and made good friends with Brittany.

"Ready to go?" Nahtaia asked as she took on her human form. "Your mom should be here any minute."

Caia looked over the room once more, making sure she had all of her belongings in the backpack Brittany brought her from home. "Yeah, I'm ready. I'm a bit nervous about what's waiting out there, though."

Nahtaia walked over to the window and shook her

head. "The crowd is getting bigger now."

"Yeah, and the hospital won't save me from them now."

"So you've been missing for a few days," Nahtaia said, thinking out loud as she seemed to do often. "What's the point in hounding you about it?"

Caia shrugged and sat on the edge of the bed to pull on her shoes. "They want to show how much they care, I guess. It's a normal thing to do here."

"If *I* had just been severely injured and gone through life-threatening situations, I would want some peace and quiet," Nahtaia admitted. "Not a group of people staring at me, patting my back for surviving."

With a laugh, Caia nodded in agreement. "I feel like humans might be more emotional than magic folk in general," she explained.

"Really?" Nahtaia retorted sarcastically. "I didn't catch that."

The door opened and Stephenie walked in. "Ready to go?"

Nahtaia and Caia both nodded, then followed Stephenie out of the hospital. The first step out of the door caused an eruption of cheers from friends and fellow students. Caia immediately broke into a sweat as she met the eyes of people she hardly knew among the handful she did. She followed her mom to the car, trying not to laugh when people patted her back, just like Nahtaia had said in the hospital. Caia looked sidelong at her Jaydürian friend, who beamed in the uproar of attention. Just past Nahtaia's head stood two others who stared at Caia with bright eyes of shock and confusion—Eric and Whitney.

For all Caia could tell, they were the only two who knew she had anything to do with Jaydür. Caia turned away from them before ducking her head into the car, hoping her eyes didn't give away the lie she was currently living. Nahtaia dropped into the seat beside her with a giggle and shut the door before the car drove off.

"Now that wasn't too bad, was it?" Stephenie asked, peering at the girls through the rearview mirror.

"I'm a survivor, Mom, didn't you know?" Caia joked.

The ride home was quick enough for her and Nahtaia to comfortably keep quiet until they were in Caia's bedroom. Stephenie worked on dinner while Brittany did homework, leaving the girls to finally sit and discuss everything concerning Jaydür.

"The two people who met Archai and saw him create a rift were at the hospital today," Caia quietly said to Nahtaia, who lay sprawled out on the bed. "They looked…disturbed."

"I would be too if I was in their shoes. If faeries and elves are as much a fantasy as you say they are, then it must be akin to watching a monster wade through crowds of people wearing the skins of human children."

Caia dropped a hairbrush, sending it clattering to the floor. "That's not what it's like at all! By the Highest...I didn't peg you as the morbid type." Picking up the brush, Caia looked into the mirror at her true reflection. Nahtaia dropped the illusion whenever they were both locked inside the bedroom alone, giving Caia a brief respite from the tower of lies she balanced on her shoulders.

"I'll have to face them soon enough, I think," Caia went on. "I don't know what to say to them. I don't know what they've told people. *If* they've told people."

Nahtaia rolled onto her belly and swung her feet up and down. "I don't think it matters what they've said anyway. You keep playing dumb, and the plan keeps working. We won't be here forever."

Caia turned and leaned against the dresser. "I haven't even seen Naoni since we got back. But I don't think we need to worry about that. She's smart. She won't show up until she knows we'll have an opportunity to talk. She knows the plan."

Nahtaia nodded, then hummed to herself. It was a song Caia didn't remember ever hearing, but it made her smile while she turned and brushed her hair, her eyes gazing into the mirror until her mind grew distant. Archai crossed her thoughts and Caia gently touched her fingers to the glass. He told her he would have no way to speak with her. But, could he still see her? She hoped he could, if only to see she was all right and ease his stresses.

A knock sounded at the door, and Nahtaia lifted her hand, creating a swirling blue smoke around Caia. Her white hair turned red. Her blue eyes faded to brown. Her glowing skin dimmed.

"Ella," Stephenie called from the other side of the door. "Dinner is ready."

"Just a minute," Caia replied.

"What are you two doing in there?" Stephenie asked.

Caia and Nahtaia exchanged grins and stepped toward the door.

"Just working our magic," Caia replied. "Gotta look presentable."

Elvish Reference

- Nidholmen - "The Chosen"
  Also used as "you" when speaking to the Voices of Jaydür.
- Níha'men - welcome/you are welcome
- It – to
- Bahlog - are/have been
- Aledhrinal - called/summoned
- Terehn - "time spirits"
- Rehnedhen - the name of the spirit parallel which includes the chambers where the Voices reside.
- Em – him
- Lem - but/yet
- Sin – in
- Nobení – death/the dead
- Fumen – smoke
- Ín - a/one
- Än – the
- Ínmi - heart
- Apan – Water
- Folc – Fire
- Mae'Ehr – Wind
- D'Irdda – Earth
- Terdhen - time
- Leget – to tie
- Eled - light
- Eled'hwen – Elven light
- Et – of
- Nobení - death/the dead
- Am – being
- Leg - tie/tied
- Fost – has/did

- Trecd – pass
- Amna - Lady
- Voka – Voice
- Scalt - rise
- Endh – alarm
- Venidh – come/be with
- Lanol – us/we
- Neu - and
- Ajundha – help/guide

About the Author

L.F Oake (AKA Lilian Oake) is an Amazon bestselling author of teen and adult fantasy. She is best known for Nahtaia: A Jaydürian Adventure, which boasts a whopping 3.7 million online hits. Born and raised in Phoenix, Arizona, she moved to North Carolina where she writes full time and is hard at work on her next book. When she is not writing, she is educating her horde of goblins in the ways of Middle Earth and Narnia with the help of her husband.

75703069R10234

Made in the USA
Middletown, DE
07 June 2018